D0710756

The Afterlife of

George Cartwright

A Novel by
JOHN STEFFLER

HENRY HOLT AND COMPANY
NEW YORK

Henry Holt and Company, Inc.
Publishers since 1866
115 West 18th Street
New York, New York 10011

Henry Holt® is a registered
trademark of Henry Holt and Company, Inc.

First published in the United States in 1993 by
Henry Holt and Company, Inc.
Originally published in Canada in 1992 by
McClelland & Stewart Inc.

Library of Congress Cataloging-in-Publication Data
Steffler, John.
The afterlife of George Cartwright : a novel by / John
Steffler.—1st American ed.
p.   cm.
1. Cartwright, George, 1739–1819—Fiction.   I. Title.
PR9199.3.S7814A68   1993
813'.54—dc20   92-16707
                                                                              CIP

ISBN 0-8050-2462-X

First American Edition—1993

Designed by Marisa Mendicino

Printed in the United States of America
All first editions are printed on acid-free paper. ∞
    1   3   5   7   9   10   8   6   4   2

For Edith and Alban

The Afterlife of

George Cartwright

1

Nottinghamshire shimmers. Fragrant, dizzy with bees at the peak of May. Turning around in the saddle, George Cartwright squints at the scattered fields – no birds within range, no sign of another person. Never a sign of another person. He lets his horse carry him on at its own easy pace, following the Nottingham road out from Mansfield, the same route he's taken every day since his death in 1819. His hawk, Kaumalak, is perched on his left fist. Sunlight pricks blue fire from the feathers of her wings, and Cartwright smoothes her iridescence: this dainty mortar shell. Songs from invisible birds beckon him forward, stirring his appetite for the hunt. For the moment, his loneliness is nearly without pain.

Sparrows splash in the puddled wagon tracks ahead, but he keeps his hawk hooded, scanning the pastures and groves, waiting for larks.

Cartwright knows he's dead, but death isn't the way he expected – although after 170 years it isn't something that troubles him very much anymore. In the last weeks of his life, riding this same well-known road, feeling his hawk unusually heavy on his glove, he had sensed the end coming and wondered what lay beyond. Not harps and angels, he suspected, but at least a brief audience with his Maker. Probably a reunion with family and old acquaintances who had already died – some he wasn't so sure he wanted to face again, but even that he was curious about. Forgiveness and understanding would likely prevail. Maybe a new incarnation in a new world awaited him, something as unimaginable as Labrador. Certainly explanations and marvels, and a few rewards. He didn't anticipate many punishments. God, he assumed, under his aura or robes or whatever, would be a manly gentleman who favoured a bit of push and gusto in his chaps on earth. But instead of any of that, he died in his room at The Turk's Head in Mansfield and woke up there, and nothing had changed. Except time had stopped, at least in his immediate vicinity, and everyone was away somewhere. All he could think to do was go hawking.

This morning, for example, like every morning, he had sat on the edge of his bed in The Turk's Head Inn – after a night of unspeakable dreams – and had thought about his unfinished affairs in Labrador, about Caubvick, the Inuit woman, and Mrs. Selby, his mistress, wondering how he might have kept them with him during his days alive. And as he sat picturing their beautiful, troubled faces, speaking to them in his mind, making them smile, and as he proved to himself once again that his bankrupt business might have been saved, his ruminations were mixed with a constant awareness of the smell of damp soot in the fireplace and of the soundlessness of the building around him, the deserted taproom downstairs, Mansfield's deserted houses, deserted streets. And then, sitting hopelessly, he noticed Kaumalak on her perch. Her keen eyes and beak. Her economical movements. Her stern looks. And in his heart Cartwright felt, with a surge of gladness, the old desire to hunt, to feel the kick of his Hanoverian rifle or the push of his peregrine's talons as she launched herself in a burst at the sight of doves. He looked out his window then at his horse, Thoroton, stabled across the courtyard, and began hurrying, whistling, getting into his boots.

Although time has stopped for Cartwright, he knows that just beneath the surface of what surrounds him it has been racing along at an insane speed. He's discovered that time is like sound – that the past doesn't vanish, but encircles us in layers like a continuous series of voices, with the closest, most recent voice drowning out those that have gone before. And just as it's possible to sit on a bench in a city reading a book, oblivious to the complex racket all around, then to withdraw from the page and pick out from the cascade of noises the voice of one street vendor two blocks away, so for Cartwright it's possible at times to tune in a detail from either the past or the ongoing course of time and, by concentrating on it, become witness to some event in the affairs of the dead or the living.

For the living, the past is always overlaid, made inaccessible by the present, but for Cartwright, both the past and the present are elusive background phenomena, subject to occasional capture. His experience as a hunter and his 170 years of practice have made him adept at nabbing rare moments by their whiskers or tails. He even stumbles into pockets of time unintentionally, the way he's often stumbled into a rabbit hole during his rambles in search of game.

Right now while Thoroton plods and the saddle creaks, Cartwright's eye is caught by a red glimmer ahead in the roadside grass. A ring dropped by some lady or gentleman? A berry? A beetle? The ruby gleam rapidly grows in size and hurtles toward him, pulling in its wake a black river of pavement and two wide wings of images: sharp-cornered brick buildings in rows on either side, poles and wires, smoke. The scarlet double-decker Trent Lines bus bearing down on him is a familiar sight. It rushes under or through him, at which point Cartwright sees it, feels its rush, but can't see his horse or himself. Groups of cars plunge through him from both directions. He seems to whirl upward, enlarged on an eddy of turbulence, feeling a mixture of horror and admiration. To ride in one of those things! The inventor and sportsman in him are aroused. And yet he's annoyed. He has spied enough on the present to know how small, how mechanical people there have become. Children of Edmund, he thinks, remembering his brother Edmund's power-loom and gunpowder engine. This is where all that led. And then remembering his own attempted inventions, he admits to himself some blame for this state of affairs.

At certain periods Cartwright has been a fan of the present, though usually a rather grudging, critical fan, following it more out of idle curiosity than love. For a while the smell of the lichen on an oak tree in Averham Park was a reliable way of getting into the Robin Hood Tavern in Nottingham, and although the effort required to trace the smell into the tavern and keep himself there was extremely draining, Cartwright had spent many hours standing by The Robin Hood's coat-rack watching television and reading the paper over the shoulder of a retired dry-cleaner who always sat nearby and whom Cartwright regarded as more dead than himself. He was actually quite interested in Nottingham Forest, the local football team, for a time – knew all the players and their statistics, laughed at the barbaric remarks of their manager, Brian Clough. But then the effort became too much, and he felt foolish, and went back to his hawk and the Nottingham road. It was lonely and predictable there on the whole, but at least it was his death, and there must be some purpose in it, he thought.

The red gleam, the Trent bus, had taken Cartwright by surprise. After a moment he recomposes himself and looks around from his elevated position over the countryside. He is out of the present again. The landscape he sees now is the familiar one, exactly as it was on the 19th of May in 1819, the day he died. To the east he sees the old family estate at Marnham and to the south, near Newark, his father's famous bridge, far from any water, like a length of Roman aqueduct, the folly that had swallowed what little was left of the family fortune and had sent Cartwright into the army and to Labrador. Buttercups and grasses festoon its parapets. A small herd of cows enjoys the shade under one of its spans.

Perhaps he's borrowing Kaumalak's eyes. This ability of his to stretch up and scan the surface of the earth is getting stronger, he's noticed. It works best, for some reason, on horseback from the top of a hill. He has seen as far east as Saxony, where he was injured by a boar for the sake of the ungrateful Marquis of Granby, and even to Minorca where he nearly died of fever. To the west he has seen Lizard Head and the Scilly Isles where more than once he came close to being shipwrecked returning from Labrador. He has seen as far as the mid-Atlantic, the same mountainous grey and yellow waves that had rolled clean over his leaking ships. But not yet as far as Newfoundland and the Labrador coast.

Cartwright rises slightly in his saddle and farts and searches the sky over the meadows for larks. No, the present causes him little envy. The past is what he can't let alone.

He turns Thoroton to the left through an open gate onto a cattle track and immediately flushes a pair of pheasants from beyond a hedge. He deftly releases his hawk's jesses and takes off her hood. She swivels her head once, unfolds her wings, and kicks back hard as he braces himself in the stirrups and throws up his arm, pushing with all his might against the amazing force.

Nottinghamshire slips from Cartwright's lap like a quilt. He watches his hands shoot out far, fingers hooked for the pleasure of catching. For feeling the quick pulse burst into bloom, red petals scattering.

His centre melts, a current of hunger surging out of his throat and eyes in his hawk's wake. His body forgotten on Thoroton's back.

Diving into a pocket of blood in the sky. Pure fugitive treasure. The motherhood under everything, even rocks and ice.

Kaumalak has disappeared in the sun. Cartwright hangs suspended, waiting, hearing a pasture gate lazily striking its post in the light breeze, pausing, striking.

Like that knocking on board the *Mary* during his first voyage home from Labrador. The sound belonged to the part of his cargo he couldn't understand; the most precious part, he now thinks, the most curious of all he carried from Labrador. The sound of beliefs fathered in people by icebergs and rocks.

Having lost sight of land east of Belle Isle, the *Mary* broke into her full ocean roll, creaking without restraint. Mrs. Selby had made a nest for herself on some bales of marten pelts by the window at the stern and was reading a book. Beside her a set of caribou antlers was lashed to the cabin wall. A tall willow cage containing an eagle swung from an antler point. Cartwright sat at a table making entries in his journal, pleased to be bound for home. Every inch of the ship was snug with cargo, the fruit of a two-year stay in Labrador.

"1772. November. Sunday 8," he had written, "Wind N.N.E. fresh. At day-break we put to sea from Chateau, and set sail for Ireland. We found a great sea in the straits, and by mid-afternoon are two leagues to the eastward of the island of Belle Isle." Pausing to match his hand to the ship's movement, he became aware of repeated knocking in the next cabin, not in time with the pitch and roll. He rose, exchanged a questioning look with Mrs. Selby, then stepped out to investigate, opened the nearest door.

The smell of the Inuit: woodsmoke and old fat. Only slightly different from his own smell after being surrounded for so long by dried fish, furs, barrels of oil from the cooked blubber of seals. Ickcongoque was lying on her back on the small cabin floor. Her husband, Attuiock, knelt a few feet from her head, chanting slowly and mournfully. Using a musket's ramrod as a lever balanced over a pewter jug, he was raising Ickcongoque's head by means of a leather thong which hung from the ramrod's end and passed under the back of her neck. Their four-year-old daughter, Ickeuna, was snuggled in Caubvick's lap, both of them fixedly watching the rite. Caubvick's husband, Tooklavinia, was asleep in one of the bunks. Caubvick turned her beautiful face to Cartwright and smiled when she heard him come in.

Attuiock chanted monotonously, his eyes shut, then opened them wide, hissed a couple of words with great intensity, and let Ickcongoque's head drop to the cabin floor. Then he began his chanting again, raising Ickcongoque's head.

Cartwright waited, watching intently, as he had done so often with these people, glad of their incomprehensible displays. Attuiock paused, looking proud and wise. "It is very good, very good," he said, pointing to Ickcongoque and his device.

"That may be," Cartwright nodded, "but pray, what is it good for?"

"My wife has got the headache."

"Ah!" Cartwright raised his eyebrows and quickly withdrew.

Three strides up the companionway, hit by the tilting bite of the air, he gripped the rail and let his laughter explode. He was rich, he knew it. The old chief's solemn face! How he loved him, his childishness and wisdom – always what Cartwright loved: dignity and fantasy combined.

Cartwright could see his success. His cargoes wouldn't completely repay his debts, but they would impress his creditors, bringing investment for his next trip out, for expanding his operations on the Labrador coast. He would speak about that with the Board of Trade. And the Inuit would bring him renown, audiences with curious grandees, people of influence – perhaps with the King himself. Some gifts of furs and curios for the men on the Board of Trade, and for Cartwright sole right to fish and hunt in the watersheds of the St. Lewis River and the

Alexis River, and eventually Sandwich Bay. And Noble and Pinson's territory as well – he would have to devour those rivals who were trying to squeeze him out. And better naval support – British law to hold it all in place. Tall doors opening everywhere to admit the adventurer-gentleman back from the Empire's outposts with proofs of supremacy. He wanted that. Thick-headed George Cartwright, the sporting dolt. He knew what his brothers thought of him. A failed soldier, forever in debt, retired young on half-pay with nothing to do and not enough money with which to do it.

He felt himself grin at the prospect of showing off England to the Inuit, watching their faces as they rode in a coach through London's streets. As they entered St. Paul's. He liked their capacity for awe, and the thought of the tales they'd take back to their people in Labrador. They looked on the English as a small tribe of landless wanderers. He wanted to show them the true proportion of things, amaze them, make them willing subjects of his rule, to both their advantages. He needed to keep them working for him, bringing him whalebone and furs; he wanted them to see that they needed his knowledge and goods in exchange.

He imagined their comic conjectures and his explanations, their blunders in high society. He was eager for this, the disruption they'd cause. He felt they embodied a part of himself returning home. He had never fitted into London society. He was happier gutting a deer. He pictured himself in London walking his wolf cub on a leash, carrying his eagle, escorted by Inuit, and felt the power they gave him – not merely because of the spectacle, but because they were his natural company. They proclaimed what he'd always harboured inside himself.

His youngest sister, Dorothy, would be frightened, filled with wonder. His brothers would be speechless for a change. In their chairs in the parlour at Marnham. Political pamphlets, inventions, and sonnets would be swept from their minds as they watched him stride about with his unimaginable friends in their clothing of skins.

It was cold and nearly dark. The crew was hauling the ship about on its port tack. Cartwright waved to the helmsman, then heaved himself below to his cabin – a lighted lamp now swinging there from an antler – and flung himself down on the furs beside Mrs. Selby. Unbuttoned her jacket, reached under her clothes.

Laughing again he described what Attuiock and Ick-congoque were doing. "Listen," he said. The knocking was still going on. "No doubt she would have a head-ache!" His fingers found more buttons, burrowed for warmth.

"Poor thing," Mrs. Selby said. "It must be leaving her people, and the strangeness of all this has made her sick."

Cartwright looked into her eyes and saw something as plain as water around rocks at the edge of a lake. Something sufficient in itself with which he could do nothing. There was also a tinge of amusement there. It seemed directed as much at him as the Inuit.

"Ah, most likely it has," he said, "but they have such a quaint conception of medicine. If they'd only ask me to bleed her, she'd be up helping to trim the topgallant sails in a minute or two."

Mrs. Selby put her book aside, a novel by Sarah Scott. It was one of the few books of Mrs. Selby's that had survived Labrador, and she'd already read it six or seven times. She took his hand out of her clothing and bit it. "You're more of a savage," she said, "than any of them."

✦

By the Nottingham road he is conscious again of the gate swinging slightly in the breeze, tapping against a post. Cartwright whistles to Kaumalak. Watches her slowly spiral in.

Out to the east the Trent is a long placid smile in a green face. Marnham, where Cartwright was born, lies just to this side of the river at the top of a soft fold.

"The land is all made here," Attuiock had remarked during his visit to Marnham. He and Cartwright were riding slowly side by side in the late-winter afternoon – meadows and hedgerows lay before them – when Attuiock turned to Cartwright with a look of embarrassed discovery on his face. "All made by man."

✦

George Cartwright, eleven years old, crouched and pushed his way through the willow thicket. His family's house was in sight at the top of the rise. With his left hand he guided his small fowling piece through the branches ahead of him, careful not to let the trigger get caught. In his right hand he carried behind him four partridges tied by their feet with a cord. A twig stung his cheek. He stepped free into the meadow and started to run.

At the top of the meadow he followed the brick-walled trench, then climbed its steps and continued running over the lawn to the window of his father's study. He peered past the reflection into the dim room. His father was there with John, Cartwright's brother, younger than him by only a year. They stood at a table looking at drawings and maps. His father's shaved head, showing a week's grey stubble, was bare of the wig he sometimes wore. His long, unbuttoned waistcoat, his open shirt, hung loosely before him as he bent forward pointing at diagrams.

Cartwright waited and listened. His father was indicating how the red lines representing turnpikes and the arches representing bridges would join with the system of canals, shown in blue, to link ports and county capitals together.

"And who shall pay for the work?" John asked. "Will the King pay for it all?"

"No," his father explained, "it will be the duty of landowning families in each district to underwrite the cost of the works, and they will then have the privilege of charging tolls to recover their expenditures and gather a profit."

"Will the roads and canals not stand vacant for want of people with money enough to pay the tolls?" John wondered aloud.

"No." His father spoke to John with gentle intimacy. "When the means are improved, the traffic in goods by land will be much greater than what it is at the present. The storehouses in Nottingham right now are filled with stockings and lace and malt that cannot be conveyed to those who would buy them. Habit is useless. There is great wealth, great wealth to be made by the man with the wits to improve the way things are done."

His father turned to reach for his drawings of bridges, and Cartwright at the window called out and held up his partridges. His father and John looked up – their eyes, their expressions nearly identical. Both for a second seemed not to know who he was. His father opened the window. "We're busy just now. . . . Well, what have we here? Oh, it's a pity you didn't have better luck. Your Aunt Elizabeth's coming, you know. One or two birds more would have made a meal."

✦

12

His mother was crying, her mouth bunched and ugly as she gave him the basket, the twisted wicker handle thick in his hands, the basket heavy with plates and food for his father and brothers. Anne, his oldest sister, pale and silent, watched from behind the cluttered scullery table. The manservant who would drive the cart, at least until Cartwright insisted on taking the reins, stood by the light-filled door, waiting, a basket in each of his hands, a vague half-smile on his face, looking at nothing.

"He's stolen your future to pay for his precious bridge. Do you know that, George?" His mother was looking into his eyes with frightening intensity, as though grabbing at him out of the ruins of her usual self. "There was a lawyer in here this morning from Nottingham. Your father sold him the Ossington house to pay for his bricks. That was my father's house. And your father knew I meant it to go to you. There won't be money for any of you for a tutor now. Army school or some wretched apprenticeship is all you'll get."

"But the bridge will bring money in, will it not?"

"Ha. That bridge is nought but one of his games."

Passing out of the kitchen garden into the carriage-drive where the horse and cart were waiting, Cartwright glimpsed the younger children beyond the orchard leading a pony. His brother William, sixteen years old but smaller than George, was lying on a rug near the garden wall, reading a book. He didn't look up from his reading. William was separate. In some ways he seemed freer, more adult than the other children; in some ways he was less taken into account than even the youngest one. He was sick much of the time, alone in his room, dining at odd hours. Because of his poor health, and perhaps because their father had once expected him to become head of the family, he was the only one to receive private lessons, although their mother was always talking of having tutors for each of her ten children.

Cartwright lifted the basket up to the servant in the cart. He wouldn't miss the house in Ossington, which he had visited only a few times; he was glad to be spared the tedium of tutors. He couldn't imagine anyone stealing his future. He was eager to drive the cart, see the country passing, and join the others down in the lowlands beside the Trent River where they were building the bridge. To be under the bright wide sky with the crowds of workers, the carters and piles of bricks.

Cartwright's father, his wig askew, his waistcoat open, was showing a group of visitors over the site, gesturing with a rolled drawing to where the fourteen piers for the thirteen arches would be situated, extolling the values of sound engineering and public works. To the east, marsh birds rose in a glittering flock. Goods and traffic would flow between Newark, Gainsborough, and Mansfield all the year, untroubled by floods, he was saying. The air was loud with the echo of carpenters' hammers. John was on top of a curved wooden form where one of the arches was being completed. He waved, called out, threw down a rope for Cartwright to tie to one of the baskets of food.

Edmund, younger than Cartwright by four years, was out at the last pier watching the engineers rigging a crane with block and tackle. Edmund had diagrams of his own rolled under his arm. In his seven-year-old voice he asked about their arrangements of levers and counterweights. The engineers paused in their work and answered him without condescension. Cartwright had set down a basket in their midst. While he listened, he took out a roasted partridge and handed Edmund a leg.

"You've got the makings of a fine officer in many respects, Cartwright." Mr. Becher, Headmaster of the Royal Military Academy at Woolwich, paused to stretch his chin high and inhale through large, snuff-blackened nostrils. "You're good in sports. The Academy Wrestling Champion. You get on well with the other lads. You're admired by many; that's clear. You could be a first-rate leader and find advancement in His Majesty's service. But, look here, you've got to apply yourself to your lessons."

"Sir."

"Mr. Ryland tells me your knowledge of Latin is no greater now than when you began here."

"Sir."

"Mr. Langley tells me your knowledge of mathematics, and of the principles of gunnery, is not what it ought to be."

"Sir."

"Our officers cannot be ignorant men, Cartwright. You seem capable enough, but I'm told you daydream. I'm also told you were absent from parade three times in the last fortnight and that you are sometimes absent from your dormitory for the whole night. Those are grounds for expulsion, Cartwright."

"Sir."

"Now I could wink at a few fallings-off of that sort if your performance here in other respects were more satisfactory. If I receive any further reports of failures in mathematics and gunnery, or absences from your duties between now and Easter, a caning is the least you'll get, in spite of your size. And I expect some progress in Latin. Think of your future, Cartwright."

"Sir."

"I don't know what – if anything – goes on in your head."

"They're letting you stay?" Kellet leaned forward over his basin of porridge across from Cartwright. "Old Becher is soft on you. Anyone else he would have had flogged and sent down months ago."

Cartwright shrugged. "He says I've got to learn Latin. Christ, I'm sick of this stuff." He stood his spoon upright in his porridge; then, grasping it like a handle, lifted his bowl sideways off the table, turned it quickly upside down in a tight circle without any spill, and set it down again.

Kellet sniggered. "You know what cook puts in it instead of salt, don't you?"

"Here, give me your handkerchief," Cartwright said.

He spread Kellet's handkerchief on the table, scraped his porridge onto it, and tied the handkerchief's corners over the mass like a peas pudding. "They'll be watching me," he said. "Put this in your hat."

Kellet whisked the moist parcel under the table into his hat. "What for?" He searched Cartwright's face eagerly.

"You know those pigeons Madame Becher feeds on the porch roof under their window? I've got a plan to get us some decent food."

The sound of boys cheering echoed up from the playing field on the other side of the building. Cartwright looked behind him awkwardly to each side. He was pulling himself upright through the leaves, clutching a vine branch with his left hand. His feet were on Kellet's bony shoulders.

His face rose shakily over the eave of the porch under the Bechers' bedroom window. Pigeons cooed apprehensively and fluttered up to the building's main roof, sending a gust of feathers and oat husks into his eyes.

He checked the window, cautiously lifted the bundle of porridge onto the roof, and opened the handkerchief. It was possible to spread the porridge over the slates like a sheet of dough. He scraped his hand clean, took grain from his pocket, and scattered it over the porridge. "Keep still," he hissed, turning his face toward Kellet.

"Oh God, I hope they're starving," Kellet moaned. "You're breaking my back."

Cartwright crouched under the eave, as deep into the vine's leaves as he could get. From time to time he twisted his head, checking the courtyard. Everyone was still at the game.

He heard a soft rush of wings above him. Mild cooing, claws clicking on slate. He waited. Heard flapping and darted his face and right arm over the eave, snatched one, two, three pigeons before they could pull their feet out of the porridge.

The air in The Swimming Dog Tavern was murky with smoke, thick with the clatter of backgammon pieces and drinkers' talk.

"The mushrooms were a good idea," Kellet said, chewing, the light from the fireplace giving his left cheek an exaggerated glow. Two nearly empty wine bottles stood on the table between them.

"Mnh!" Cartwright agreed, dipping bread in his plate. "Astonishing what you can do with a wad of porridge. Just add some wine and onions and plenty of peppercorns. And Meg to cook it of course."

Kellet and Cartwright laughed and clinked their

glasses together. "To Meg! To Madame Becher! To porridge!"

Meg, who had just served them their pigeons, took the earthen baking dish back to the fireplace. "I'll leave the last one here on the hearth to keep warm," she said. Then she returned and stood at Cartwright's side, her hand at the back of his neck, her right hip touching his shoulder. Cartwright put his hand on her waist and looked up into her face.

"Do you think my friend Kellet here could stay the night too? What about Theresa? Will she be by?"

"Oh, I should think." Meg smiled openly at Kellet's red face. "We'll see the young gentleman safely housed."

✦

A wide tilting column of smoke is jutting into the sky from just beyond the crown of the meadow he's in. It must be a farmer burning old hay. He urges Thoroton forward. During his whole time since dying he's never encountered another human, not one he could talk to. He's looked in on the living, invisibly, often enough, but his own customary realm has always been empty of all but animal life. Where did his family go in their own deaths? His soul, or whatever he is, has lingered near home. Why haven't theirs? In all his ghostly hunts and rambles through the familiar countryside he's never crossed paths with his parents or with any of his four brothers and five sisters. Eventually he's bound to find John or Catherine or one of them sitting under a tree or walking some lane as lonely and baffled as himself.

The smoke just over the rise mounts into the air with unusual volume and energy. Reaching the crest of the meadow he stretches up in his stirrups to see its source,

18

and finds he's been tricked into the present again. The smoke thunders up out of the five cooling towers of the power station that stands on the site of his old family home. There is a railway below him and a highway with windshields glinting in the sun. He should have thought of this. He's seen those funnels often enough. As though some experiment of his brother Edmund's lurched out of control, swallowing the house, pinning the landscape in its cogged and levered arms.

He strokes Kaumalak's breast, then turns Thoroton back down the meadow, out from under the looming presence, into a sprinkling of birdsong.

In late December 1779, approaching his fortieth birthday, back from Labrador, exhausted, his business in ruins, his relations with Mrs. Selby at an end, Cartwright had made his way by carriage from London over the muddy roads to Marnham.

Passing through Newark, alone in the carriage, he looked for his father's bridge in the distance. Dykes and canals had drained the Muskam marshes into the Devon and Trent. To make a shortcut and avoid the toll which the bridge's current owner was trying to impose, the driver chose a humpy track to the east of the bridge, across what used to be swamp.

Cartwright counted thirteen vague arches in the evening rain. Already grass and brambles seemed to be crowning them.

At Marnham his father had embraced him tearfully, struggled to open Madeira wine, his hands trembling constantly, talked breathlessly of his latest financial schemes, plant-breeding, shares in Doncaster mills, his voice thin and brittle.

Since his father's sister, Lady Tyrconnel, had recently

died, only their daughter Catherine, their old servant Mary, and a cook were living at home with his parents now. His father led Cartwright into the conservatory, its floor and tables strewn with pots and boxes of earth. Whispering, he lifted a small potted plant and invited his son to stroke its leaves. The old man plucked a leaf, nibbled part of it, and offered the rest to Cartwright, whom he watched expectantly.

Cartwright's mouth puckered.

He had bred it himself, his father said, blinking rapidly. A thornless, edible thistle. It would alter the course of history. He was weeping again. "It will release the poor from hunger and reverse God's curse on Adam. It is a great step toward the recovery of Eden, which now must be the whole object of man's endeavour."

Black plumes pulled sideways in the wind. Cartwright has seen so many over the years, over the landscape, from chimneys and tall stacks. Coal mines, cloth mills, breweries. The cooling towers at Marnham, on top of his old house. These glimpsed billows and skeins often seem to detach themselves from their settings and come after him. Shapes like faceless banshee women, black rags streaming, hovering over his head. Reminders of Caubvick's hair.

Even Kaumalak diving sometimes is a black plume.

"Give me your hair," he had begged Caubvick. "It has to be burnt or thrown away."

Her long black hair, unusually coarse and glossy, almost like a horse's mane – he had loved to dig his fingers in it, feeling her body's pull like a river's current. It had seemed to spring not just from her skin, but from her whole history and the land that had made her. The fever had lifted it off like a wig. The potent mane was attached to a scalp-shaped layer of scabs and dried skin. "Give it to me, in the name of God," he had pleaded repeatedly as they sailed toward Labrador. "It's full of death. It will kill your people."

But Caubvick, bald, hollow-eyed, her face pitted with sores, had locked her hair in her trunk and would not give it up. As though she were guarding all that remained of her beauty.

He should have forced her, weathered her screaming, her devastation, and taken the trunk, broken it open and flung her pestilent hair into the sea. Except he knew she'd have thrown herself in after it.

He had taken so much from her already, and was grateful she had survived to spare him from having to face her people alone, explain alone what had swallowed their relatives, how he had let them slip. He wanted to handle her gently, not rob her of what little she had left.

It was like something fallen out of his hands from the brink of a cliff. He could see it falling, but could not snatch it back. The most precious thing. Falling down and down. His arms were not long enough.

Hawking and spying over the land, listening in on other periods in time, getting tangled in parts of his life and disentangling himself, finding himself back on the Nottingham road – this jolting process makes up Cartwright's days. And then there's the night, and his journal.

He never thinks of his journal until it's dark and he's in his room in The Turk's Head Inn and Kaumalak is asleep. The loneliness, the immobility of time seem to be crushing him. He's sure he's about to implode, metamorphose into some horrible thing. And then the crisis of torment passes, and a dullness sets in, and his apathetic gaze passes over his journal on the table by the extinct hearth. He takes up one of its volumes for no particular reason, becomes intrigued by some old entry, and forgets where he is again. Sometimes an idea it triggers prompts him to take up his pen and add a new passage. Sometimes he sits up all night, filling his journal's pages.

For a long time now he has continued to write in it, examining his peculiar version of being dead, recording his excursions into the current age, his luck at hawking, his memories.

It used to be, he now realizes, that when he was alive he enjoyed making entries in his journal almost as much as he did hunting. The sense of importance, the ritual gave him great pleasure, the times by the fire in the Lodge in Labrador when Mrs. Selby would hush the others because the master was writing. He enjoyed reassembling events, picking out some pattern in what had gone on, and capturing happenings in words. It was not so different from hunting, or so it used to seem.

Now, when he writes, he does so with much less order and purpose. Who will read it after all? How long will it go on? He finds himself rewriting passages almost word for word. Some evenings he only reads old entries. Sometimes he simply sits thinking with a volume in his hands and falls asleep. Is he pulling things together, making sense of his life? He can't tell.

2

1819. May. Wednesday 19.
Wind S.W. light.

When I was fourteen, I thought that India would be the door by which I would come into wealth and honour and discover my character as a man. I expected it to transform me.

Like all my fellows at the Royal Military Academy at Woolwich, I took it for granted that if one could survive the four- or five-month journey out, the advantages of being posted to India were immense. The army there was at the service of the East India Company, and although we were told that competition with the French in that part of the world had been growing, we believed that troops in India were employed in a kind of permanent guard duty rather than in marching against other well-trained armies of equal or greater strength – such as would be the case in Europe. The East India Company itself, being rich and of special interest to the men of power in our government, was a good organization with which to be involved. There would be opportunities for special services and rewards, and for forming useful associations. And in any case India was a land of fabulous wealth in disarray, where a commissioned man could enrich himself through his own dealing, or – failing that – could at least indulge himself in sport and exotic pleasure. The tiger hunting and harems were thought to enlarge one's conception of the world.

I am surprised when it occurs to me how infrequent and meagre my memories of India were during my later years, considering how readily I now can recall even small particulars of my experiences there. When I am riding on open ground I have only to look to the southeast and search far back in my memory, and my gaze seems to travel through both time and space into the very corners of the rooms I frequented at Madras when I was sixteen years old. Even the sounds and smells return to me with astounding immediacy. Yet it all seems more foreign to me now than it did when I was there. Scarcely part of my life as I've come to think of it.

Either India's door did not fully open for me, or I was fortunate to enter and exit as I did. Many went in and never came out again.

Killed a partridge just off the Newark road outside Mansfield. A fine day.

✦

In late February 1754, having graduated without honours or distinction from the Royal Military Academy, Cartwright went to Gravesend, on the sea-smelling lower Thames, to board the East Indiaman *Dodington*. The ship, bound for Madras, carried thirty-two guns, and her hull was painted with rows of false gunports so that from a distance, and flying the correct flags, she might be mistaken by inexperienced pirates for a sixty-gun ship of the line.

Kellet, Cartwright's friend from the Academy, was also making the voyage and had already loaded his belongings on board the ship. The two friends, together with eleven other cadets, were quartered in the gun room under the quarter-deck in rows of makeshift bunks. They shared the room with a few East India Company clerks, or writers as they were called, and the lieutenants accompanying a contingent of recruits going to join Colonel Aldercron's regiment at Fort St. George, the East India Company's factory at Madras. The six lieutenants had arranged canvas partitions around their bunks. The 128 recruits were packed into three tiers of hammocks in the between-decks toward the bow of the ship.

Cartwright waited in Gravesend for over a week while supplies and Company merchandise were loaded. The captain and chief officers also sent large quantities of personal provisions and trade goods on board. Some of it – casks of beer, crates of clocks – appeared in the gun room between the rows of bunks, but the lieutenants complained, and the things were removed again. Chickens were stowed under the poop deck, sheep and pigs penned in the lifeboats. Insurance agents and hawkers, ship's agents, customs men, Company officials and army officials came on board every day. Naval officers ransacked the ship several times in search of sailors who'd deserted the Royal Navy. Parties of friends and relatives visited the crew and petty officers at all hours. Cartwright and Kellet took a room in one of the dockside inns, but the extra expense and the fear of losing their bunks forced them back on the ship again.

The *Dodington*, with her gilded, trumpeting figurehead, took possession of Cartwright's imagination like a queen. The dockyard clutter, the foul harbour water in which she was moored, the confusion and crowds that covered her decks, none of that could conceal her superb spirit from his eyes. The oiled beams over his bunk seemed bravely experienced and dedicated to action. He admired her curved deck, like a well-caulked barrel, and her smell of pitch. He was eager to get to sea, after his pointless studies, out into the world where such ships and such men as himself belonged.

The day before they embarked, his father showed up to give him some last advice and some gifts. He had already paid for his son's passage and meals – the army didn't take care of these things since Cartwright wasn't commissioned yet – but to help round out his diet his father had six dozen bottles of wine, some cheeses, hams, and pots of jam carried on board, and himself helped to find places in the gun room to store his purchases. Some went into a trunk under the bed of one of the Company writers, who agreed to give up the space in exchange for a share of the wine.

1819. May. Wednesday 19.
Wind S.W. light.

It was my father who chose my career in the army. I didn't object. I had no alternative in mind.

"What do you say to Woolwich and an army commission? You've always been keen on shooting. Colonel Aldercron has offered to help and is confident that if we make appropriate arrangements it should be possible to buy you an ensign's place immediately, a lieutenancy in a year or two, and a captaincy whenever one becomes available after that. And then you can carve very nicely for yourself, as all officers above captain I've ever known have clearly been able to do."

Colonel Aldercron's regiment, the 39th of Foot, my father explained, had the reputation of being a "lucky" regiment. This meant that it had good connections with the Horse Guards and the Secretary of State for War and even with the Board of Ordnance – it was virtually unheard of for a regiment to have favourable relations with all three of these governing bodies, and as a result it enjoyed a comfortable residence most of the time at Limerick. True, it had been ordered to join the Gibraltar garrison for three years in the late twenties and afterwards was nearly sent to Jamaica – the place synonymous with yellow fever – but this is where the good connections came in; everything was put right at the last minute, and the 39th was recalled to Limerick. It looked like a stint in India might be at hand, according to Aldercron, but this wasn't necessarily a bad thing, especially when the alternatives were taken into account.

Being the founder of the Nottingham militia, my father had a lot of military connections of his own and a great deal of inside information. He urged me at all costs to avoid the 38th Regiment of Foot which had been rotting in the West Indies since 1716 and the 9th and the 18th which had been condemned to Minorca and Gibraltar since 1718.

Listening to his gossip and counsels, it was easy to believe that the army offered a worthy and colourful career. But it soon became apparent, once I'd become a cadet and was off in India, that this was only true for those with money and influence enough to purchase advanced commissions. John, who was always my father's favourite, and Charles, my youngest brother, I couldn't help noting later, were steered into the navy, which was clearly a much more prestigious and glamorous line of work. My elder brother, William, had a nominal place in the Treasury arranged for him, although I doubt that he knew where the Treasury was. Edmund, of course, went to Oxford and became a clergyman and a poet, until his real inventive genius asserted itself.

✦

On the 6th of March, Captain Bolts boarded the *Dodington*, and, together with the *Falmouth*, another East Indiaman, set sail following an escort of two frigates which led them out of the Channel and across the Bay of Biscay.

Captain Bolts was a short, thick-set man with small eyes who carried his jaw at an angle and strutted, showing his belly off like a bag of coins. On their first morning at sea he put the crew and passengers through the required gunnery drill. Only five guns could be run in and out at their ports for loading and firing. The rest were buried in cargo. A merchant with goods on board protested this lack of readiness. The captain called him a sot and put him in charge of a gun. Handspikes, sponges, and rammers were distributed. The use of the train tackle and side tackle was demonstrated, gunpowder charges and shot were handed around. Since the crew would be busy aloft in any emergency, Bolts explained, the passengers would have to manage the guns.

One recruit was injured when the ship heeled and a gun carriage rolled over his foot. Another was slightly burned when his friend gave him a pipe of tobacco mixed with gunpowder. Three cannons were successfully fired. One of the sheep on deck died of fright.

The ship's rudder tiller passed through the rear of the gun room and clanked incessantly. In rough weather off Galicia seawater poured through the openings around the tiller and through cracks in the cabin's walls, soaking the bedding and clothes. Cartwright and Kellet were both very sick for a day and then got used to the motion.

After eight days they reached Madeira. The cadets hoisted their clothing and bedding into the rigging to dry and along with everyone else went into Funchal in the lighters to buy wine and fruit. The solid land, the steep streets were voluptuous underfoot. There were birds in the flowering vines, music from taverns.

In a small street high in the town, Cartwright and Kellet discovered two of the ship's recruits with their breeches off, grappling with one another in the dirt in front of a wine shop. There were a few laughing spectators, and at first Cartwright took it for some sort of wrestling match. Then he saw the erect cocks and the efforts of one to mount the other from behind. The soldiers were both half-starved-looking – one of them seemingly lame or deformed in the legs – and both were drunk to the point of crab-like awkwardness. This sort of thing was not new to Cartwright, who had been in boarding schools for many years, but he knew it to be an offence punishable by death and never expected he'd see two grown Englishmen going at it so carelessly in the open street. He lifted a chair from a doorstep and struck the two of them with it across their backs.

The soldiers' captain to whom Cartwright reported the incident took him aside and ordered him to keep quiet about it. His company was already below muster, he was in debt for the cost of their uniforms and provisions, and losing the two recruits would also mean losing their stoppages – the amount he deducted from their pay – by which, if all went well, he'd recover the money he'd spent on them and make a profit. "Now, if they were trying to desert," he said, "or hurt one another, I'd take it more seriously." The voyage would likely kill them in any case.

The *Falmouth* reached Madeira a day behind them and was still there when they left. Out of Madeira they caught the trade winds and headed southwest. The ship's officers and crew as well as the civilian passengers all had stores of liquor and wine which they drew on throughout the day and also sold to the soldiers, whose pay was just enough to keep them drunk.

The soldiers seemed to be mostly paupers and criminals out of London jails. Their eyes were blank or full of cunning. Their mouths either gaped or smirked. Cartwright knew they were dangerous, and that he'd soon be commanding a group of them, but the feeling they gave him was more repulsion than fear. Many were sick or inclined to cringe before their superiors, and Cartwright, who was nearly six feet tall at the age of fourteen, assumed he could thrash any one of them who dared to oppose him. Every few days one or two died and had to be stitched into a piece of sail cloth and dumped in the sea. There were fights and thefts and floggings.

Cartwright wanted to learn how things were done in the army and paid close attention to all this. He stood on deck and listened while a young captain named Henry Tolly spoke to his company after a flogging. Tolly reminded his troops of their duties, the need to uphold the regiment's honour and the glory of England. He explained the army's authority over their lives and promised punishments much worse than what they had just seen. He extolled the security that the army offered them together with opportunities for personal gain and promotion. Finally he mentioned their daily rations of rum and biscuit and their uniforms, which alone, he pointed out, had saved many of them from naked beggary. To Cartwright's surprise the men cheered. Their expectations and their willingness to cooperate, he saw, were not much different from his own.

Rats ate the cheese his father had given him.

They crossed the equator at longitude 31° west, and all first-timers underwent Neptune's rites. Some were stripped and hung by their heels from the ratlines. Buckets of water were thrown eveywhere, although few had been dry to begin with. A young woman who joined the ship in Madeira, and was going to India without a Company Court of Officials' permit, struggled and cursed comically, then laughed as the water streamed down her hair and dress. The merchant, who had disagreed with Captain Bolts a number of times over some trade goods in their joint possession, was forced to run naked while the crew whipped him with knotted handkerchiefs. The merchant slipped and fell, then grabbed a sailor's knife and chased the captain, threatening to disembowel him and strangle him with his guts. Bolts fled to the quarterdeck, then immediately reappeared with a saber, offering to cut the merchant's pizzle off and stuff it into his throat. "I'm sure you've had the taste before," he roared, "but never your own!" Henry Tolly and the ship's chief mate stepped between the two and tried to dismiss the incident as a jest, but the merchant, his blotchy buttocks jiggling, vowed to bring charges before the Madras Court.

Sometimes the sea was blue and white hounds yelping and bounding in a vast hunt. Sometimes the waves were rocky uplands come to life, on the march somewhere. Cartwright was stunned by the size of the earth and its stretches of emptiness. He doubted his memories of the land. He closed his eyes, and waves invaded every image that came to mind. The hills above Marnham had been merely painted on silk, a thin layer swaying over bottomless depths. He and Kellet squatted in the gun room, drinking wine, trying to eat hardbread and jam. Their mouths were full of sores. Their joints ached. At night Cartwright lay awake listening to Kellet crying in his sleep.

They sighted then smelled the island of Fernando de Noronha where they would load fresh water and get news from other ships. They went ashore and stumbled against the ground, lay on its tipping face.

A few days later they entered the sugar port of Bahia. Like a ghost ship, Cartwright thought. The hawkers and taverns offered so much, but his appetite was only for sleep and the smell of earth. Green food, fresh food. Musicians came on board and men with slave women whom some of the soldiers and sailors paid to use. Cartwright bought a melon, cut it, buried his face in its glowing orange flesh.

At Rio de Janeiro they stopped for a week and a half, nursing their scurvy, buying fresh food, hiring crew to replace those who'd died. Portuguese ships loaded and unloaded strings of black slaves chained together by their necks. Cartwright was mesmerized by their naked pliable-looking limbs, their amazing apathy. It was as though their souls had flown out of their captured bodies and stayed in the forests where they had lived. Bodies awaiting the will of their new owners.

On a tavern terrace he and Kellet finished a platter of beefsteaks and called for a third jug of wine. The twilit harbour necklaced in lights rose up like a beautiful woman opening her arms. "I shall live here forever," Cartwright said. "I have found my home."

Southeast of Rio they hit the roaring forties, west winds that set the *Dodington* on her nose, snapped her rigging, exploded her sails. In the gun room a set of bunks collapsed, breaking a lieutenant's arm. Fever broke out among the recruits. Coming up from their cramped quarters they reeked of vomit and excrement. Nearly every day bodies were thrown into the sea.

Cape Town presented itself like a miracle after all hope for anything like it had passed. Its tiers of gardens and orderly homes, its well-rooted citizens, who had no conception of being at sea, driving their carts of produce in the morning sun. Here they stayed for nearly a month, trying to cure their diseases while the ship was being repaired. Captain Bolts advised Cartwright to tie some garden loam in a handkerchief and hold it close to his nose. "The smell of earth," he said, "is scurvy's cure."

Cartwright and Kellet ate fruit they had never heard of before and drank new wine. They had their clothing and bedding cleaned and wrote letters which the first homeward-bound ship would take in the fall.

"Honoured Madam," he wrote to his mother, "I have had the good fortune to make the acquaintance of Captain Henry Tolly of the 39th Regiment of Foot also bound for Fort St. George on the *Dodington*. He has given me much valuable counsel and assures me that an ensignancy must soon be available after our coming there. I keep tolerably well, although the salt water has devoured my shoes. . . ."

The *Falmouth* arrived a week and a half after the *Dodington*. The two groups of passengers, most of whom had never met before, embraced like relatives, and spent hours exchanging similar tales.

In town was part of a British regiment waiting for

transport to England. The ship on which they were travelling from Bombay had been taken by pirates eight months before in the Mozambique Channel. The stranded officers' eagerness to be home, their cryptic allusions to India, and the condescending pity they showed the cadets – whom they referred to as poor Griffs – were troubling, but also intriguing. There was something attractive about the experience they'd had, however horrible and unlucky it might have been.

Cartwright and Kellet talked every day of taking a carriage to Table Mountain, but never went. In their second week they felt well enough to explore the town. There were trellises, potted flowers on walls. The black girl Cartwright followed upstairs coiled and uncoiled her arms and legs around him like soft vines. Her body was the entrance to a garden. A flower opened between her legs enveloping him.

On the tavern verandah Cartwright and Kellet leaned in their chairs, singing loudly, squeezing their girlfriends' waists, making them laugh and show their fabulous teeth. The remains of fish, chops, fruit, bottles of wine were scattered over the table they rested their boot heels on. The green harbour lifted up like a gorgeous face. "I shall live here forever," Cartwright said slowly, looking deep into Kellet's eyes. "I have found my home."

At sea again, east of the Cape strong winds and the Aghulas current nearly drove them into the African coast. At dawn the *Dodington* swung southeast no more than a quarter mile from rocks. Cartwright stood on the steep deck with a group of passengers, holding tight to the rigging, and cheered. The skin on his face seemed to shiver and blur as though he had seen his life stop and change direction before him.

Near the Comoro Islands they spotted a privateer in

the distance, approaching them. Captain Bolts ordered the cargo cleared away from twenty guns, and Cartwright joined in, helping to move crates and barrels. Bolts hoisted his collection of naval flags and steered directly toward the privateer, which turned and made full sail to escape from them. Everyone on the *Dodington* drank to their lucky victory, although most also grumbled about the captain's recklessness.

They called for a day at Johanna Island, in the Comoros. Many were sick again. Many were quarrelsome because of the dangers and the length of the trip. Natives came in dug-out canoes and scrambled aboard offering things to trade, chickens and fruit, mostly, and cowrie shells. One heavily tattooed islander insisted on having an officer's wig in exchange for a small girl. Soldiers finally lifted the man and threw him over the side. Cartwright leaned on the rail and laughed with everyone else while the bedraggled savage swam ashore. His pleasure in this was not very deep, but he accepted how things were done, and the sense of being British and strong was important so far from home.

They sailed straight on in a kind of delirium, finally passing the Maldive and Laccadive Islands. A third of the original crew had succumbed to disease and exhaustion. Some actually passed away in the rigging and fell to the deck, injuring others. Forty recruits had died. After the first dozen or so deaths, the bodies were no longer stitched in precious sailcloth, but were dropped in the sea in their clothes. Uniforms were kept to be sold again.

Like everyone else, Cartwright saved one set of clothes to wear ashore and otherwise went nearly in rags. He had reached a kind of equilibrium, brown, skinny, pleased with himself in spite of his weariness, as though he could sail forever. They rounded well to the east of Ceylon, then cut back for the Coromandel coast on the southeast trades.

Fort St. George at Madras was a squat collection of buildings on a beach with breakers foaming in front. There was no port. Outriggers came to carry the passengers and the cargo ashore. Cartwright and Kellet dragged their trunks containing their few remaining belongings up on deck. The voyage had lasted almost six months. Without speaking they watched the boats come out from the brown and yellow land. It was not what Cartwright expected. It was all a mistake.

The heaviness, the unbearable load, the body four times its normal weight, pulled toward the ground, longing for greater ease, broader abandonment than the narrow barracks cot could afford. Feeling the blood pushed into his face in his long contractions, his lips and eyes near to bursting, Cartwright was certain he'd swallowed the egg of some hideous animal that had hatched inside him and was growing, taking over his body as a second shell. His face was about to split, curl back in two halves to reveal one of those fanged heads he had recently seen carved on a native shrine.

There were voices beside his bed, a tilting, a change in the light. "Welcome to Madraspatam. You've got the 'Griffin's greeting.' Everybody who comes here gets it. If you live, you'll be a regular Indian like the rest of us."

In the morning outside the gate of the fort the merchants from Black Town spread out their goods. Oddly dishevelled men in the midst of their wealth. Diamonds from Golconda, pearls from Tuticorin, rubies from Burma, sandalwood from Mysore, grain, spices, saltpetre, calico. Many officers bought and traded small gems, won them and lost them at cards, hoping through shrewd deals and good fortune to work their holdings up to a few fine stones that would make them rich in England. Cartwright did as the others, impressed by their talk of carats and brilliance. Lieutenant Squarry was pointed out to him across the parade ground, a man with a Burmese ruby worth £2000. The first thing he was told about Captain Bennet was that he had more pearls than any soldier under the rank of general.

Cartwright bought a small diamond, which others assured him was of very good quality, though to him it looked like a piece of salt. He staked it on a game of whist, hoping to win a larger gem, but lost it. He repeated this experience several times and then became bored with the huddled showing of prizes, the fussy tension around private trunks and hiding places. He had heard of the hunting in the hills to the west, of the tigers there and the deer and innumerable birds. He bought a French rifle in the market and persuaded Kellet, who had done much better at gem collecting, to sell some of his pearls and equip himself to join in trying for deer.

Along the roads, arched over by banyan trees, the air was filled with the chortling and screaming of parrots, green streaks as they swooped, criss-crossing, from branch to branch. Among the leaves countless bats hung by their claws making a piercing noise. The guide, a wrinkled, scholarly looking man, stopped, pointed his stick at one of the bats, waited for Cartwright to observe it and then lean close to receive his words.

"This fowl," he said, raising his voice over the shrill-ness, "engendereth in the ear."

Cartwright looked back and forth from the bat to the guide several times. "How . . . ? How are the young born then?"

The guide studied his face for a moment.

"In the ear!"

Near a village, stopping for lunch, Kellet uncorked a bottle of beer, the white foam spilling out. The local people, seeing this, spoke together excitedly. The guide explained: "It is not the sight of the drink flying out of the bottle they speak of, but the question of how such liquor could ever be put in."

"Ah, the marvels of England," Kellet said. "More. More to come." He handed bottles of beer to the two men standing nearest to him.

There were dinner parties and dances every night at the homes of the Company's senior officials or the rich English merchants. Their city houses had dozens of servants and large banquet rooms illuminated by chandeliers. Their country houses were set among gardens of jasmine, mangoes, and plums where the guests could dine in pergolas screened with muslin and hung with coloured lamps. Musicians played, and uniformed guards patrolled the grounds, firing their muskets periodically to frighten bandits away.

The cadets and officers were always invited. Food and drink were cheap, and the soldiers' uniforms were highly appreciated. There was a shortage of single English ladies, however, and the soldiers often found themselves standing in groups, holding cheroots and glasses of punch, watching others flirt and dance. The unmarried ladies who had made it out to Madras, with or without the Company's permission, were hunting for wealthy husbands, and so automatically overlooked the soldiers as though they were potted plants. The most the soldiers could hope to get from the single ladies, unless their jewel-trading was flourishing or they were developing lucrative business connections, was exercise on the dance floor and maybe, if they were extremely handsome and lucky, a short, secret affair.

Many married ladies had more to give. They picked their lovers from among the cadets and young officers, perhaps gave them small sums of money to help pay their debts, and introduced them to people in business or the Company council who might help to advance their careers. The soldiers, aware they were being played with, flirted and flattered with theatrical charm, trying to get whatever they could.

✦

1755, September 18

Honoured Sir,

I have recently obtained a commission as ensign in Colonel Aldercron's regiment by the death of Captain Lyon. I am highly satisfied with my position and hopeful that, if the opportunity arises and the means are available to me, I shall be able to advance to lieutenant within another year. Fevers are frequent here, and I, like the others, have often suffered, but have developed some resistance I believe through the use of cotton undergarments and the drinking of infusions made from medicinal plants. The heat surpasses my ability to describe it. There are many wonders and curiosities among the people, their customs and buildings, and in the natural world, which you would enjoy. But for all that, life in the garrison is often tedious. There is a large number of English here in the town, who live much as they do at home, except with more gaiety. I hope this finds you, Mother, and all the family in good health. The purchase of my commission has come near to exhausting the last of my resources. I shall be most grateful if you could help to restore my ability to take full advantage of the opportunities here.

Your devoted son ever,

George

✧

The Company factors worked from nine in the morning till noon, then dined and napped and dressed to go partying. They had separate servants to care for each of their needs, even hookha-bundars to service their hookhas and light them after dinner or keep them drawing well while they lay calmly puffing under the hands of the perruquier. All the English, apart from those in the army, dressed in elaborate style, flowered coats and waistcoats, brightly dyed stockings and shoes. The ladies' evening wigs were heaped in three tiers with combs and ringlets at the sides, their bodices were cut to reveal the edges of the nipples of their up-thrust breasts. There were pages with parasols and fans, costumed bearers with silk-lined palanquins. In the cool of the morning, parties would have themselves carried out with baskets of cold meat and wine to picnic on carpets and cushions in the groves of mango trees.

The soldiers were forbidden to go out of the fort in anything but their regulation uniforms. Many times Cartwright packed his long limbs into a small palanquin and had himself jogged out through the dust to some

40

fragrant garden party, sweating and cursing in his braid-loaded coat.

✦

3 June 1756

Dear George,

We have today received your letter of last September, and rejoice in the news of your good health and your successful obtainment of a commission. My special congratulations.

We are all well, and life in Marnham proceeds much as ever. Edmund has so far convinced his masters, and all of us, of his abilities as a scholar that I am resolved to send him to Oxford for his further education. My hope for John, when he has concluded his studies at Heath, is that he will consent to stay at Marnham and make his career in managing the estate in my place. Elizabeth plays with charming skill on the new clavichord. Mr. Crawford, whose family are drapers in Nottingham, has asked to marry her.

Unfortunately, my investment in the Newark carting firm has not proved as fruitful as I had reason to expect it would. Nor has the business of the Muskham bridge been resolved, although I believe some progress in that area can soon be expected. The problem is a general blindness to the advantages of improved transportation.

Providing for your brothers' careers, yours also, and for your sisters' marriages, is a worthy charge on the family's small resources. I shall continue to do all I can to promote your concerns in your far corner of the earth, and pray you are not disappointed.

Your loving father ever,

William Cartwright

A lady redolent of spiced punch whispered to him about her predicament. Her husband, when she married him a year ago, had recently made a fortune selling glassware through raffles and lotteries. He was now busy losing it at cards. Her breasts brushed Cartwright's coat as she spoke.

There was a stone bench behind a hedge beyond the last lantern. Lying down on it she gripped Cartwright's silver-trimmed lapels and dug her shoe heels into the sides of his bare buttocks. Rocking and twisting against him she made a surprising amount of noise which the shrill night insects and the rasping musicians conveniently covered. Then she sat up, pushed him away, and vomited into an urn of chrysanthemums.

There was always a disagreement between the way Cartwright saw himself and the way others saw him. Given his family's former wealth, his connection with Lord Tyrconnel, his father's respected place in Nottinghamshire, Cartwright considered himself equal at least to most of the English in Madras. Superior certainly to the little merchants' and factors' wives who let him toy with them and treated him like a penniless soldier-boy. But the disagreement went deeper than that. Cartwright knew that others often thought him boorish or dull. It was expected that country gentlemen like himself would be addicted to hunting and sports, but his fondness for getting dirty was too extreme. He seemed to come into his own sitting up in the branches of trees or chasing wild pigs. And he did these things without the usual sporting mannerisms, the air of fellowship and ritual. Instead, he seemed alone, aiming his gun, rushing ahead through the underbrush, absorbed in an instinct or passion all his own. It was the same when he wrestled or played fives with his fellow officers. He was unbeatable, but he went further than necessary to win. He wasn't playing so much as going wild, in a very efficient way. The officers were in awe of him, but dismissed his threat to their own sense of superiority by thinking of him as barbaric, peasant-like.

And even the most rustic country squire was expected to be able to display good manners in polite company. Cartwright could do this, but half of the time he chose not to. In the middle of dinner he would jump up and insist on trading his coat for a native musician's or servant's jacket and then talk at length about the superiority of Indian clothing to the kind of thing his fellow diners were wearing. Or he would try to organize a game of skittles using melons and empty bottles, or he would imitate the movements of animals, or suddenly turn and leave the room during a dance, abandoning his partner in the centre of the floor. The fact that these people took so seriously things that often irritated and bored him made him look down on them. The fact that he disregarded the things that they valued made them look down on him.

But Cartwright was never completely cut off from others, because he could also be amusing and talkative. At times he could spark a general sense of fun, urging people into outrageous antics, competitions where men climbed pyramids of furniture, races in which ladies rode on teams of men. He would appear at friends' homes with gifts – not always dead birds – and invite them to go with him in a boat on the river or to witness a festival at a neighbouring village. He would tell hunting stories, and ladies would listen, finding his ruggedness colourful. But the precise details he used to elaborate his tales, the horrors and ordeals he described, the passionate gleam in his eyes, would tell them finally that he was not presenting the stories in an effort to win their favour, but out of a private obsession of his own, and they would feel vaguely offended by him and turn away.

In any case, Cartwright never cared much for the English women in Madras. He preferred Portuguese ayahs and the ladies in dim Indian houses with grass-screened windows dampened for coolness and nearly bare rooms with tea and small glasses of arak on a tray.

He and Kellet went on hunting trips whenever they could, sleeping at night in hammocks in village gardens or forest trees. Their hunting tunics, waistcoats, and blouses, dirty and unbuttoned, they finally exchanged for native shirts. Eating from broad leaves by campfires, they talked with local men. "Have you ever killed a tiger? Why do you wrap your head in cloth? Why do you have so many gods?"

But apart from birds and a few wild pigs, game was scarce in the neighbourhood of Madras, and it was rarely possible to get a long enough leave to permit an excursion to the Eastern Ghats. The Mahrattas were said to be gathering in the Deccan. The French were said to be planning another attack.

Lying on his barracks cot in the afternoons, Cartwright was sometimes overwhelmed with boredom. He had never imagined time could stop like that. He heard the tile roof cracking in the sun, flies buzzing, cicadas shrilling in the trees at the compound's edge. Cicadas, he found, had the power to bring time to a standstill, the power even to turn it back. He was sure, as he listened to them, that he heard the sounds of an afternoon from a thousand years ago. He could hear bits of whitewash, bits of clay fall from the wall in tiny grains.

Devika had long black hair in a braid. She wore a thin silver ring in her left nostril, and her eyes were remarkably full of health, completely at ease with whatever they met. Vigour and business were in her eyes, and amusement. But no mockery or arrogance. They seemed to Cartwright like black birds in the wild going about their affairs with frank appetite.

She entered the room still speaking loudly over her shoulder to a woman outside, perhaps a relative, who was cooking over a small fire, preparing food for a group of children playing with masks on sticks. It was always like this where Devika lived. An old woman, nearly blind, would be spreading wet clothes on a scaffold of canes beside a wall. A child would be milking a goat or feeding chickens. A farmer would be standing over his basket of greens entertaining a group with some story of rural wonders. Everywhere there were looms and women weaving and bunches of plants drying under cane canopies and boys prodding at skeins of thread in tubs of dye. Devika wove muslin and mended the officers' uniforms.

She was still speaking over her shoulder, involved in what was happening outside, as she turned to Cartwright and began to unwind her sari. Her eyes when they touched on him did not glance down or distance themselves or put on a mannered seductiveness. They took him in fully, they seemed to enjoy what they saw. His being so fully alive. His anticipation of her. He felt like a section of river, a young horse.

✧

It was rumoured that France was sending Dupleix to Pondicherry again with six ships of the line and three thousand regular troops to mount another attack on Madras. Cartwright drilled a company of sepoys, trying to teach them the art of rolling musketry – march, halt, load, fire, march, halt, load, fire – the invincible, ugly routine. "You are not individual warriors! Imagine you are the spokes in a giant wheel! Together you will roll over your enemies, crushing them!"

Their faces seemed to change every day, half the company somehow slipping out of the garrison each night, and replacements, brothers, cousins, slipping in. "Tell that one in the front rank he must fire with one knee on the ground, not standing – unless he wants his head blown off by the man behind him. . . . What's the matter with him? He was doing it properly yesterday."

"Sir, he was not here yesterday."

When the Viceroy of the Deccan, Nizam-ul-mulk, died, his estranged son, Nazir Jang, seized the treasury at Aurangabad and proclaimed himself viceroy. Nizam-ul-mulk's chosen successor, his grandson Muzaffar Jang, was thus displaced and went to Satara hoping to win the support of the Mahrattas in claiming his right to rule the Deccan. Meanwhile, Dupleix, the French governor of Pondicherry, was scheming to undermine the position of the hostile Nawab of Arcot, Anwar-ud-din, who was a supporter of Nazir Jang. Dupleix paid the ransom for Chundah Sahib, the son-in-law of the previous Nawab of Arcot, who had been languishing in a Mahratta prison. Once freed, Chundah Sahib also began travelling about the Deccan trying to persuade the Mahratta nobles to help him win back the Carnatic from Anwar-ud-din. Chundah Sahib and Muzaffar Jang, with their similar causes, met and joined forces in order to wage war against both Anwar-ud-din and Nazir Jang. As they had hoped, Dupleix sent General d'Auteuil with four hundred French soldiers and two thousand sepoys to assist them. In the pass near Ambur, Anwar-ud-din, with his ally Mohammed Ali, the ruler of Trichinopoly, met them in battle. Anwar-ud-din was killed and his army defeated, but Mohammed Ali escaped to Trichinopoly where he was joined by a British force of two hundred men from Fort St. David under General Cope. Nazir Jang then began to move his army of three hundred thousand toward the Carnatic to attack Muzaffar Jang and Chundah Sahib and to punish the French in Pondicherry. Cope and Mohammed Ali joined forces with Nazir Jang. The French army mutinied, Chundah Sahib fled, Muzaffar Jang was captured and put in chains. His uncle, Nazir Jang, satisfied with his victory, returned to his palace in Arcot and disbanded most of his army. Chundah Sahib then regrouped his army and together with a French detachment under d'Auteuil attacked Nazir Jang and Mohammed Ali in Arcot. Many of Nazir Jang's nobles had been turned against him by the schemes of Dupleix, and one of them, the Nawab of Cuddapah, decapitated Nazir Jang and mounted his head on a spear. Muzaffar Jang was released from his chains and proclaimed the new Viceroy of the Deccan. But soon after, while marching with French forces under Bussy to the capital of the Deccan in Aurangabad, Muzaffar Jang himself was murdered by a rebellious noble. Bussy immediately declared Muzaffar Jang's uncle, Salabat

Jang, the new viceroy, and the march to Aurangabad resumed.

In Madras everyone was talking about the new writer, a Mr. Livingstone, who wore his hair so heavily larded with pomade that the rats, attracted by its smell, bit through his hairnet while he was sleeping and ate up all his hair.

Devika would turn in the doorway, the dark warmth rising in her face, her braceleted arms unwinding the light cloth.

✦

A small gecko patrolled the wall above their cots. Distant cicadas sharpened the silence.

"What I ought to do, Kellet . . . is take care of my family's land. My father would just as soon not be bothered. But he wants my brother, John, to take it on . . . although John wants to fight for Frederick the Great or join the navy. So he thinks. There's always so much going on at Marnham, so much every season that has to be done. And there's sense in the work. Not like these merchants here . . . or the army. They're always at tug-o-war with someone else. Most likely whoever they call their friend."

"Listen to you! You'd be bored at Marnham. And nobody likes a tug-o-war more than you."

"I mean . . . disguised tug-o-wars. And I couldn't be more bored than I am here."

"My father says a man is either a peasant or a thief. And I don't want to be a peasant," Kellet said.

"Really? Is that why you joined the army? To be a thief?"

"I joined so I could retire. I've got two brothers between me and my father's estate. I'll have money enough to live on whatever happens. But my father says you have to have something to retire from. Captain or general is something the village will tip its hat to for fifty or sixty years."

"My case is different." Cartwright looked out the window, the sun on the empty parade ground. "I'm doing it for the money, I'm afraid."

✦

It was the moment he'd come for.

When the news came to Madras that the Nawab of Bengal had taken the East India Comapany's fort at Calcutta and killed over a hundred and twenty British soldiers by locking them in a small airless room, the council at Madras immediately organized an expedition to recapture Calcutta. Admiral Watson, who had recently brought his fleet to Madras with Robert Clive on board, was willing to commit all his ships to the operation. Colonel Aldercron, commander of the 39th Foot in which Cartwright had been made an ensign, agreed to take his whole regiment to Calcutta provided that he was made commander of the expedition's operations on land. Aldercron considered himself strictly an officer in His Majesty's service, answerable only to the King and the army's governing bodies; he disliked taking orders from the East India Company and its presidencies' councils, and would not promise to return his regiment to Madras at the governor's request. The Madras council, afraid of a French attack, wanted to see the expedition led by someone who would continue to be responsive to their own needs. Since there was also some doubt about Aldercron's knowledge of Indian warfare, the Madras council refused to appoint him as commander and chose Robert Clive instead.

Aldercron was furious. He was jealous of Clive's successes and regarded him as a fraud, an opportunistic clerk, not a soldier at all. Aldercron would not permit any of his troops to serve under Clive and even ordered a detachment of Royal Artillery, already on board ship, to disembark.

Cartwright saw Aldercron leave the council chamber and stride to his quarters followed by a group of silent, embarrassed officers. Aldercron's face was white, he cleared his throat and spat repeatedly as he walked.

For four days Aldercron stayed in his quarters in the fort. A few individual councillors called on him, but were unable to change his mind. At last Admiral Watson, who had long since readied his fleet to depart, had himself rowed ashore and walked alone through the garrison to Aldercron's door. Aldercron couldn't refuse Watson's request for troops because Watson was another high-ranking officer in His Majesty's service, not merely an East India Company agent. He agreed to contribute three of his companies, provided they served only as marines under Watson's command, not as land forces under Clive.

Which companies would be chosen to go? Like everyone, Cartwright wanted to be included and was afraid. He wanted to be one of the ones with stories to tell. The garrison, already boring, would become a shameful place, a foolish place for those left behind. Of course if he were selected to go, he might be killed in any number of ways, and the expedition was bound to be strenuous and unpleasant at the very least. But the only way to win fame and rewards in the army was to be in on some victory, and there was always the chance of spoils or a share in a ransom fee.

News of which companies Aldercron had picked to send with Watson flashed through the fort in one wave of excited running, opening of doors, and shouting. Cartwright's company was not one of the chosen ones. So that was that. He stood staring blankly at his cot. And then had to pass a sleepless night listening to the singing and shouts from the barracks of the men who were bound for action.

The following morning, he watched the lucky officers assembling their troops on shore, conducting them out to Watson's fleet. Crossing the surf, the open transport boats were pitched almost vertical on their sterns, water breaking over the backs of the troops, the officers standing upright, their faces expressionless. Many were men Cartwright had scarcely noticed before. They looked suddenly handsome and important. The real affairs of the regiment, it struck him now, the achievements, the consequential alliances, had been taking place somewhere completely beyond him.

✧

"What are you keeping in there?"

"Never mind." Kellet turned his back to Cartwright while fitting the lid on a large biscuit tin which he quickly slid under his cot.

Cartwright tried to reach under the cot, but Kellet tackled him around the waist and pulled him away. Cartwright laughed and wrestled with Kellet, who fought with more determination than usual. He pushed Cartwright backwards over a wicker trunk, but

Cartwright finally pinned Kellet by sitting on his back and pulling his leg up by the ankle. "It's a collection," Kellet said. "Stop it for Christ sake! It's just a collection of things."

While Kellet tucked his shirt into his breeches and buttoned his cuffs, Cartwright opened the tin. On a layer of cork lined with light blue damask there were rows of insects held in place by pins. Cartwright glanced at Kellet. As far as he knew, Kellet hated bugs. It was one of the reasons he longed for home. "Just imagine," he used to say, "sleeping without a mosquito net . . . putting your boots on without any danger of being killed by a scorpion. Everything here bites or stings. I'll bet even the butterflies are poisonous."

Kellet moved over beside him, looking into the tin.

"I started with the ones that were biting me." He pointed to rows of fleas, bed bugs, ticks, mosquitoes, bees, wasps, scorpions, centipedes, and spiders. There were even nearly invisible lice.

"Then I got interested in the bigger ones. Rhinoceros beetles, scarabs, locusts, cicadas. Roaches of course. These ones are all coleoptera. This is a death's-head moth. It squeaks like a bat when you catch it."

Cartwright placed the lid carefully on the tin and handed it back to Kellet. "Jesus Christ," he said, "we've got to get a tiger before we get out of here. Or the fever or Madame Mendonca's arak finishes us."

"They're too far away," Kellet said. "We'll never have time to go after them."

✦

Devika's soft arms moving in waves, unwinding the thin cloth. "My cousin says you are robbing us. I say you are giving me many pagodas, but he says you and your people are taking more than you bring. You must leave your clothes for mending with my aunt and not come into the house again."

"Will you miss me if I stay away?"

Her face strange, surprised at the question. "No. I have many things. I never think of you when you are not here."

✧

While most of their regiment was up in Calcutta earning riches and glory, Cartwright and Kellet were sent out from Fort St. George in charge of a company of sepoys and British soldiers. Their leader was Captain Pelham, who was suffering from dysentery. Their job was to help the Nawab of Arcot gather his taxes from the citizens of a mud-walled village in the hills west of Madras.

The column they led was composed of a few dragoons, sixty foot-soldiers, two eight-pound guns carried by elephants, an ox-cart baggage train with Indian drivers, and a straggling collection of water carts, litters, hand-pulled barrows, herds of sheep.

The road out of Madras was a sleeping creature that woke up and joined the column. It rose and attached itself to faces and clothes, wagons and animals, colouring everything like the land itself a burnt rusty beige. The column moved muffled and screened from the countryside in a caterpillar of dust. The men's eyes blinked surprisingly white, their mouths cracked open pink in identical masks. Even up in the forested hills the valley dust followed them, hovering around each of them in a separate cloud.

Cows, camels, fakhirs, beggars, children, musicians,

prostitutes, vendors of water and food that were in the road or under the banyan trees beside it, rose up and joined the column as well.

Cartwright and Kellet rode in front where at first the dust was thinnest. The sick Captain Pelham had himself carried in a closed palanquin behind the dragoons.

Word of the company's orders and destination spread back through the troops to the baggage train and the followers. These last, non-military members of the expedition, being familiar with the road to the village, took shortcuts across open fields, behind cane brakes, and waited for the column of troops to catch up with them. An old woman riding a donkey led the way in choosing the shorter routes. She was followed by the ox carts, the water carriers, the various vendors, spectators, and herds of animals.

When Pelham saw his own baggage train waiting in the road ahead surrounded by a ragged bleating horde half hidden in dust, he went mad with rage. He crept from his palanquin, bent and stiff, and approached the ox carts, screaming at them to keep to the rear and follow the road. Not trusting anyone to relay his orders in the midst of such confusion, he hobbled into the brown clouds himself, gesturing and bellowing his commands to the dust-coated porters and drivers individually. They nodded and smiled, pleased with his demonstration.

An hour later they were resting again at the top of a rise in the road, their oxen placidly chewing, waiting for the troops to catch up with them.

Pelham raved with such exertion that the sweat streaming on his face formed mud rivulets like grotesquely swollen veins. Cartwright helped the captain back into his palanquin, then asked the carters to tell him who was the best guide to the region's trails. The old woman on the donkey was pointed out. He invited her to ride between himself and Kellet, and after distributing water to the troops, he ordered the column to proceed, following the woman's chosen route.

The tax-dodging village lay at the head of a valley of green terraced fields. Although the company reached it a full day ahead of schedule, the villagers seemed to be ready for them. No sound came from behind the mud walls, which bristled with muskets and were lined with guards.

The British gunners, each coughing inside a thick brown cloud, unloaded their guns from the backs of the elephants and set them up. At a signal they fired two balls into the main gate. A spout of dust, chaff, and squawking chickens flew up, and the gate and much of the adjoining wall collapsed. When most of the dust had cleared, a flag was seen waving over the rubble and a small sing-song voice was heard.

Two elderly white-robed men climbed over the shattered gate carrying a wooden chest. The Nawab's tax collector who had accompanied the column, always several miles behind in clearer air, arrived just at that moment and without pausing had his palanquin bearers carry him forward to inspect the offering.

Although the tax collector was himself Tamil, like the villagers, because he was on state business he would speak only in Persian, and communicated with the villagers through his interpreter.

Not taking any chances, Cartwright had the cannons loaded and aimed again and led a detachment of troops into the village. The place was deserted. The bristling muskets were merely carved sticks. The guards were straw effigies with painted masks. Cartloads of grain, baskets of cheese had been left in a central square for the Nawab's men.

The elders, followed by the tax collector with his

bearers and retinue, came jostling in amongst the British detachment. The tax collector stepped from his palanquin to personally sniff the cheeses and probe the carts of grain with a gilded staff. A disagreement flared up. The tax collector returned to his palanquin, waving his hand dismissively. The elders surrounded his silk-curtained vehicle, howling, gesturing tragically. Cartwright asked the company's sepoy translator to investigate. The sepoy spoke to the elders and to the tax collector's interpreter who in turn bowed and spoke to the tax collector behind his curtains.

After a lengthy exchange the sepoy returned, stamped, saluted smartly in an explosion of dust, and made his report. It was a question of transport, he said. The elders claimed that the village men were away on business in the hills and unavailable to drive the carts which were in any case village property and were to be either unloaded there or returned, according to written agreement, after the Nawab's men had borrowed them. The tax collector refused to accept the goods until delivered. He said he would have the British demolish the village unless drivers were found.

"Tell them," Cartwright said, "that we'll bloody well not destroy anyone's village, and that we do not take orders from the harem master there in his travelling bed. But to complete the arrangement that was made, we'll drive the carts to Madras ourselves. It saves boot leather. If the villagers want their carts and oxen back they can send people to get them."

Captain Pelham struggled out of his litter, still enveloped in dust, objecting to what he called this dishonour to the regiment and the King. They were not mere drivers and carters, he cried. "But we are mere assasins and bullies," Cartwright said. He brushed past Pelham and ordered their men to hitch the carts to whatever animals could be found, and to take turns riding in with the grain and cheese.

Pelham dogged Cartwright's footsteps, repeating feverishly, "You'll pay for this, Cartwright. This is misconduct, this is a breach of our standing orders."

"It's better than making them march in this heat," Cartwright said. "Let's get away from here."

✦

In July 1757, after only three years in India, the 39th Regiment was recalled to Ireland. Colonel Aldercron's connections were again serving him well. The Madras council wasn't unhappy to see them go. Reinforcements, fresh faces were on their way.

Cartwright rode out through the breakers with a detachment of men in a small boat as he had watched so many others do, trying to stand upright, trying to keep his uniform dry. The coast spread out gradually, the background hills rising into view, the same sight as when he arrived, but now articulate with names and associations in every feature. And yet aloof. The whole place awhirl with its own affairs, its feuds and imperatives. None of it paused to watch him go.

1819. May. Wednesday 19.
Wind S.W. light.

My old friend Kellet. Without him how lonely I would have been.

And yet I always felt he was inferior to me, mainly I suppose because he was physically smaller and less expressive. But his father was wealthier than mine and more generous, and he had a way of winning favour. This I never understood since to me he seemed somewhat insipid.

When the three chosen companies of the 39th returned rich and glorious from Bengal, there were gaps in the ranks to be filled. Kellet, through the good graces of his father and his own good fortune in dealing in gems, was positioned to take advantage and immediately purchased a lieutenancy. He urged me to accept a loan in order to do the same, but, as none of the captains had offered an opening to me, I declined. There was nothing for me to do but congratulate him. Fortunately we were not in the same company, so I did not have the mortification of serving directly under him. And although our friendship cooled and our circle of associates began to divide, we continued on sociable terms even during the voyage home.

3

In Madras, the night was like velvet a perfumed lady had worn. It had her body's warmth in it and her smell.

On the terrace, a young woman was playfully calling to him. "Mr. Cartwright, climb up and find my fan for me, please. These others are too mean. And too cowardly." The "others" – two officers from Cartwright's regiment – began tickling her and threatening to pull on certain ribbons in her dress. In a game of keep-away, earlier, one of the men had spun her grass fan too high overhead, and it had disappeard in the dark boughs of a mango tree, beyond the glow of the coloured lanterns. Cartwright stepped from the lighted doorway, grasped a low branch and disappeared upwards, in the direction the fan had gone.

When his eyes had adjusted, the fan was easy to see and to retrieve. He rustled along a thick limb and reached to take it, and then noticed, not ten feet from him, a pair of whitish-green eyes. It was a leopard, stretched on a neighbouring branch, its tail hanging, swinging slowly, curling up at the tip ever so slightly at the end of each pass. Holding the fan, Cartwright crouched and watched the leopard. The leopard watched him.

"Have you got it? . . . What are you doing up there? Don't pull *that*! Fly down, Mr. Cartwright! Save me from these brutes!"

"Cartwright cannot save you. He has fled. His lust for you has transformed him into an ape!"

The squeals and laughter continued below, no more noticeable than the sounds of the insects. The leopard's tail swung and curled.

"Cartwright! . . . *Cartwright!*"

"Christ. He really has gone. What a peculiar bugger."

The terrace had emptied, but the tall ballroom windows behind it still thrived with light and activity. Music now flared up, like a stronger form of the light and laughter. The leopard, he noticed, had turned its face to the window. Cartwright arranged his heels more comfortably on the branch and did the same.

Ladies in gowns, poised uniformed gentlemen, spun past the window. Bodices. Slippers. Tunics. Satin coats.

Like a flower. Or a kind of toy.

The past clamours and poses in Cartwright's mind, and he sketches it in his journal's pages, labours at details in a kind of trance, his hand leaving its trail of small script.

The candles flutter and drip – he always burns two, set in holders of pewter and narwhal tusk, one near his page, one on a shelf to his left – and his pen scratches loudly over the paper. There is usually no other sound. Kaumalak sleeps on her perch in the shadows behind him. On a pile of folded maps on his desk, a round silver medal gleams in the candles' light.

Some nights the wind moans and talks in the chimney and the shutters creak. When this happens, which is very rarely, Cartwright surfaces out of his journal and pays attention, hoping the wind will grow and develop into something emphatic. Howling and banging. Lashing broadsides of rain. Jolts of lightning giving a greenish glimpse of the courtyard in its midnight life, with bats jerking through backward turns in the streaming air, and rats scuttling down walls. The earth opening, the curtain of the visible world being torn aside. Some vast fundamental change. But the slight sobbing and rattling always die gently away. If he opens his window and leans out, what he sees is a starry, moonless sky, the dark outline of roofs and trees. The earth is completely black, completely still.

He is practically never tired. He sleeps for the sake of variety or because his thoughts have become too repetitive or have stopped. When he stays up writing through the night it's because some memory or idea has occurred to him that seems new or rare and following it, capturing it, gives him the feeling of growth. In the back of his mind is always the notion that some insight, some as yet unthought thought or unremembered memory is needed to complete his life and allow him to get on with his death. He feels certain that where he is now cannot be the end.

1819. May. Wedneday 19.
Wind S.W. light.

Through the retirements and promotions that took
place once the 39th had returned to Limerick, and with
my father's cooperation, I was at last able to purchase a
lieutenancy. Aldercron held the option to buy back most
of his officers' commissions for a set fee and sell them
again to the highest bidder. Although my father admired
the man and thought him a benefactor, I knew that
Aldercron was doing us no special favours. The price of
my lieutenancy was very high.

I also knew that this was the last large contribution
toward my career I could expect to receive from my
father and that I would have to go the rest of the way on
my own merits and through my own financial arrangements. He did of course continue to help me by exerting
influence and arranging introductions through our family and his circle of associates. And for this I was grateful.
Although in the end I suppose it never did me much
good. And even at the time I always suspected he
reserved his best efforts for John.

In any case, I got my commission from Aldercron and
went looking for Kellet, who was quartered in another
building, thinking to share my good news and renew
our friendship on a more equal footing. I discovered him
already partying with a group of senior officers. He was
celebrating the fact that he had, that same morning,
purchased a captaincy from Aldercron – and for less than
what my lieutenancy had cost.

We congratulated one another and shared a couple of
drinks, but I was angry and embarrassed. I felt I was
intruding where I had not been invited, and I soon went
away.

After that, I would listen to Kellet addressing his company or giving his subordinates some task, and the sound of his thin, piping voice would fill me with contempt. I knew that I was a better officer, stronger, more decisive, more skilled at arms, and with a far finer voice and manner for giving commands. It astonished me that no one laughed behind Kellet's back – the junior officers seemed to respect him as much as they did the rest of the captains and senior men – and that so little notice was taken of me.

Contrary to the opinion many had of the army, it often seemed to me to be a haven for idlers and charlatans. The unequal rewards for service frustrated me, the repetitive talk in the officers' mess filled me with impatience. I preferred to be out riding or at least visiting inns in the countryside if I wasn't involved in active duty of some kind. Yet I had no alternative to the army in mind. I assumed I would have to learn to advance within it, on its terms.

Later, when I mentioned these frustrations to my brother John – we were sailing together to Newfoundland – he urged me to make them public, write letters to papers, publish a pamphlet exposing the army for what it was and recommending an end to the system of purchased commissions and the other abuses whereby the senior officers enriched themselves, and the Crown and the nation were robbed. John himself had begun to do this sort of thing, write letters to papers criticizing injustices, recommending reforms. He was still in the navy at the time, and it surprised me that he thought he could both defend his country with arms and attack it with opinions.

He argued that as long as he appealed to truth and justice – on which he said we had to believe our nation was founded – he should have nothing to fear. I was more practical. I saw no reason to bring trouble on myself. Nor did I have the eloquence to frame my complaints in such a way as to win other people's support. Or the appetite. The idea of making my dissatisfactions public struck me as cowardly if not traitorous, as though going over the head of the King to the mob. The King and the highest men in the country, I believed, were essentially just and honourable, and we had to support them because our nation's pride and strength depended on it. Lower men, the captains and generals in places like Limerick, might be corrupt and lazy, but the men at the very top certainly were not, and if I could only make myself known to them, through the right connections, I would be recognized, and any wrongs which I might bring to their attention would be addressed.

I believed in government by gentlemen. But, although I was hurt by the army's treatment of me, I was not much concerned with the general issues of truth and justice. I simply wanted to get ahead. John felt secure, perhaps, in attacking people in power because our family's lands had been promised to him and he knew he wouldn't need to depend on a naval commission all his life.

I am ungenerous. John was braver than I.

And yet, was he wiser? What has giving the vote to the rabble achieved? I have peeked in on the present often enough to know that little has changed. Some of the old injustice is gone. There is less disease, and people have more machines with which to amuse themselves. But this is unjust in another sense. Considering the way they live, they deserve disease. In their greedy millions they are choking the earth. They will never vote themselves under control.

I am ungenerous again.

1819. May. Wednesday 19.
Wind S.W. light.

At Limerick I constructed in my imagination a social fortress to advance my cause in the midst of my enemies. I pictured an invincible configuration of allies in the classic star-shaped trace, like Vauban's citadel in Strasbourg. I of course was at the citadel's centre. My father was in the bastion in one of the star's points. John was in another, advancing my cause through his association with Lord Howe. Colonel Aldercron, I continued to hope, would hold another of the points. My aunt, Lady Tyrconnel, held another. Although living in my father's house in retirement since her husband's death, it was remarkable how many favours she could procure through her correspondence. Various other friends and relatives constituted my forward defences – my ravelins and hornworks – but I was lacking a fifth major point to complete my star.

And this is where Aldercron surprisingly came to my aid. Perhaps he felt some discomfort at how I'd been treated. Or recognized my genuine hunger for action. Perhaps he merely wanted to be rid of me. There was intense sympathy in England then for Frederick the Second of Prussia who, in an effort to carve out a nation for himself, was waging war against France, Austria, Russia, Sweden, and Saxony. Apart from Portugal, which was of no account, we British were his only ally. Everyone was mad with admiration for his bravery. Even John was caught up in this passion. When John finished his schooling, my father and aunt wanted him to stay at home in Marnham and learn to manage the estate (William, my older brother, was incapable, and I was off in India, and had apparently also proved myself unfit to be chief heir), but John would have none of the insipid career they had planned for him, and ran away intending to join the Prussian army. My father's steward caught up with him in Stamford and persuaded him to return home. In any case, everyone's head was full of the battles of Zorndorf and Minden, and so when Aldercron sent for me and asked if I'd care to be transferred to serve as aide-de-camp to the Marquis of Granby, Commander in Chief of the British forces in Germany, I was beside myself with joy. The Marquis of Granby would be the fifth point in my citadel's star.

To be aide-de-camp was no promotion in rank as such. Nor did it entail a rise in pay. But the opportunity it presented for me to prove myself, to acquire experience and rise through new associations with men of power, was vast beyond calculation.

I invited Kellet and other friends to celebrate in sharing a case of brandy with me. But he, and everyone else, was strangely subdued. I suppose his exalted position with Aldercron, who was likely to stay ensconced in his Limerick garrison for an indefinite time, was not as satisfying to him as it had recently seemed. It often appeared to me during my life, in situations of special success on my side and others', that I generally gave more congratulations than I received.

✦

Woodsmoke. Campfire smoke. Rubbish, fences, straw, fruit trees, pieces of barns and carts, all smouldering in piles. The smell of shit coming from everywhere, the latrine trenches, roadside ditches, every thicket and bush near to the camps. Wet dirt churned up by hoofs and feet. Gunpowder smoke. The salty clinging taste of it. Cannon smoke, musket smoke in the clothes, in the food, in back of the throat. Horses. Rotting meat. Bones that the butchers and sutlers had strewn around. The bodies of thousands of badly buried men, dug up again by dogs.

This mixture of smells – smoke, shit, mud, horse, decaying meat – was the smell of Germany. For years Cartwright lived in it like a mood, a state of mind. Like weather that never changed.

Years later on a filthy village corner in Nottinghamshire, close to a butcher shop, he caught a brief, analagous smell and was instantly back near Kassel in a sprawling autumn camp, feeling with new understanding the same stripped numbness, the same fear and suspension of time he'd lived with then. But the recollection had carried a strange attraction and pleasure, too. It was part of his youth he was smelling. The last of it. It was an ordeal he'd lived through and boasted about and forgotten and falsified. A whiff had confirmed how abnormally bad it had been.

The horse he'd bought on disembarking in Bremen had been stolen one night near Fritzlar, saddle, bridle, and all. His servant had not taken enough care in guarding it. Now he had to quickly borrow money to buy another, and had sent his useless servant, after scolding and cuffing him, to fetch one of the agents of a London bank who followed the troops. He would have to agree to a ridiculously high rate of interest since his chances of living to repay the loan in person were not good. But it didn't matter. He needed a horse to accompany the Marquis of Granby to a conference the next day with the field marshal, Prince Ferdinand of Brunswick. He would have to have his coat laundered, too, and the washer-wagons were miles away. His servant would have to take care of that while he dealt with the horse traders.

Granby was relentlessly fussy about how his aides-de-camp were turned out. The Prussians, he said, were always perfectly groomed and splendidly mounted, and accompanied by equally impeccable servants, and he wanted to show that the British were not inferior. But how could anyone stay clean in this mud and soot? One minute slogging through bogs and wheat fields, wading across rivers, sleeping in his clothes under a wagon, and the next minute having to show up shaved and brushed in his best parade uniform. This was fine for princes and rich men with their wardrobe wagons and teams of valets, but for simple officers like himself it was ruinous. Granby had already loaned him money to outfit his horse. He was really a very kind and generous man. But he couldn't go back to Granby for money again. Not so soon. He would even have to borrow to pay his servant and buy him better clothes, which the fellow would likely run off in as soon as he'd got them on. But there was no other way. He would have to dress and play the part if he wanted to be among rich and important men. And that was the only way of becoming one of them.

How many times has he crossed the Weser River, the Diemel, the Eder, the Schwalm, the Fulda, the Werra, alone delivering messages or shepherding hundreds of men? Wading chest-deep with his guns and powder over his head. Riding a frightened horse, plunging and churning among other frightened horses, heaving and stumbling up banks, riders and animals falling on one another, harnesses tangled together. He has crossed the same river four and more times in the same day, manoeuvring, chasing the enemy, falling back, following Granby's or Ferdinand's plans. He has run into the water, slipping and falling, dodging musket balls.

He has plunged in, glad for the coolness, drinking handfuls in the heat of July. He has inched into the black current when the shore was edged in ice, felt the first rush over the tops of his boots, cold striking his balls, erasing all but his face in pain. He has reached into his wet coat pockets at four in the morning, unable to sleep by a dying fire, and found small fish still alive there.

Herding men back and forth over rivers and fields, through forests and ruined villages. Slow, ragged men. Their faces as blank as those of the slaves he'd seen at Rio de Janeiro, their souls having deserted, unable to wait for their bodies to take the chance. Most of them sick. Rounding up stragglers, beating them. Shouting encouragement. "You are the 50th Foot! . . . A proud, old regiment. Much feared by the French! Lord Granby has promised each of you a free ration of beef, and a quart of ale, when you get to Hoxter tomorrow night!"

Falling back to avoid attack, the troops sometimes stampeded in terror and crashed into the hordes of camp-followers that were always close behind, trying to match the army's movements. Many officers' families were there in caravans. There were sutlers of every kind in wagons and tents, selling food and drink, clothing, shoes, and weapons. There were horse-dealers, butchers with herds of cattle, flocks of sheep. There were lawyers, money-lenders, couriers, musicians, portrait painters, brothel tents, bath tents, restaurant tents, taverns, doctors, and booksellers. The panicked cavalry, followed by the artillery – their guns and ammunition carts bouncing behind teams of horses – piled into the sutlers' vehicles, locking wheels, upsetting wagons and caravans. Horses went down on their haunches, shafts and axles snapping. Cattle charged through tents and campfires, children and half-dressed women running, avalanches of china, bottles, books, lines of laundry dragged off on dragoons' helmets, on horns of cows. The shouting. The yanking at harness, the whips, the braying and neighing, the dust and smoke. With the foot-soldiers, red-faced, burdened with packs and muskets, still to come, driven back by the galloping French.

Frau Hauptspiel's Café Musical was a large tent which could only be entered through a caravan richly furnished in velvet and hung with lamps. In one corner of the tent a string trio – elderly, wigged musicians – played more or less constantly each night. At the opposite end a man in apron and clogs grilled skewered pieces of meat on a brass brazier. To one side there was a long table set with bottles of wine and brandy, cheeses, fruits, and hams.

Cartwright was struck at once by the beautiful ladies in low-cut frocks and high, impeccable wigs. He was troubled at first, thinking that either he or they were in the wrong place. They were equal at least to the wives of the major-generals. Their expressions were haughty, almost stern, but they sat with the Prussian and French lieutenants, most of whom had their waistcoats and shirts unbuttoned and were clearly drunk, especially the French. The ladies were even feeding some of them bits of food or helping them drink.

When Cartwright and his friend, Lieutenant Croft, had taken a table, an especially aristocratic-looking woman whom he'd overheard speaking French came and sat down with them. Would they like to order champagne and food to celebrate the pleasure of life and their obvious good fortune as men at arms? She spoke with a faint London accent. Cartwright and Croft laughed and took her suggestion. Without smiling she gracefully urged them to loosen their clothing, since it was very hot, and in fact she did the job herself, standing behind each of them, touching her bosom to the backs of their necks and stretching her smooth white arms in front to unbutton their coats.

The French officers were arguing loudly amongst themselves about which of their generals, Broglie or Soubise, was more incompetent. One of them ordered a bottle of brandy for Cartwright and Croft, then approached their table. "My dear English friends, are you not sick of this countryside? I am sure you do not wish to own it or to die here. Nor do we. There are things we would rather be doing at home, in spite of the pleasant company one sometimes encounters here. And what do we stand to gain personally? Our generals of course, if they can convince the King's ministers that they have done well, will divert an even larger share of the national revenue into their pockets. As for me, the most I can hope for is to escape this autumn without having lost any of the more useful portions of my anatomy. Why not sign a treaty of peace of our own?"

He sent a waiter out to buy paper and pen, and when they arrived drafted an agreement to cease hostilities in the name of reason, brotherhood, and the universal right to peace. He signed his name, Henri de Vaux, and handed it to Cartwright. Croft furtively shook his head and whispered, "No, no, this is trouble."

Cartwright accepted the pen and signed in large letters: Henry Kellet. The Frenchman read his signature. "Congratulations, Mr. Kellet." He clapped Cartwright's shoulder and shook his hand.

✦

1819. May. Wednesday 19.
Wind S.W. light.

I always imagined I'd marry one day. Marriage seemed to me a feature of maturity and success, both of which I supposed I'd eventually achieve. But I couldn't conceive of marriage, in my own case, without an estate and large family to dignify it and give it purpose. I saw no point in marrying for romance or secure female companionship. I never had any trouble getting all the female company I could fit around whatever else I was doing, and I never had enough money to support an estate and family.

I pitied the married officers who dragged their wives behind the army in small caravans. They seemed to have accepted their poverty, forfeited the dignity of deferral. Their marriages seemed merely contracts, without any trappings or substance. Anyone could keep a woman in a wagon. To be married to one was an unnecessary disadvantage. Even John's and Edmund's marriages struck me a bit this way. A man and a woman stuck in a small house. Even given a couple of children. What's the purpose? It's not large enough.

In a way my life was a continuous effort to earn the estate at Marnham and restore the old family – all ten children, the servants and various relatives – to correct the mistakes my father had made and make it flourish again. This seems a paradox in view of my actions. When our father died, I was astounded – John even more so – to discover that in his will he had left the estate to me. But the lands were so heavily mortgaged, and I myself was so financially burdened at that point, that I had no choice but to sell the estate to John, on the understanding that when I was able I would have the right to purchase a portion of it back again. John in fact was not an entirely eager buyer. He had wanted the property, but expected it to come to him free of charge, and was himself doubtful of being able to pay the debts and keep it intact.

I was blamed for abandoning my responsibilities. But in fact I was wandering farther and farther afield trying to find the means to reclaim it and restore it all. Meanwhile, John's efforts proved no better than mine or my father's had been; it fell irreparably apart, and I withheld myself from wherever I happened to be until it was too late.

What about love?

I was afraid. Or it was impossible.

If I'd forgotten Marnham and married Caubvick, my estate would have been all of Labrador. My family would have been everything alive there. Even now those unclaimed kin clamour in my chest.

✧

1819. May. Wednesday 19.
Wind S.W. light.

How I miss weather.

1819. May. Wednesday 19.
Wind S.W. light.

Weather is change, the symptom of the world being alive. Weather is the emotional aspect of time, the earth's basic behaviour. It's the language of the past that speaks directly to our minds without our even knowing it. It's a traveller, more familiar than any uncle, any brother or friend. It's always arriving, bringing news, bringing an idea of life somewhere else. It's always gathering as it goes. Always eager to leave, to see something beyond, to have an effect.

Here the weather is forever perfect, at the peak of May. The way it was the day I died.

More than food, more than people, I want clouds coming. Yellowish brown clouds. Purple clouds, the air bursting with nerves, the ocean above, all that has ever lived condensed in a wind. The smell of rain before it hits.

1819. May. Wednesday 19.
Wind S.W. light.

My oldest and most valued possession is my Hanoverian rifle. I marvel gratefully at the fact that it, along with my animals, has accompanied me into my present state. I have had it and used it constantly since 1761. It's often saved me and others from starvation. It stands in the corner behind me now as I write. Its touch is the same to my hands as it always was. Whatever the state of my own strength and effectiveness, its has certainly not diminished. I bought it from the Prince of Brunswick's personal gunsmith, who had not made it himself, but who assured me, as I think to be true, that it was made by the gunsmith to the House of Hanover, a man of exceptional skill who had recenty died. I always thought it most likely that the Elector of Hanover, our King George III, who was about my age, would have the mate to my piece in his own collection. In my one meeting with the King I attempted to raise the subject, but was prevented when one of the Inuit, whom I had with me at the time, did something which made the dog that the Duchess of Bedford was holding in her arms begin to bark.

With the help of my Hanoverian rifle, and given the fact that I was skilled at arms since boyhood, I was able to outdo all the other officers in the British contingent in Germany in contests of marksmanship.

I overheard Granby once refer to me as a regular sporting squire. He said I'd do well commanding a squadron of Highlanders or jaegers, whose job it was to creep into the woods and pick off enemy sentries and officers. It was a compliment in a way. Yet it also sounded as though he were saying I was too coarse for anything else.

I was always puzzled by how little value the army placed on military skills.

✦

Sometimes Cartwright's attention would wander off and linger in the branches of a tree just at the moment when his arguing fellow officers finally agreed on some plan, or just as a general's rambling remarks concluded with a command, and Cartwright then would be suddenly conscious of everyone else pulling their riding gloves on and walking away, and he would stride quickly to join the group, confused, embarrassed to have to ask what was going on.

There was the occasion when Granby sent him galloping to General Bulow to confirm the time of their combined attack on the French. The directions Granby had given him were incomplete, or Cartwright had missed something Granby had said, and he lost his way in the cloud-filled woods on the Desenberg hill. As he was trying to find his way back to Granby and his own troops, he heard cannon and cheering. Anxious and flustered, he rode out of the fog and into a clearing on the side of the hill facing Warburg just in time to see Granby burst into view below him, leading the whole English cavalry straight at the French in a wild charge. Granby was waving his sabre, his tiny bald head gleaming in the sun.

Unlike the British and Prussian armies in Germany, which baked bread in portable iron ovens that could be quickly assembled and disassembled, the French army would accept only bread that had been baked in traditional ovens of brick. They obtained their bricks by tearing down local houses, then had to devote a couple of weeks to constructing their ovens. Since bread was the only ration the armies regularly provided for their troops, regiments could never conduct manoeuvres more than five days' march from their field bakeries, and for this reason the French army, anchored to its massive hearths, was much less mobile than its enemy.

On a number of occasions Cartwright was involved in the capture of French bakeries. They would take the numerous bakers prisoner, steal the wagons of flour and whatever bread was available, and blow up the ovens. Later they'd exchange the bakers for an equal number of British or Prussian prisoners. The bread, being better than what their iron ovens produced, was highly prized and normally distributed among the senior ranks or sold to sutlers who in turn sold it to the troops.

Once, in taking a bakery, Cartwright's company also surprised a party of French officers seated under a pavillion at a long table spread with a linen cloth and set with crystal and silver. The officers were drinking wine and waiting for pans of lamb and vegetables to be baked in the nearby oven. Cartwright's men politely disarmed the French who then invited the British to wait and dine with them when the food was cooked.

Cartwright and one of the French officers recognized each other. "Ah, Mr. Kellet," the man said, "is there no end to this farce? We have signed a treaty of peace, I thought."

The French and British officers drank to one another's health and ate together. Later, when no one was looking, Cartwright returned de Vaux's sword to him and allowed him to walk away.

The idea was, once committed to battle, never to think defensively until it was too late to save yourself. All the necessary defensive measures had already been taken, presumably. That was the job of the generals. They spent weeks marching their armies around, feinting and dodging, trying to avoid being outnumbered or having their supplies cut or being surrounded, divided, surprised, or losing their path of retreat. When the chances of not being defeated looked best, the generals sent out a portion of their troops who were expected to advance in a block straight at the enemy as though the enemy's guns were firing only blanks. After long, ponderous defensive manoeuvres, encounters were usually decided in bursts of reckless posturing, suicidal attacks.

Battles of this kind were won by the troops with the most discipline and the least concern for their lives. The ideal soldier was one who had been robbed of his individual identity and driven insane in a special way, so that his officer's orders and the routines of marching and firing would be more real to him, more immediate in the midst of combat, than the enemy's cavalry charges and cannon balls.

Cartwright drilled his company to accept death as part of the routine. "You soldiers in front, when I've given the order to fire, and you've fired your muskets, I want you to fall down right where you're standing, as though shot! And the rest of you behind them, when I give the command to march, I want you to march over them! Step on them if need be! But don't for Christ sake trip on them!"

The French guns had been unexpected. They had been hidden behind a clump of willows. The quick retreat of the French infantry was obviously part of the trap, but the British cavalry didn't think of that and went chasing them, exposing the flanks of the infantry unit Cartwright was leading.

Cartwright marched his men forward in a prescribed rectangular block: six long rows of men, the first three rows, or front line, separated by a space from the three rows behind them. The French pulled their cannon into the open, three hundred yards to his right, and started firing. The bolts of flame, the rolling clouds of smoke, the claps of noise he could feel in the earth, punching the soles of his boots.

Amazingly, he could see the cannon balls coming, skipping over the sod. Some skimmed overhead, buzzing loudly. One struck into the end of one of his rows of soldiers and bowled the men down like skittles. Another ball did the same. Cartwright tried to get his troops to hold their formation and wheel to face the guns. It was the only way to go on the attack. If they moved quickly they could overwhelm the guns and capture them. He advanced his troops a hundred paces, halted, fired a volley, marched, and fired again. At first the cannon balls did less damage since those that were accurate were hitting his lines at right angles, and the lines were only six men deep. But once the range had shortened, the French switched to grape-shot and cannister.

Immediately after his company fired its second volley and were striding out of their own smoke, Cartwright was knocked off his feet. He was unable to breathe, his mouth stretched open, his body shuddering. He was sure the ribs on his left side had been broken in like the staves of a barrel. The front of his coat, his left sleeve, were soaked with blood. He was aware of men running by him, above him, horses too, his own cavalry. Then the guns were quiet, except for muskets farther away.

He was breathing again. There were birds gliding in the clear sky straight above. Almost like the sight of home. He watched them for a while as though he'd abandoned himself. And then he thought perhaps he didn't have to die. Perhaps if he wanted to, he could get up and walk. He got to his feet. A piece of shot had cut across his ribs and glanced into his arm. He could open and close his hand, but blood continually dripped from his fingertips.

He walked past men from his company, some sitting or crouching, holding parts of their bodies and cursing repeatedly. Some looking foolish and embarrassed by their wounds. Others, the ones the large balls had hit, looked as though they had exploded from within. Cartwright was astonished by how clean and bright their innards were compared to the shabby uniforms, the dirty exteriors with which he was familiar. Their bones and tendons, the insides of their skins gleamed surprisingly white. Their muscles had been sheathed in clear membranes, just like deers'. The faces of the dead had the appearance of delicately fashioned masks dropped by actors onto discarded costumes at the close of some play. They were not soldiers anymore. They were all that was left of horribly misused men.

✦

1819. May. Wednesday 19.
Wind S.W. light.

I saved the Marquis of Granby's life under circumstances that were not honourable from his point of view, and although he was grateful to me, as of course he had to be, I think he never forgave me for it. I also think this is one of the reasons my service to him as aide-de-camp proved so fruitless to me.

After the incident I made a point of never alluding to what I'd done for him, but of behaving as deferentially and obediently as I always had. Yet under the surface of our apparently normal intercourse I could feel him thinking something to this effect: "Here is this great oaf, so proud of his skill as a marksman and woodsman, pretending to honour me, but all the while feeling superior because of saving my life. I must show him that I expect as much from all my servants. I have no special debt to him." The result was that while he continued to seem as generous and affable as ever in small matters, in the larger issues of promotion and the assignment of duties, he put me last.

My rescue of Granby took place while I and a couple of his other aides-de-camp were accompanying him on a boar hunting expedition arranged by Prince Ferdinand. A number of other senior Prussian and British officers were present, together with all of our servants. Some German jaegers had been sent ahead to scout for signs of boar, and the rest of us had dismounted to await their return. It was June, and Granby had only recently returned from his winter's leave in England. Ferdinand, who had been fighting the French since April, was clearly annoyed with him for joining the summer's campaign so late, but Granby pretended not to notice. He was joking, telling stories, and he kept ordering his servant to offer brandy to the other men. Granby himself was nearly drunk.

All at once an enormous black boar sprang out of the forest from the direction the jaegers had gone. Granby was closest to it, but facing away from it. Seeing the rest of us exclaim, he turned just in time to receive the charging beast's snout between his legs. He was thrown onto his back, and the boar in trying to gore him caught his tusk in Granby's sword hanger and began shaking the Marquis from side to side and pushing him along the ground like a terrier with a rat.

There was an outcry of alarm, but some also laughed – perhaps Ferdinand among them – and I'm sure Granby heard.

I had learned to kill wild pigs, using only a knife, by jumping on their backs when the dogs had cornered them. Some jaegers had taught me the trick the previous summer. I leapt on the boar's back and drove my dagger behind its shoulder blade. The action seemed only to anger it more. It broke free from Granby, turned on me, and got its head between my thighs. I held it off as best I could and struck it several times more with my knife to cause it to weaken more quickly. I thought I was sure to at least lose my private parts, but was lucky to suffer nothing worse than a cut on my right thigh.

Granby, although he was dirtied and disgraced, was unharmed.

I was much admired for my actions and was often toasted and praised for them afterwards. By the Prussians mostly, who called me Herr Meister Jaeger.

✦

Cartwright had been watching the back of a flour wagon for six hours, ever since dawn, the high wooden box lurching precariously over the humps and gullies along the Weser River road. Appointed to guard a convoy of supplies, he was riding with three dragoons at the end of a line of wagons, listening carefully, glancing over his shoulder from time to time. To their right the rising slope was covered in trees. Below to the left were more trees with the light from the river showing among their trunks. Every few miles there were clusters of half-ruined cottages, ragged women watching the convoy from in front of sheds.

Just past a small village, enemy hussars were suddenly there behind them, galloping, firing their carabines, drawing their swords. Cartwright's dragoons spurred their horses up through the trees and vanished, and Cartwright did the same, jumped at the edge of a field and let his horse run on, stretched himself under some ferns beside a log.

He heard muskets and shouting, another horse running through bushes very close by. Then nothing more.

Small ovals of sunlight moved through the leaves above him, filling their fine branching veins with yellow light. Ants climbed up the stem of a fern onto the mossy log. A woodpecker tapped with clear resonance somewhere nearby. A squirrel with a very full tail passed in slow wave-like leaps along a branch overhead. It had a nut in its mouth. Cartwright was struck by the thought of this sanity, this vast undemonstrative order continuing outside the confines of his life. Something lovely and enduring that he longed, with a painful surge, for his life to match. The Weser road, with whatever was left of the convoy, was merely a scratch on the face of the earth he could walk away from. Why not desert, leave the war with its unnecessary imperatives behind?

And then what? Live in a tree, eating nuts? Where would he go? He could desert, but he couldn't transform himself into leaf or squirrel. He would have to continue to live in the human world, and that world held only one place for him.

He sat up, looked over the ferns at the empty forest, feeling small, foolish, disconnected from everything. Birds were chattering overhead. He picked up his pistol and cocked it. The squirrel was bounding back up the tree with another nut. Cartwright moved his pistol in time with the squirrel and fired. It spun through the air like a scrap of fur. The birds were gone.

Cartwright made his way back down through the trees. Some of the convoy's wagons were burning. Most were off the road in the bushes or on their sides. The horses had all been stolen or chased away. A few of the drivers were dead, their bodies already stripped of most of their clothes.

Women and children were filling barrels with flour, using blankets to bundle up cheeses and tins of lard. Cartwright chased one young woman down toward the river, and caught her by the back of her dress, pulled her down, and kneeled over her, pinning her arms. Her eyes, he thought, were more angry than afraid. "So. Stealing," he said. "And running away." He put his hands on her breasts and tried to unbutton her dress, but she twisted and hissed violently, and he had to laugh and give it up. *"Geld, Geld, und viel zu Essen,"* he said, patting his coat pocket.

She lay still a moment, then nodded, looking him in the eyes with hard contempt. He got up to unbutton his breeches and allow her to lift her dress.

✦

1819. May. Wednesday 19.
Wind S.W. light.

An aide-de-camp to a commander in chief was always supposed to be in the sure line of promotion, but at the close of the German War, in spite of my service to Granby, I was still nothing more than a lieutenant in the 39th Regiment. It seemed I would have no choice but to return to Limerick. This was disappointing enough, but when I learned in a letter from my father that a couple of junior officers in my regiment had been permitted to purchase commissions over my head, without their ever having been offered to me, I called on Granby at our base in Bremen and protested to him in person. He regretted my predicament, he said. He had no control over the allotment of commissions in my regiment, which were based on available places. I was a favourite of his, he said, but clearly Aldercron's captains had favourites of their own.

However, to spare me the humiliation of serving under those who had recently been my subordinates, he offered to arrange for me to retire on half pay with a settlement of £250. I accepted.

Granby had a reputation for generosity. He held my arm and whispered about the representations he'd make on my behalf to the Horse Guards and the Secretary of State for War. I came away feeling grateful for his support. The feeling didn't last.

The £250 went immediately into paying debts I'd contracted through having to keep horses and servants in order to attend Granby in the required style.

✦

Perhaps it wasn't only Granby's grudge against me that was at work. Perhaps I was turning away from the army in any case, but with no idea of what I was turning toward. The more experienced I became in military affairs – and the more I became like the other soldiers – the less appetite I had for the army's work. The less fit I was for it. I see this now, but I don't know why it was.

In any event, my career was dissolving before me like smoke, and for no clear reason I could discern. I was angry and resentful, but also, in part, relieved. I would no longer have to endure the army's mysterious and unfair ways.

What then to do with my freedom? I couldn't return to Marnham and my family's advice and condolences, and their comfortable talk of county affairs. All I could think of was to keep away from polite society and devote myself to sport.

4

In the spring of 1765 Cartwright moved to Scotland. He assumed he could live more cheaply there, do as he pleased, and enjoy an abundance of game in its woods and streams. He took with him his horse, some trunks of clothes and sporting equipment, and a lady he'd met at a card party in London. He rented a sooty manor house in a valley above Loch Leven, purchased old furniture in the nearest village, also a horse for his lady friend and three brace of dogs, and hired two servants. He referred to this entourage as his family.

His army pension, two shillings and fourpence a day, wasn't enough, however, to pay his servants and keep his family fed. He planted lettuce and cress, ordered his servants to gather firewood in the scrubby hills, and himself went fishing or hunting every day to furnish the table with food.

The lady spent most of her time sending the servants for water, heating it in the fireplace, washing her silk dresses and underclothes, and drying them on a line strung from a window latch to an apple tree across the weedy terrace in front of the house. She refused to live without coffee and wine.

"I don't care what it costs! What else is there for me in this place? You're out with your dogs all day chasing through brambles like nothing more than a big dog yourself!"

Cartwright responded by imitating a dog, bounding toward the lady on all fours, his tongue lolling to one side, attempting to nuzzle his face between her thighs. Instead of laughing she sidestepped him, snatched her skirts out of his grasp, and got the table between the two of them, where she kept it by dodging from side to side.

"Stop being a fool!" she shouted. "I'm perfectly serious about this! I went to call on the Cameron ladies today as you suggested. Fine company they are! You should see the pair. Wool shawls from head to toe, stinking of bad milk and wet sheep. And I could hardly see them, their house is so dark. Nor could I understand a word they said."

He bought her a virginal, most of whose keys worked. But when he was out hunting she broke it apart and burnt it to heat water to wash her dress.

The servants, in spite of their small wages, contrived to be drunk most of the time. They had an unusual capacity for sleep, and a peculiar, rumpled, trailing way of wearing their clothes.

They would stand very rigid by the sparsely laid table

when Cartwright and his lady dined, and would make a great show of uncovering the platters on which they served the scrawny partridges or small trout that Cartwright had caught.

When he'd had enough of their "Wine, Monsieur? Salade, Monsieur?" he would throw something at them or strike them with a riding crop – the dogs springing up from under the table and filling the room with commotion – but the servants, floundering among fallen chairs, would only laugh, covering their heads, and feign intense agony, crying "Ooch, *nay!*" and "Och!" with exaggerated Scots intonation.

With the approach of winter, the trout and partridges vanished, the lettuce froze, and the house became unbearbly cold. Cartwright dismissed his servants, who pretended to be stricken with grief. He auctioned his furniture, sold his horses, and returned to London by sea with the lady and dogs.

In London, he deposited the lady at an inn run by her sister and brother-in-law. Her sister held her at arm's length, studied her hair, her dress. "Oh, my poor darling!" she breathed, and embraced her with a sob. The dogs he sent to Marnham by coach. He then spent a few days walking the streets, visiting acquaintances, all of whom seemed to be in the middle of urgent business of one sort or another. The city was too expensive to stay in. Unable to think of anything else to do, he took a coach to Plymouth where his brother John commanded a small cutter assigned to intercept smugglers.

"George! What a surprise. How are you keeping?"

"Oh fine! Free as a bird. Spent the summer in Scotland. Fabulous hunting. Ought to take you and show you sometime. Good company too. Nice piece of a wench to pass the nights with. London gal. Just said goodbye to her. . . . Well, I've just got a day or two.

Expecting something from Granby very soon. Will have to get back and speak with him. What about you?"

"Oh well, it isn't much, but we're kept pretty busy here. You'd be surprised at the number of smugglers on this coast."

"And you catch them, do you?"

"I should say! In the past four months we've taken more smugglers, more contraband too, than any ship on record."

"And you shoot at them?"

"Look, I'll show you our guns. This little punt is deceptive."

"You surprise them? You chase them? At night?" Cartwright's voice rose with excitement as he followed John out of the shipping office onto the jetty.

"Mm, and in daylight."

"If there's room on board I think I could spare the time to sail with you for a day or two." Cartwright's eyes darted up and down over the cutter, noting its gunports, its abundant sails. "I'd love to see how it's done."

"You're welcome, of course. There's room, I believe. But . . . I doubt that there's room on the pay master's list, at least right away."

"Oh, don't bother with that. I've got my army pay. . . . John! This is the life!"

Being under no one's command, Cartwright would sometimes lie half the morning in his berth on the cutter, which was called the *Sherbourne*, while the crew's feet thundered back and forth on the deck overhead. At other times he would rise with the morning watch and stand supervising the work, advising the men to coil the ropes more neatly or steer the ship closer into the wind. He was not popular with the crew.

Being experienced with artillery, however, he took an interest in the ship's guns – four long nine-pounders – and after a little practice, by timing his shots with the ship's roll, could dismast smugglers' craft, using chain-shot, from an unheard-of distance. He would strip down to his blouse and breeches, set his wig aside, and aim the guns and manage the linstock himself. He made a point of taking out only the masts and rigging, leaving the ships' hulls with their cargoes and human lives untouched.

When John was discharged from the *Sherbourne* the following spring and promoted to first lieutenant on the *Guernsey*, a fifty-gun man-of-war, Cartwright went with him and shared his quarters on the new ship. A few eyebrows were raised, but Cartwright acted the affable gentleman, talked of India, the war in Germany, Granby, Aldercron, Watson, Clive, and space was made for him. He was able to dine with the senior officers at no expense.

The *Guernsey* was bound for Newfoundland where it spent every summer guarding British territory against the French. Cartwright later wrote in his journal: "Having no particular engagement, and hearing that bears and deer were plentiful there, I felt so strong an inclination to be among them, that I accompanied my brother on that voyage."

John, who had grown resigned to Cartwright's companionship and knew that some of his recent success on the *Sherbourne* was due to his brother's gunnery, made no complaint.

Newfoundland's governor, Sir Hugh Palliser, was on board. During the crossing Cartwright talked with him about colonial enterprise, especially the trade in fish, furs, and oil. The coast of Labrador, Palliser told him, was rich in these things, but scarcely exploited.

"Why?" Cartwright asked.

"The summers are short. Ice and the Eskimos have chased away the few of our people who've tried to establish premises there." Palliser clenched his teeth and thrust out his jaw after every few words.

"Were they well equipped for the climate, I wonder. Did they try to make peace with the Eskimos?"

"The climate I think isn't really the issue. But given the isolation and the precariousness of existence there, the Eskimos' hostility is the crucial thing." He inhaled sharply and held his breath. "The pattern of warring with them was started some time ago, no doubt by our side, when the first ignorant fools who went there found it easier to shoot the Eskimos than try to come to some peaceful agreement with them. However there's still hope for Labrador, to get in there and do things properly." He closed his eyes, the lids fluttering, the cords at the sides of his throat forming deep troughs. "On the Island of Newfoundland I'm afraid things are already out of control. Too many settlers there, killing the Indians whenever they can. It's not only unjust and un-Christian. It doesn't make economic sense! Instead of living in dread of Indian attacks, they could be *trading* with them. They could have the Indians out working for them, out in the forest bringing them furs . . . in exchange for simple goods . . . but they're too stupid to see that!"

Breathing harshly, Palliser hoisted himself to his feet and limped back and forth in the cabin. Cartwright watched him respectfully. It was widely known that Palliser had been badly injured during his time as a naval captain when an arms chest blew up in front of him.

"Isn't it possible to bring in laws to stop our people murdering them?"

"Laws. . . . Our good British and Irish ruffians have

been hanging about these coasts for over a century without laws. Who's to make them obey? The place is immense! But of course you're right. In fact I'm planning a system of small coastal forts, for a number of reasons. To secure the area against the French . . . *and* the New Englanders. To regulate the fishery and supervise settlement." He drew his lips into a wrinkled white bud. "And to protect our people from the natives, and vice versa. . . . The only thing now is to let the natives know of our good intentions. Relations are so bad, we've no way of talking to them."

In October, Cartwright, along with his brother and all the *Guernsey*'s officers, was invited to dinner at Palliser's house in St. John's. The naturalist Joseph Banks was there. Banks had spent the summer as a passenger on the naval frigate *Niger* and had just come from Chateau Bay in Labrador where he'd been collecting specimens while a crew of marines built one of Palliser's small forts. Banks presented Palliser with a couple of walrus tusks and some bird skins as gifts.

James Cook was also at dinner. He'd been surveying the southwest coast of the island that summer and had brought his ship into St. John's harbour on his way home to England.

After the plates were cleared away, Palliser, Cook, and Banks unrolled charts on the table and got out various notebooks, sketches, and specimens of plants, furs, and rocks. They talked late into the night, drinking wine, discussing their summer's adventures and discoveries. Cartwright looked on, saying little, but feeling a strong affinity for these men. Their conversation and confident manners seemed to pull his own interests and character into focus. What they were concerned with, studying nature, mapping the wilderness, was just a loftier version of what he himself had always loved. He began to feel less like a failed soldier and more like a person with valuable knowledge of wildlife, travel, and war, the natural companion of men such as Banks and Palliser.

Newfoundland changed the contents of Cartwright's brain. The basic image, the background material his mind came to rest on before he slept or when he had stopped thinking of any particular thing was now the landscape of Newfoundland. The coastline. Black glistening water leaping in white foam along endless rock. A wall of dark spruce trees hiding a world of Indians and animals no European had seen. Scotland was nothing to that. Nor India with its thousands of princes and villages. The cold appealed to him. The icy water and wind. It seemed free and aloof, preserving a secret few would be strong enough to learn.

1819. May. Wednesday 19.
Wind S.W. light.

When I returned to England after my first visit to Newfoundland, word came to me that the Marquis of Granby had obtained a company for me in the 37th Regiment of Foot, then stationed in Minorca. In spite of the bitterness I had felt on leaving the army, my first reaction to this news was delight. It was a relief to know that I'd not been completely forgotten. My time in Scotland and in cruising with John, it now seemed, had been but an interlude between appointments, and not the start of a lifetime of aimless wandering.

On reflection, however, and especially considering how matters unfolded in Minorca, I saw less reason to rejoice at the Marquis's efforts on my behalf. To begin with he made it clear that the captaincy in the 37th Regiment had become available, unexpectedly, through the death of Captain Slack, who died in consequence of a wound he received from the last shot that was fired by the French army in Germany. This gave me some sense of the position in which my concerns were ranked in Granby's mind. All the scores of British captains who died in the German War were replaced, without a vacancy ever having been found for me. But at the very end of the war, as an accident, a Captain Slack was killed by a stray bullet, and, since everyone else was occupied, I was given the chance to take his place. In Minorca. The notorious naval base my father warned me to avoid. No wonder Slack's commission was on the block.

Nevertheless, Granby had done me a kindness which I was in no position to refuse. Perhaps he'd intended to help me all along when the opportunity arose. Perhaps his conscience had begun to trouble him on my account. Although I had not been as broadly public in my complaints as John had recommended, in my private speech and correspondence I had not refrained from giving a true account of my service to Lord Granby and of my dissatisfaction with its outcome. Perhaps, as I intended, the comments of others on my retirement made him uncomfortable.

✦

In the summer of 1767 Cartwright joined his new regiment in Minorca and within a week was sick with malaria, just as his father predicted. Everyone got it. Some died. Most were reasonably healthy between attacks. Cartwright never got well again while he was there. His weight, which was usually over 190 pounds, fell to 140. He was virtually always in bed, or longing to be. The other officers and the men in his company remained almost complete strangers to him. Only his personal servant, an old soldier named Charles Atkinson, cared for him, giving him water, helping him to the chamber pot when his fever was at its worst.

The sound of the regiment's routines drifted into his room, distant and echoing, boiling up with meaningless volume at times, then stretching again into feeble strands. The life outside seemed conjectural, unreal. He sank and floated, passed through layer after layer of matter, soft textures that rolled like bolts of cloth underneath him, coarse ones he fell through for hours like a gravelly sea. He could die, he realized, and no one would notice or care. The laughter and banging doors, the rattling equipment and shouts would go on just as they went on now. He would have to get out of there if he wanted to live.

He dreamed of the cold water of Newfoundland, the open sea far from the fetid port of Minorca with its pestilent air. He would be clean there and strong. He had the impression the sun itself in Minorca was rotting him, breeding larvae in everything. Even in rocks and the woodwork of buildings. The faces that peered at him, opening their mouths to talk, were hollow, about to collapse on themselves like wormy gourds.

On a rainy day in February he got out of bed. Charles helped him dress and took him to the Lieutenant-Governor's house where Cartwright asked for permission to go home, and to bring Charles with him.

The passage back to England was slow. When the ship was at sea his sickness lifted, returning when they entered a port. They arrived in Spit Head at the end of April and discovered the *Guernsey* there, his brother still first lieutenant, and the ship again under sailing orders for Newfoundland. He immediately wrote to Granby requesting leave to recover his health. Charles agreed to follow him as his servant, and Cartwright wrote to Minorca to arrange his discharge. When they boarded the *Guernsey*, Cartwright was shaking with fever again, but with happiness also, knowing that somehow he'd been saved.

As they sailed west to Newfoundland, into the fogs and the cold air, Cartwright's health returned, he gained weight. When, after six weeks, the *Guernsey* reached St. John's, some of the passengers had begun to show signs of scurvy, but Cartwright strode the deck from end to end, thumping his friends on the back, loudly promising to befriend the Beothuk Indians and eat a bear.

✧

With Kaumalak hooded, inert as a stuffed hawk on his wrist, Cartwright searches the sky over Kirkby Forest, southeast of Mansfield. Specks of birds drift very high. Impossible to tell what kind. The pastures before him have an annoying emptiness, a posed neutrality, like camouflage, like the backs of hands concealing a face. It seems the edge of the woods might even be trembling a little with the strain of withheld breath, suppressed laughter.

But Thoroton's leisurely rolling gait soothes Cartwright, transmitting a lulling motion up through his back, into his nodding head. At least there is this companionship. Thoroton is a beast of exceptional equanimity and regular habit. He's always eager for exercise when Cartwright approaches him with his bridle and saddle. He whinnies low in his throat and nuzzles his master's neck. A slow walk through the country lanes is what he enjoys, and a chance to browse on fresh grass. When the sun is low in the west and it's time to return to the stable, he enjoys that too, the prospect of oats in a bucket and a rub with the curry comb. He knows his own way home from anywhere within a day's ride from Mansfield, and moves steadily along, leaving Cartwright free to relax in his own thoughts or absorb the sight of the lengthening shadows, the bronze aura the sun casts around everything, the swirling clusters of flies like dancing sparks.

If Cartwright happens to look out the window of his room at night, down into the courtyard, Thoroton's head will be there poking over the lower half of the stable door, the starlight reflecting softly in his eyes. The horse's expression will be one of calm understanding, of reading things. And Cartwright will say to himself, "I wonder what goes through that creature's mind?"

Kaumalak, on the other hand, Cartwright thinks he understands. The bird is either lit or unlit, like a lamp. When she is unlit she sits asleep, uncompromisingly shut off, her bird nature suspended, or kept alive in a deeply interior dream. When she is lit, which is whenever she is awake, she is all appetite. There is no middle ground, no domestic self behind her theatrics. Cartwright identifies with her. He feels she expresses his own will, his own insatiable cravings. She's like a companion to whom one might say not only, "Let's go hunting," but also "Let's get drunk," or "Let's get fucked," or "Let's kill the bugger," and "Let's get out of here."

If Kaumalak expresses something essential of Cartwright's mind and character, Thoroton expresses a feeling he has for his body, and for what there is of his father's body in him, and for all his ancestors, those unknown people who passed their physical life on to him.

Cartwright rides Thoroton now to the top of a meadow near Coxmoor Lodge and turns his head to the west. Kaumalak, hooded, sits motionless on his wrist. There is a row of trees at the meadow's edge, then the roofs of Kirkby in Ashfield and South Normanton and Alfreton, Crewe, Chester, the Cambrian Mountains, Ireland, the Atlantic Ocean, a blue mist on its far curved reaches. For the first time he can see Newfoundland. Cliffs and surf. Cape Spear, probably, a dusting of green on top. The matted spruce forests farther west. Conception Bay, Trinity Bay. The glassy black water he sailed on with John.

Where is Labrador though? He strains upward and forward eagerly. But he still can't see that far.

1819. May. Wednesday 19.
Wind S.W. light.

John was the articulate one and quick to look for credit and acclaim by committing his thoughts and deeds to print.

When we reached St. John's in 1768, I visited Governor Palliser whom I'd met on my previous voyage to Newfoundland and with whom I'd discussed the plight of the island's Beothuk or Red Indians – the Indians so called, Palliser had explained, because of the ochre pigment they used to adorn their bodies and possessions. They were close to extinction already at that time. Knowing of Palliser's wish to protect the Indians and establish a friendly trade with them, I proposed making a personal expedition up the Exploits River into their territory to open peaceful communication with them, and, if possible, to bring back to St. John's a few whom we might train as interpreters and who might teach their language to us.

I wasn't in a position to formally lead such an expedition, being an unofficial visitor, and especially since most of the route lay by water; but John was. We talked the matter over with him, and he agreed to assume command of a schooner which Palliser would put in our charge, and to man it with nine of the *Guernsey*'s crew.

When we had nearly completed our expedition – having ascended and descended the Exploits River and returned to Twillingate in Notre Dame Bay – my brother fired off a letter to Governor Palliser by way of a report on our achievements. John showed me the letter at the time, and sent it ahead in spite of my objections to many of the points it contained. Ten years later he published the bulk of the letter together with other information in a pamphlet entitled "A True Account of the Wild or Red Indians of Newfoundland." Unwilling to embarrass my brother or create a division between us, I didn't dispute his version of the expedition in my own account, which I published as part of my journal in 1792.

In his account, John wrote that on the fifth morning up the river, having worn out our shoes, Charles and I and three of the seamen were forced to turn back. And I agreed with this in my *Journal of Transactions and Events*, admitting that the rocks had chafed the stitches through and set the soles of our shoes at liberty. What I did not mention – and what John refused to believe – was that later that same day those of us who had turned back discovered a recently abandoned Indian settlement. In it we found dried caribou skins from which we fashioned new shoes of a rough but serviceable design. We also found a birch rind canoe with paddles, and in it proceeded up the river hoping to rejoin the rest of the company. We paddled until well after dark, the moon being full, and without knowing it, passed the place where John and his party were camped. We stopped for some sleep, then continued at dawn, thinking John and the others were still ahead of us. By the time we reached the river's source, which is the large body of water we named Red Indian Lake, we realized we had overtaken the others in the night. I was extremely excited, however, at the discovery of this beautiful lake, never before visited by Europeans. We had found the secret refuge of the Beothuk Indians.

There was evidence of extensive settlement on both the north and south shores, but most of the dwellings were empty and appeared not to have been occupied for some time. Their owners, if they were yet alive, were no doubt in their summer quarters near the sea. Notwithstanding our disappointment, we left knives, needles, and thread as gifts in the house showing most evidence of recent use.

After camping for two nights rather apprehensively and in stormy weather, we turned back to the river. John's and his comrades' footprints were visible on the sand where the river issued from the lake. It was as far as they had come. We paddled quickly downstream, and this time, designing to play a trick on them, we deliberately passed their camp in the night and hastened down to Mr. Cousens's house on Exploits Bay where we awaited them, feasting on the roasted joints of a black bear that I shot on the evening of our return.

John refused to believe our tale in spite of the evidence of the Indian canoe and deerskin shoes. He maintained that he was the discoverer of the lake which he insisted on calling Lieutenant's Lake – after himself.

There were other small irritants in John's letter which I

have not been able to forget. He gives a detailed account of the ingenious structures the Indians had erected along the river for directing the migrating caribou into locations where they could easily be killed. John at first had no idea what these fences, sewels, blinds, and platforms were for. It was I, being an experienced hunter, who first perceived their purpose and explained it to John. In neither his letter nor his pamphlet did he accord any credit to me for enlightening him.

✦

Newfoundland seemed to Cartwright endlessly open, inviting. He imagined himself plunging into its clear, healthy space, consuming it, swelling to fill it. It gave him a sense of vigour he hadn't known since he was twelve years old. He wrote in his journal about the great pleasure he took in gorging on salmon and bear steaks grilled over open coals. "Nothing," he said, "whets the appetite equal to good exercise, sleeping in open air, and drinking water." He slept deeply with reassuring dreams in all kinds of terrain and weather, and woke eager to resume his pursuit of the stream or coast he was following.

The scale of the place and the lack of people appealed to him. To travel at all was to explore. To visit a crew of salmoniers was an expedition. Strangely, the huge, scarcely mapped land didn't dwarf people. It made them large and significant. In London, people were what you ignored, a stream of anonymous faces. In Newfoundland, they were rare. Each was a town, a county in himself.

Cartwright wanted to go where others had not been. To return to Red Indian Lake, measure its length, climb the mountains he'd glimpsed to the west of it. To travel the coast of Labrador past where the place names stopped. And the thought of the native people obsessed him. What was unknown, unmapped for him, for them was home. The people were more unknown to him than the land itself. They were the heart of the land, he imagined, and to know them would be to fully discover the land. He believed he could win their confidence, study their customs and language, teach them European skills. He liked the idea of mating his culture and country to theirs, bringing the two continents into contact, with himself as the bridge. Perhaps he could become their great leader.

He felt a sense of importance in Newfoundland. Gentlemen there were scarce, and while Newfoundlanders on the whole were less deferential than the lower classes in England, he did stand out. He was honoured and shown favours wherever he went. Whoever the people in power happened to be, he was one of them. If a naval ship was in the vicinity, he was invited to dine on board, a wherry and crew were provided to take him shooting ducks. His simple presence was taken as serving the British cause.

And best of all, it was nothing but sport. It was what he most loved to do. If he took a mistress and dogs and went hunting in Scotland, he was merely an idler, and no one wanted to hear of him. If he took his mistress and dogs and went hunting in Labrador, on the other hand, the King himself would send him honours and men-of-war.

It was sport that could make him rich. He met men who owned fishing and trapping companies with stations in Fogo and Twillingate. They were wealthy men, owners of fleets of ships. They were looking for partners who could manage new stations in Labrador.

At the end of the summer, Cartwright returned to England, retired from the army a second time, and spent the next year and a half borrowing money and discussing his plans with the Board of Trade. He got in touch with Francis Lucas, a man with ideas like his own, whom he'd met on both of his trips to Newfoundland. Like Cartwright, Lucas also had recently quit his military career. He'd been a naval lieutenant and was familiar with Labrador. In the fall of 1768 he'd brought an Inuit woman to London and had learned some of her language before taking her back to her people the following spring.

Cartwright and Lucas agreed on a joint venture, and in March 1770 went into partnership with Perkins and Coghlan, a couple of Bristol merchants who owned the largest fishing company on Fogo Island off Newfoundland's northeast coast. Perkins and Coghlan would furnish them with supplies. Lucas would try to cultivate trade with the Inuit. Cartwright would start up a fishing and trapping station at a site Lucas knew of on the Charles River in southern Labrador.

It was a good site, Lucas promised. It didn't matter that Nicholas Darby's efforts to start a business there had failed three years earlier when Inuit, in revenge for some offence, had killed three of his workers. It didn't matter that Darby and his crew had then murdered twenty Inuit before fleeing the place. These things could be patched up, Lucas said.

5

Cartwright had spent a dull April morning accepting small cups of coffee from a man who lived on Cavendish Square and who hoped to invest in the Labrador trade. Mr. Couts paced his parquet floor as he and Cartwright talked about audits and dividends. When the topic of risks and insurance arose, the would-be investor squinted and drew his mouth up in a dentured grimace. "What about . . . *pirates*?" He squeezed the word out like an infected splinter. "What about . . . shipwreck . . . cannibals?" Cartwright played down the chances of loss. Mr. Couts listened, tilting his head, working a finger between his gums and the rim of his false teeth.

They concluded their affairs at last with a couple of

signatures and a handshake. Tucking his papers into his waistcoat pocket, Cartwright nodded to his servant, Charles, who'd been standing patiently by the door; it was time to alert the driver of their hackney-coach that the master was on his way.

At the bottom of Holles Street, Tyburn Road was jammed with crowds and carriages heading west. It was hanging day. Cartwright gave Charles some coins and told him to take the afternoon off. He then paid the driver, and himself plunged into the throng on Tyburn Road. For a couple of pence he was welcomed into a coach packed with young men.

At Tyburn, where the gallows stood, Mother Proctor had already rented every space in her viewing stands. The crowd was pressing in from behind. In front, people on one another's shoulders were blocking the view. Cartwright bought some gingerbread and then for a shilling acquired seating space on top of a coach which afforded a good view of the executions. As he hadn't seen a hanging in London for several years, he decided to make his business appointments wait.

The executions were about to begin. The first convict, a toothless thief, was too drunk to speak clearly, and his voice didn't carry well. He seemed to think he was making a brave show, pointing aloft and striking his chest, but the crowd was dissatisfied and pelted him with pieces of food. The noose had not been adjusted properly, and when he was hoisted up it slipped over the back of his head and allowed him to fall. He made a wriggling effort to escape, but the crowd held him back, and soon the hangman and constable had him again and fitted the noose more tightly around his neck.

Someone was shouting. A woman, stepping out of a crowded coach near to where Cartwright sat. "What is this man guilty of?" she cried out. "You make his misfortune your savage amusement, and call yourselves a civilized people! Each of you who enjoys this spectacle should submit to a like punishment!" There were jeers, shouts of "Shut it!" "Hang yourself!" Some threw pieces of turnip and roast potato.

Cartwright was intrigued. She was a good-looking young woman, oddly dressed in a high-bodiced grey silk dress and carrying a large yellow shawl. She pushed her way out through the crowd away from Tyburn, and Cartwright slipped down off the coach and followed her. Some urchins continued to pitch bits of rubbish in her direction. Cartwright chased them away, but she took no notice of him.

"Do you believe crime should go unpunished then?" he asked when he'd caught up with her.

"Of course not. But the punishment should suit the crime, and be less prejudiced against the poor. Death for what that man did is preposterous. Deportation would be a blessing given the state of affairs here."

"You sound bitter."

"Leave me alone."

"It's strange for a lady like you to be alone in a place like this in the first place. But to decline innocent company is stranger still."

"I'm a strange person. And that's how I'll remain to you."

"Why did you go there if you find the proceedings so opposed to your taste?"

"I was taken against my will by the idiot driver of the hackney-coach I was riding in. He pretended to be caught in the crowd. He knew he could make more money renting his roof to people like you than by taking me to my destination. He even demanded I pay him for taking me there."

"Are you married?"

"No."

"Are you . . . a governess?"

"Exactly – you sound like my brother. A woman is either married or a governess, or a burdensome spinster. Or a . . . disgrace."

"A strange coincidence. I was just thinking that in *your* views you remind me of *my* brother John – a great critic of how things are done."

"Then it's your brother I ought to be talking with, not you. . . . Until recently I was living in France, where changes are coming and people are not afraid to look at things with fresh eyes. We English pride ourselves on our liberty, but I find we could learn a thing or two from what's happening over there."

"What took you to France? And why have you consented to return to this pitiful place?"

"I was there as governess to the child of a wine merchant. But the child died. And I find myself now in the house of my brother who urges me each morning to find myself either a husband or a new charge. Which is what I was attempting to do before becoming entangled in the sport you were enjoying so much."

"Attempting to find a husband, you mean?"

"No. I was in Reeves Mews, answering an advertisment for a governess."

"And were you successful?"

"I wouldn't have accepted the position had it been offered me."

"Why?"

"The people were odious. The woman with her ring of keys and litany of injunctions. I must needs change my wardrobe and the cut of my hair before teaching French to their foolish girl. . . . Slavery has various forms. Only great wealth confers liberty in this self-deluding land."

"Would you like to leave it again?"

"Fervently."

"And you're looking for employment?"

She didn't answer.

"I'd like to leave it too as it turns out," he went on, "though more for opportunity and adventure than to escape hangings and haircuts. I'm . . . my name is George Cartwright. I'm forming a company to trade in furs and fish in Labrador, and I need a lady to . . . to manage my domestic affairs for me. Would you be interested?"

She stopped and looked at his face for the first time. Studied his eyes and lips.

"Labrador?" she said.

"Yes. I've been there. Near there. It's wonderfully . . . wonderfully full of . . . space. It cured my ague. And my melancholy."

They were silent for a while, as they made their way down the edge of Tyburn Road.

"I'm Mrs. Selby," she said. "When do you plan to leave?"

✧

On the 25th of May, 1770, Cartwright began his first voyage to Labrador. He was accompanied by Mrs. Selby – who had bid good riddance to England – and by his servant Charles Atkinson and a man from Nottingham named Haines, who, having been a gamekeeper at Averham Park, understood animals and knew how to live outdoors, at least in England. Completing his entourage were six foxhounds (three male and three female), a pair of bloodhounds, a greyhound, a pointer, a spaniel, and a couple of tame rabbits.

It turned out that Cartwright had to buy two ships to cross the Atlantic. To begin with, Perkins and Coghlan had sold him and Lucas an expensive eighty-ton schooner, the *Enterprise*, to use in crossing the ocean and running their business in Labrador. But before either Lucas or Cartwright could get to Bristol to board the ship, Perkins and Coghlan sent it ahead to Fogo with supplies of their own. Lucas, who arrived in Bristol ahead of Cartwright, then sailed with Coghlan in another ship. And when Cartwright, with his retinue, finally reached Bristol, Perkins was waiting for him with the news that all the ships destined for Newfoundland that season had already sailed. The only thing Perkins could suggest was that Cartwright help buy a second ship to take them across. Cartwright could then turn his share in the ship over to Perkins and Coghlan in exchange for a slightly higher percentage of future profits. This was how business with Perkins and Coghlan went.

After forty-three days they landed at Fogo Island, off the northeast coast of Newfoundland. The *Enterprise* was there being repaired for the trip to Labrador.

Cartwright filled the time by taking his people and dogs on board a small sloop and going from island to island in Notre Dame Bay hunting foxes and caribou. With his pocket telescope he also scanned the shores for signs of Beothuks. He was still disappointed that he hadn't encountered any on his trip up the Exploits River two years before. He continued to hope that he would be able to capture some, to convince them by force of his peaceful intentions, and, as a result, become famous as the man who led them out of their savage obscurity. He pictured himself displaying his willing captives before gatherings of scholars, explaining their novel grammar, their curious lore.

He did spy Indians in the distance, camped on an island, and was all for taking his men and the boat's crew and surprising them at night. But as Charles was the only one willing to go along with his plan, he reluctantly gave the idea up.

In Fogo, Cartwright hired workers: five woodsmen, six furriers, a cook named Nan O'Brien, a cooper, two carpenters, a boy as carpenter's helper, a mason, and a blacksmith who was Nan O'Brien's husband. He also bought goats, a pig, and several chickens.

Just before leaving Fogo, Mrs. Selby tripped on a sparsely planked landing-stage and broke her leg. The break was not serious. Cartwright set the bone himself and made a splint. Mrs. Selby cursed loudly, not because of the pain or because she feared being lame in the wilderness, but because she wouldn't be able to stand on deck and enjoy the trip. She had loved the crossing from England in spite of its length. She'd spent whole after-noons at the rail watching the sea. At least three times, when Cartwright was standing on deck beside her, she had looked at him with a kind of thrill in her eyes and said, "You can breathe out here."

The weather was clear and warm during the days they sailed in Notre Dame Bay, and although she was angry with Cartwright whenever he talked of capturing Indi-ans, and complained of having to wait while he chased his dogs through the thickets on every island they came to, she was happy and excited by everything she saw. During their few days on Fogo she'd made friends with a young widow who sold spiced herring and rum, and painted small pictures of harbours with fishing-families at work. "People are different here," Mrs. Selby said. "I don't think they care for a lot of our laws."

She had two trunks of books with her, but during the crossing had left them untouched, planning to save them until she was settled in. During the four-day journey from Fogo to Labrador she got Charles to open one of the trunks, and, lying in bed, her leg heavily wrapped from ankle to knee, she read Frances Brooke's *The History of Emily Montague*, putting the book face down on her stomach every few paragraphs, hoping to make it last as long as she could.

Before leaving England, Cartwright had exchanged several letters with Mrs. Selby and visited her a few times to get acquainted and discuss preparations for the trip. They rode on horseback to Hampstead together. They walked in Vauxhall Gardens. There, when he put his arm around her and kissed her, she disengaged herself and went on speculating about the kinds and quantity of footwear to take. At times Cartwright had wondered whether she was the right choice. She was not purely a drawing-room creature, as she'd demonstrated by her ability to manage a horse, and by her general adventurousness, but he didn't know how she'd take to living in a cabin during the winter in Labrador. He didn't know for certain how he'd take to it either, he reminded himself. And that made it all the more important to be sure they could share the same bed. That was really the point of having a housekeeper, after all. He tried to be blunt about this. "The winters are very cold there, I'm told. And sleeping alone is apt to have fatal results."

"Oh I imagine with furs and feather-beds we'll survive. And we can all take turns tending the fire. It's a new land, and new methods and ingenuity are required. As you said yourself." She grinned.

The sort of lady companion he usually took hunting with him would certainly keep him warm at night. But how would he survive that kind of woman's company cooped up for eight months of winter in a small house? Mrs. Selby's company he enjoyed. He liked her opinions, her reactions to things, although he always disagreed with them. An outspoken woman was an amusing novelty. The other things would work themselves out naturally, he decided.

At the inn on the way from London, and at Bristol, Cartwright and Mrs. Selby had separate rooms. But when they boarded the ship, Cartwright insisted that the lack of space required them all to share accommodation. "This is our berth," he said, opening a cabin door. "And we're lucky to have it to ourselves."

Naked, she lay very gently against his body, her fingers at either side of his neck. "Is this the work you expect of me? I can do more than this."

"You'll need to once we get over there. But we have to be friends."

"Will I be a partner then? Or a servant like the rest?"

"A partner. And a servant both."

"This needs more discussion then."

❖

On the 28th of July, Labrador lifted out of the west with the slow dawn. Cartwright's first impression was of something prehistoric, more primitive even than Newfoundland. Under the grey sky the coast with its headlands and islands seemed black, made purely of rock thinly covered in moss and low spruce. It was rugged, without being lofty or grand. Hills, plateaus, and canyons stretched north and south as far as he could see, but they all seemed low, like creatures huddled and hiding their faces, or raising only their foreheads out of the sea.

Country of bones, Cartwright thought. The very beginning or the end of things.

Lucas pointed out the bay they were headed for. The valleys he said were more fertile, richer in trees than it first appeared.

Sir Edward Hawke, First Lord of the Admiralty, and Commodore Byron, the new governor of Newfoundland, were delighted that someone had come along who was willing to occupy Nicholas Darby's old station on the Charles River, after the unfortunate outcome of Darby's efforts to start a business there. Hawke and Byron sent two sloops of war to Fort York in Chateau Bay, about thirty miles south of the Charles River, to wait for Cartwright's arrival and offer him guns and encouragement. Cartwright loved the approval of powerful men and also loved to display his gentlemanly unselfishness, which he knew would increase their approval. When the *Enterprise* called in at Fort York, he dined with the captains on board their ships and turned down their offer of arms, saying he already had enough of his own.

A Lieutenant Davyes, whom Cartwright had met on the *Guernsey* two years before, was now commander at Fort York. He presented Cartwright with a New England whale-boat, then opened two hogsheads to show him the huge hams of white bear pickled in brine which he was about to send as a compliment to the governor in St. John's.

Lucas was the only one with any experience of Labrador. He piloted the *Enterprise* into the mouth of the Charles River, led their small flotilla of punts and whale-boats upstream, and indicated where Darby's settlement had been. There were tiny, almost invisible buildings at the foot of a brushy hill. The newcomers penned their animals in what was left of a couple of sheds and put up tents for themselves.

In the first nights they camped there, Cartwright's people were terrified of being attacked by Inuit or bears. The ones who had never heard loons before believed their cries to be those of spirits or savages.

While Lucas sailed the *Enterprise* up the coast looking for Inuit with whom to trade, Cartwright set his crew to cutting wood and constructing buildings.

His colony consisted of twenty-two people. Mrs. Selby and Nan were the only women. Since the success of the venture would depend most on the work of the furriers, Cartwright chose the one with the greatest experience, a man by the name of Milmouth, to be his headman. The English gamekeeper, Haines, was older than Milmouth, but since Haines had no experience of North American animals, Cartwright realized it would be a mistake to set him above the Newfoundland crew. Most of the hired men were in their early twenties, although Bettres, the carpenter's helper, was only fourteen years old. Charles, at fifty-three, was the oldest person in the settlement. In Labrador, he would serve less as Cartwright's domestic servant and more as a general worker, helping with hunting, carpentry, gardening, whatever the circumstances required.

Cartwright paced the site and drew up plans for a group of buildings. Highest up from the river, commanding the best view, would be the main building, his residence. It would feature a cooking and dining area large enough to serve all his people on special occasions. Two storerooms and a bedroom for himself and Mrs. Selby would open off the main room. A long structure containing quarters for his men would lie close to his house. It would include eight small chambers, each with from two to four beds, and a common cooking and dining room where the men would prepare their meals. Cartwright's cook, Nan, and her husband would have a cabin of their own. There would be storage sheds near the river, a carpentry shop and smithy, a couple of latrines, a wharf for small boats. There would be no point in constructing a permanent wharf, Milmouth told him. Floods and ice would be sure to sweep it away.

Nan and most of the men wanted a palisade. For a moment Cartwright recalled the star-shaped bastions he used to build in his imagination, with their scarps, counter-scarps, glacis, ravelins, and demi-lunes. He had the workers; now would be the time to realize those dreams. But no, he was sick of all that, and he didn't want to hide behind walls, he wanted to see what the country had to offer, get out into it, invite it in. He imagined Inuit joining him – erecting their tents or whatever fascinating dwellings they used – enlarging his colony on the banks of the Charles. Perhaps a village, a city would grow there. He didn't want limits to his domain.

But the first thing Cartwright constructed was a crutch for Mrs. Selby. With it she was able to make her way along the bank of the river and fish for trout. Later he carried her on his back through a low spruce thicket onto an open hill where they picked berries and enjoyed the view. "My God!" she said, rubbing her forehead and neck. "What are these flies?"

On the morning of the 2nd of August, there was a half-inch of ice in the bucket outside their tent. In his journal Cartwright wrote: "Whether this be the last of the spring or the first of the autumn frosts, I cannot yet determine."

Only at times was Cartwright discouraged by the blackflies in Labrador. Being accustomed to the bites of fleas and lice since childhood, the venom of these new creatures did not irritate him. He grew desperate only when the flies swarmed so densely around his face that he found himself inhaling them. Or when they bit his forehead and temples in such numbers that his blood flowed into his eyes. Eventually, at the height of the blackfly season, he adopted the Inuit practice of greasing his hair and exposed skin with animal fat. He experimented by making an ointment of powdered red ochre mixed with melted fat, and found this more effective than plain fat. On this basis he theorized that the Beothuks coloured their bodies with ochre not for cosmetic or religious purposes, but to ward off flies.

As an old man he would expound this theory in a lecture to the Royal Society in London. He provided a demonstration in which he greased his left hand with some of his red ochre ointment and then introduced it into a large glass jar containing a piece of honeycomb swarming with bees. The bees clearly avoided his russet grasp. He invited his audience to repeat his action with their hands unprotected, or protected only with common lard, a tin of which he placed on the table before him. As no one accepted his invitation, he grinned crookedly, showing his few remaining teeth, and said, "Thank you, gentlemen. I take that as eloquent approbation of my theory."

✦

Cartwright wakes up in his room in The Turk's Head. He's been sleeping at his desk, his head on his opened journal. He has been dreaming of hunting in Labrador. He'd shot a large white owl on the tip of a spruce tree, and the ball had severed its legs. The bird had floundered in the air, legless and bleeding, and then swooped directly toward him so that its face loomed up disk-like and surprisingly big. It was an owl's face, with its startled, severe eyes, but also a human face. Human in essence, or in his feeling toward it. The horror had wakened him.

He rubs his eyes. The candles are still burning. Although they drip they never get any shorter. He looks at his journal, the last entry on the page. John. He dips his pen.

1819. May. Wednesday 19.
Wind S.W. light.

I hadn't been on the Charles River more than a couple of weeks when early one morning just as I was about to sail for Chateau I met my brother John coming up the river in a whale-boat. John was still a lieutenant in the navy and had been made deputy commissary to the vice-admiralty court in Newfoundland. This meant that he had the task of trying to sort out the endless wrangles among fishing company owners and among the owners and their crews in places like Trinity Bay. I could see right away that he didn't look well.

John was there on the Charles River, officially at least, because Admiral Hawke had put him in command of the schooner, *Ranger*, to bring me a gift of some extra carpenters and supplies. Of course the idea for the voyage was as much John's as anyone's. He wanted to share in the start of my venture, and he wanted to get out of court duties in Old Perlican. His mission to Labrador was a perfect excuse; on the Charles River he was beyond recall. He managed to stay until the end of September, at which point there was only time enough to get back to St. John's and board the *Guernsey* for its return home.

On his way up, John had stopped in at Chateau, where, hearing of Mrs. Selby's accident, he located a surgeon's mate on one of the ships anchored there and kindly brought him along to attend to her.

The carpenters and seamen he'd brought with him we set to work alongside my people, and John and I went shooting, together with Mr. Langman, his first mate. Having the *Ranger* at our disposal, we often took a small crew and sailed the coast to the north, drawing a rough map as we went and naming every river, island, cove, and headland we came to after family members and friends. One very bald island with a small indifferent harbour where we passed the night I called Granby Island. It was like being children again.

✦

"Cartwright."

"Yes."

"My position is housekeeper?" Mrs. Selby asked.

"Yes."

"Then you'll have to give me something to keep. So far there's little to distinguish this place from the huts they've made for the goats and the pig. Imagine this earth floor in the winter. The cold and damp will kill us before Christmas."

"You're probably right. I'll have them put in a wooden one. I was meaning to anyway."

"You're away hunting all the time with your brother. You don't watch what these fellows do. Look how they've built the chimney. It ought to be made of stone till it clears the roof. We'll have the house flaming around our ears, the way they've done it. Sticks and clay. It looks like something the beavers would slap together with their tails. And we'll need at least one more chimney in here. I want one for the copper alone. We'll need the hearth just to heat the room and for people to warm themselves and dry their clothes. Nan and I can't be trying to cook there with that going on. So why don't we put the kitchen at the other end?"

"I see what you mean."

"And we ought to have a trench between the back wall of the house and the hill. When it rains, the water comes under the wall."

"Anything else?"

"Yes. The walls and roof are too thin. We ought to double their thickness if we want to keep out the wind."

✧

1770. August. Friday 24.
Wind W. fresh.

This morning we left the *Ranger* at anchor in Gilbert's River while my brother and I went in his whale-boat up Porcupine Creek, which we found to run about three miles to the westward and to be very narrow.

Mr. Langman went on shore at Olivestone to roast a haunch of venison and bake a venison pastry. Just as the food was ready, the woods caught fire, and burnt with great fury, which forced Mr. Langman and his assistants to make a precipitate retreat. He saved the venison and implements of cookery, but a boat's sail and a few other things were considerably injured by the accident.

Friday 31.
Wind N.E. little.

We sailed at daylight and anchored again off the east end of a handsome, wooded island which I named Cartwright Island. There, all the shooters landed and stationed themselves across the middle of it, each placing himself within proper distance of his neighbour. After sending the two boats to lie off different points, we dispatched a few sailors into the woods with the hounds. In the afternoon a young hind passed within shot of my brother, but he didn't see her. An hour after, I saw her again, standing up to her belly in a pond which was above a mile below me. There I got within distance and killed her. In the course of the day I shot three curlews, three grouse, and an auntsary. The rest of the party killed four grouse, one curlew, one auntsary, and a whabby.

September. Monday 3.

Early this morning both boats were equipped, and we took all the hounds along with us and sailed to Langman Island, but found no deer there; nor is that a likely place for them to continue on, for it is a steep narrow ridge of a hill covered with bad woods and destitute of proper food.

In our investigation of the coast and islands to the north of Cape Charles, we have encountered no sign of Eskimos. John and I both, several times, have sighted what we took to be dwellings, or evidence of human industry, and have directed our craft close to the place in question, only to be disappointed each time. I hope, for

John's sake, we will meet with some Eskimos before John's duties compel him to leave.

Wednesday 12.

At daylight I got four of the men from the *Ranger* to work on shore. To prevent being flooded by the melting of the snow in the spring, as the hill rises very suddenly at the back of my house, I resolved to have a drain cut parallel to the upper side of it, and another from each end of that down to the river.

Monday 17.

All hands were employed today as follows: six men in the woods; three on the drain; two carpenters slitting the planks; one at work in the house; another nailing battens on the paper which was put upon the store roof; my brother, the mason, and Charles, in setting up a copper in the kitchen; two men were employed in bringing tree roots out of the garden and piling them up for firing; Mr. Langman and Bettres in building an oven a little distance from the house; and I was engaged in making four canvas bags for the purpose of bringing home venison, and also in scraping the otter's skin.

Friday 21.

Mr. Langman completed his oven today. Having taken out of the oven the supports which he'd made use of to turn the arch upon, he was making a fire in it in order to bake a pie, when alas! down it fell; to no small mortification of us all.

Sunday 22.

My house not having yet been distinguished by any name, we called it Ranger Lodge, in honour of His Majesty's schooner which was moored before the door.

Mr. Langman began another oven.

Sunday 23.

The kitchen chimney, being a wooden one, and the roof of the dining room took fire today; but it was extinguished before they received much damage.

Tuesday 25.

Mr. Langman finished his second oven, and we baked a pie and a pudding very much to our satisfaction.

The roof of the house took fire today from the heat of the stove funnel.

Sunday 30.

This morning Mr. Langman killed a porcupine upon the hill at the east of the house; and, although his hands suffered some injury in its preparation, he succeeded in baking it in a pastry.

My brother left me this evening to return to St. John's.

As we have not yet encountered Eskimos, I begin to fear they no longer inhabit this region of the coast.

Before boarding ship, the surgeon's mate gave Mrs. Selby's leg one last examination from top to bottom, pronounced it cured, and urged her to discard her crutch.

✧

1819. May. Wednesday 19.
Wind S.W. light.

I always thought of John's visit with me in Labrador as the happiest time we ever passed together. He was excited about my enterprise and proud of me, and I enjoyed showing him over land that I already thought of as mine. Differences arising from loans and the division of our father's estate sometimes clouded our relations in subsequent years. It was not until toward the end of my life, when he helped me in building and testing a number of inventions, that we again enjoyed one another's company so unreservedly.

And yet, now that I think of it, John was unwell during his whole stay. He was always eager enough to join me in following rivers or tramping the barrens for birds, but he was pale and thin, and I often had to stop and wait for him. At night, over glasses of rum, he was never light-hearted. He railed against the navy's backwardness and fumed at length about a newly invented chain-pump which he said had been shown to empty bilges twice as fast as the usual pumps, but which had been scorned by the men in charge of outfitting the navy's ships. He vowed to write letters on the topic when he got back to England.

We embraced when he left. To me he felt thinner than ever. He wished me success and, then, looking over my shoulder at the land, he said he doubted he'd ever return to that part of the world.

✧

"I refuse to refer to this place as Ranger Lodge. I'll call it the Lodge, or simply Lodge, if you like."

"What? For Christ's sake. *Why?*" Cartwright, who was hanging bunches of Labrador tea in the rafters of their house, stepped down from the bench and stared at Mrs. Selby. "How can you always question my actions?"

"The loyal tribute, I think, is out of place."

"That is ingratitude. The *Ranger* was sent here for our benefit at His Majesty's expense."

"His Majesty knew nothing about it," Mrs. Selby said calmly.

"This is only your bitterness."

"Your pious loyalty is neither honest nor handsome."

Reddening, Cartwright drew himself stiffly erect. "You will not speak to me like this." He used his military voice.

"You're acting on your own behalf here, not the King's," Mrs. Selby went on. "And I think we're more alone than you suppose."

"All the more reason then to honour the King and the nation that give us our strength."

"It's our own strength we'll have to rely on here."

One night in early October, while Cartwright and Mrs. Selby were stewing curlews in a pan at the hearth and the chimney was moaning overhead, two men from the *Enterprise* opened the door of the Lodge and stepped into the firelight. The wind was a bugger to row against, they said. It had kept them down on the anchored ship all day. They were surprised that Captain Lucas wasn't already there, drinking hot rum at the fireside. Lucas and one of his sailors had gone ashore that morning to make their way to the Lodge overland.

Cartwright rushed out and ordered Charles and a couple of others to build a large fire on Battery Hill above the house, and he stood beside it, the sparks and flames pulled horizontal away from him, checking his watch, firing his gun every fifteen minutes. At five in the morning Lucas and his companion pushed their way out of the spruce trees, drenched in bog water and mud, nearly speechless with cold.

"I've got some for you," Lucas said.

"Some what?"

"Eskimos."

Five days to the north Lucas had found an Inuit settlement and persuaded one of its chief men to bring his family to spend the winter near Cartwright's post, to establish friendly trade. He had them on board the ship, nine of them, along with their boat, their sled, their dogs, kayaks, and other things. They'd want to make their home down near the sea where seals were plentiful, not up on the river where Cartwright was.

Lucas couldn't stay long. A few days, a week, was all

he could spare, he said. He was shaking, unable to hold the mug Cartwright put in his hands. The *Enterprise* would be useless – would be wrecked – on the Labrador coast in the winter, with the rivers and bays all solid ice. To make the ship pay for itself he'd sail it to Portugal now with a load of Perkins and Coghlan's fish, then down to the Caribbean with wine and cloth, then back to Newfoundland in the spring with sugar and rum. And to Labrador. To bury Cartwright's frozen bones.

Three Inuit men came up the river in kayaks. The older man was Attuiock. Lucas had explained that Attuiock was a kind of chief and a kind of priest, and that among the Inuit the chiefs and priests were often hard to distinguish from other people.

With Attuiock were his young brother Tooklavinia and his nephew Etuiock. They shook Cartwright's hand and smiled. Cartwright showed them the buildings on his station, his boats, and introduced them to all his people, some of whom at first were afraid to approach the Inuit. The Inuit seemed familiar with European boat-building and carpentry and took little notice of it.

The goats and the pig, however, held their attention for a long time. They squatted close to the animals, sniffing, pointing to various parts of the creatures' bodies and talking together calmly and steadily.

Nan and Mrs. Selby served them a breakfast of hotcakes, boiled trout, and coffee.

Lucas had left Cartwright a simple handwritten Inuit vocabulary. Inuktitut, Lucas had said it was called. Cartwright at once began to put it to use and tried to enlarge it. He pointed to various objects, utensils, articles of clothing. He gestured to suggest different actions and wrote down approximations of what the men said.

"I want . . . your . . . words," he said, consulting Lucas's sheets. He repeated his sentence, pointing at the three men, then making his fingers flutter in front of his mouth and pretending to snatch the fluttering entities and clutch them to his chest. Attuiock looked somewhat alarmed at this demonstration, but Etuiock and Tooklavinia rolled on the floor laughing.

The rest of Attuiock's family comprised his wife Ickcongoque, their three children, Tooklavinia's wife Caubvick, and another woman who was either a servant or slave. Attuiock brought them to visit the following day. Since Cartwright's people hadn't seen children for a number of months, they doted on Attuiock's young ones, offering them buttons, pieces of sugar, bread with partridge berry jam. With their children there, the Inuit seemed less fearsome, and the gift-giving was as much an act of gratitude as a sign of affection.

"They're very jolly people," Mrs. Selby said, "and very easy to please. . . . But their harsh way of life, their diet and so on . . . being so different, so much less . . . refined than what we're used to, at least *were* used to in England . . . leaves its inescapable mark on them."

"They'll change, I think, slightly, with time." Cartwright said. "It's one of the things we have to offer them in exchange for their goods. Our knowledge, our habits, I mean."

"I wonder, though," Mrs. Selby said, "what use our habits will be to them, except to make the Eskimos more acceptable to us."

"To be civilized is worthy in itself." Cartwright spread his arms as though offering himself as an example. "It's the duty of the civilized man to elevate the savage."

"It's our duty, I should think, really, to leave them alone if we can't accept them as they are."

"*You* are the one who was complaining about them just now!" Cartwright exclaimed. "And we *can't* leave them alone. We're in their country. They're one of the reasons we came here."

"Why can't we work on our own without involving them?"

"Because they know the country. And they're numerous. Trading with them for furs will be much more practical than doing all of the trapping ourselves. And in fact, I rather like them as they are. There's an uncorrupted nobility about them. They're certainly no worse in their outward appearance than my own woodsmen here, or the people I lived with in Scotland some years ago. I'll visit them at their camp tomorrow and invite them for supper."

✦

1770. October. Friday 12.

Early this morning I went to pay a visit to the Eskimos. Of all the people I ever yet heard of, the Eskimo, I think, are the most uncleanly. They even exceed the accounts which I have read of the Hottentots, for they not only eat the guts of an animal, but with a still higher gout for delicacies of this kind, they devour even the contents! Their tent was highly impregnated with the effluvia of such savoury dainties. At the farther end, a little raised from the ground on pieces of boards, were abundance of deer-skins and garments on which they both sat and slept. The rest was well filled with vessels for eating and drinking, bags of seals' oil, part of the carcass of a seal recently killed, fat, guts, fish, and a great variety of other good things, all lying in glorious confusion, on which their dogs and themselves fed promiscuously. The whole was nauseous in the highest degree, and I was obliged to quit the place without much reluctance. Afterwards, I walked upon the cape land where I killed a pair of eider ducks, a grouse, and a ptarmigan.

✧

In dark November, Attuiock sat in the chair across from Cartwright, his hands propped on his knees, staring at the floor. Each of his slow breaths came out as a sigh. Cartwright waited to hear what was on his mind.

His house was bad, he said at last. His family was not well. His youngest child had died. There was not enough food.

Cartwright wondered if it had been a mistake to separate the Inuit from the rest of their people. Would they be a burden all winter, expecting him to provide for them? Would they be any use? Had he and Lucas, in some subtle way, disrupted their capacity to survive?

He offered to build him a new house in whatever location Attuiock chose. He gave him hardbread and salt pork. Then he remembered something Lucas had brought back as a curiosity from his journey up the coast: a leather sack filled with fermented oil and pieces of fat. That, Lucas had said, was the Inuit notion of pudding. Cartwright had hung the thing on a spike in the woodshed and forgotten about it. He got it now and presented it to Attuiock, half afraid that Lucas had been playing a trick on him and that Attuiock would be incensed by the gift. But Attuiock accepted it and, seeming faintly comforted, took it to share with his family.

Cartwright and Mrs. Selby discussed the affair.

"Why did you give it to him if you thought it was bad?"

"Lucas assured me they like it. And I wanted to please him. I suppose it's no worse than cheese, when you think of it. Or that German stuff, sauerkraut."

✦

Cartwright wakes up fully dressed on his bed in The Turk's Head. He's been having the fire dream.

John's first mate, Mr. Langman, had been baking pies in his misshapen oven behind the Lodge. Cartwright had seen the pies as Langman prepared them. They contained small fur-covered animals, curled up, probably sleeping rather than dead. The coals Langman had raked from the oven were scattered around. Cartwright walked on them, squeaking them under his boots. When they shattered, they were bright orange inside.

Someone shouted, and Cartwright looked up. The bushes behind the Lodge were on fire. Cartwright took up a shovel and beat at the flames. He shouted to Langman and Charles and Mrs. Selby to bring water. But the whole hillside was blazing. He clambered up through the acrid smoke flailing at small crackling trees.

From the hill-top, as far as he could see, the country was burning, curling up, contracting, like a sheet of paper in flames on a grate.

6

Here is what Cartwright sees when he sits at his desk, thinking of nothing: boulders, light brown, their sides creased like elephant hide. On top of each, like a cap, and sometimes draped from one to the other in a continuous cloak, is a layer of black peat, five or six inches thick. Over the peat grows a tangle of moss, ferns, and miniature shrubs. Erosion has cut the peat at the edges as clean as sliced cake, exposing thousands of tiny dead roots and twigs matted together. History of all the growth since the recent glaciers. All the summers' work.

The rocks stand at the border of a pond, their bottoms disappearing into water which looks black from a distance, tea-coloured up close. There are trout in the water, long bronze shapes half made of shadows. The bottom is out of sight.

✦

In his first winter in Labrador, Cartwright didn't know what to expect of the weather. He attached his Fahrenheit thermometer to the outside wall of the Lodge and recorded its readings every morning and evening along with the wind's direction and speed and the condition of the skies. Having been told that the winter would be colder than he could imagine, he kept expecting it to get much colder and forced himself and his people out in snowstorms and bitter winds to develop their tolerance for the climate. "If we cower indoors in this kind of weather," he wrote, "it being still only December, and the mercury not having reached the bottom of the glass by any extent, how shall we have the courage to do our work and get our food in the more severe conditions which are sure to come?"

As the winter progressed, he gradually learned that the worst weather lasted no more than three or four days at a stretch and was always followed by sunlight and temperatures not much below 0° Fahrenheit. And since traps were hard to find during blizzards and game was scarce in the spells of extreme cold in any case, he finally realized by the middle of March that it would have been only sensible to spend the most inclement days indoors.

There were problems with frostburn. Cartwright hadn't known what frostburn was. He would go out wearing fleece underwear, wool coats, and fur capes, and come back sweating and feverish, but with white frozen patches on his feet, fingers, and face. "The effect of frost," he wrote, "is to cause flesh to ache or sting as though being burnt and then to become numb; but the effect of thawing is painful to a far greater degree." Attuiock showed him how to thaw frozen skin using tepid water or the gentle warmth of another person's body, and cautioned against ever heating the frozen parts too rapidly in front of a fire.

Attuiock advised him on how to dress. He gave Cartwright caribou socks, sealskin boots and mitts. Mrs. Selby borrowed a parka from Ickcongoque and copied its design. Always inventive, Cartwright made modifications of his own, attaching various flaps of wool and fur to the garment Mrs. Selby made for him, so that he could cover or uncover parts of his face and neck as the weather and his exertions required. Because he would often walk twenty or more miles in a day on snowshoes, he found Inuit trousers too warm, and instead wore thick wool breeches and woollen wrappings below the knees.

His livestock suffered. The chickens' feet froze. The pig was frostburnt and had to be eaten well before Christmas.

Cartwright and his crew of furriers studied the animals of the area, then laid out a series of traps for marten, foxes, and otters. When most of the inland waters had frozen, but before the snow had covered them, he used skates to visit his traps, following an intricate system of ponds and brooks. He had brought the skates with him from England with no special use for them in mind other than pleasure. In Labrador, he strapped them to leather boots in the usual way, and then covered the boots with fur spats for warmth. Where his path took him away from the frozen ponds and brooks, he unstrapped his blades and slipped on snowshoes – "Indian rackets," he called them – which he otherwise carried on his back. In this way, he could check all his traps in less than half the time it had taken him walking on land.

Cartwright invited Attuiock to watch: he put on his skates, clattered onto the ice, and swept across Punt Pond with a few long, easy strides, then turned, glided back, and came to a stop in front of him with a small shower of ice. Attuiock was speechless. He understood the construction of sled-runners very well; the possibilities for fun and speed using foot-runners like Cartwright's seemed to set his imagination on fire.

Cartwright asked his blacksmith, O'Brien, to fashion a pair of skates for Attuiock. Because of Attuiock's soft footwear, it was necessary to attach the blades to wooden soles with vertical pegs at the sides to strap to his ankles. Attuiock dubbed the contraptions his "foot-sleds," and within a couple of days he was as proficient a skater as Cartwright was.

When Attuiock demonstrated his new skill to his family, he took a whip onto the ice with him and pretended to be driving an invisible team of dogs. His wife and children, and the few woodsmen and furriers who'd gathered to watch, fell about, wheezing with laughter. He shouted and acted as though the dogs were out of control, jerking him right and left, spinning him around, stopping suddenly, even making him go in reverse.

Cartwright's furriers were doing well, bringing in foxes, martens, otters. But once the furs were removed, what was left of the animals was barely enough to keep his people fed. His dogs were beginning to starve.

Cartwright went to Attuiock, who was no longer in

need since the winter seals had arrived, and begged some meat for his dogs. Attuiock threw a couple of frozen seals on his sled, hitched up his dogs, invited Cartwright aboard, and drove him along the river shore to the Lodge.

It was a kindness he repeated throughout the winter without being asked. He seemed to think nothing of it. Although Cartwright's people were not fond of seal, it was sometimes the only food they had.

Now and then Attuiock would call on Cartwright and stay the night. The two sat in front of the fire sipping hot, watered rum through pieces of sugar. With a small but rapidly growing number of English and Inuktitut words that they both understood, and with plenty of pantomime, there was very little they couldn't discuss.

"Is there no river where you can hunt and fish in your own land?" Attuiock asked.

"No. They are all in the camps of other men."

"Here there are many seals. Many fish and animals. You will be well."

"But why do you not catch seals? They are easy to catch and good. The animals you hunt are small and hard to catch. There is little meat on them and their skins are too small for clothing."

"In my country, people trade much money for those furs."

"What is the money for?"

"To trade for the ship that brought us here. To trade for the traps, the flour, rum, sugar. To give to my people. To trade for my own camp in my country."

"It is easier to hunt seals."

✦

"Do your people have whalebone, Attuiock? Can they get fox furs and marten furs to trade with me? Look. I have thread and needles, beads and hatchets to trade. Take this thread. For Ickcongoque."

"We have whalebone. We can get small furs. When I return to my people in the spring I will speak to them."

"You have clever things, Cartwright, but your people are few and weak. And you have no home. You are always wandering. We Inuit are strong and very many. We could kill you all very easily. But if you are peaceful you can stay. You will be well here."

"My people are many more than yours, Attuiock. They are the strongest in the world. They have more ships, more houses, big, big houses. You cannot dream them. I will take you and show you."

"Why do you white men smell bad?"

"We smell bad!? *You* smell bad."

"No. We smell good. You smell bad. Like the animals you brought here. The ones that froze."

"You must please the animals or they will go away from you. I have watched your trappers. Perhaps they offend the animals they have killed."

"How is that?"

"People are always in danger, because everything we kill is made of souls. Everything we eat is made of souls."

"What do you mean?"

"Everything is a man inside. When seals or caribou die – it is the same even for trees – their souls come out, and they look like people. Only they still think like seals or caribou. If we offend the souls of the things we kill, they will take revenge on us."

"Lucas told me that you are a priest – an angakok – as well as a chief."

"Yes."

"What does an angakok do?"

"I will show you sometime. I can chase away evil spirits. I can bring back people's souls."

"How is it done?"

"I have a powerful torngak to help me."

"What is that?"

"Mine is an owl. It can see where the seals and caribou are. . . . I also have secret words that are very strong."

"How did you become an angakok?"

"It began before I was born. A white owl dropped a rabbit beside my mother while she was carrying me in her body. When I was young, spirits came to me in the night. I would speak in my sleep, torngak words that only an angakok could understand. I would walk in my sleep and wake my family up. I would piss on them in the dark.

"When I was old enough, an angakok in the village began to tell me what to do. Each summer I would go to a hut in the hills and stay alone without any food. All day I would sit outside and rub a small stone against a large one, like this, around and around. And I would say secret words.

"When I had done this long enough, after many days, Torngarsoak in the shape of a large white bear came out of the lake below where I was sitting. He came straight to me and ate me slowly, limb by limb. I was only a skeleton lying there. And then my torngak came to me.

It was the white owl. It sat here on my ribs, and its life went into me, and I watched the flesh come back on my bones, first one leg, then the other, then my arms and belly, just in the order Torngarsoak had taken it off. My clothes came back on my body too. And I got up and went back to the village."

"Were you an angakok then?"

"No. I had to learn many more things from the old angakok. I had to learn the torngak language and how to travel into the land of souls.

"Finally, the old angakok came to the hut where I was staying alone. He came with a knife to try to kill me. It was the custom. If he could kill me, he would eat my liver and have control of my soul. If I could escape, it would mean I was finally an angakok like him.

"The chase lasted all afternoon. We went around and around the hut, down to the lake, around the hill and back to the hut again. We both had the power to go right through walls, so we would go in through the door of the hut and out through a wall, or in through a wall and out through the roof to surprise one another. At times he was very close to catching my clothes, but I could leap very far, even when the strength in my legs was gone. At last the sun set, and the old angakok sat down, and I walked to the village to announce myself."

"That you had won?"

"All that I told you was done in secret. None of my family knew what I was doing in the hills. I went into their house and said, 'I am an angakok.' I commanded them to put out the lamp so I could give them my proof.

"I called my torngak to speak in me and made him fly through the house so my family could hear his wings and feel them, and his claws, on their faces and hands."

✦

It was so cold at times the eyes of flying birds froze solid as beads, and the birds tumbled out of the air as though shot. The winter weather, even at its best, was like one continuous storm. To go out required special precautions. Indoors was the only safe place to be.

Cartwright was surprised how the weather invaded even there. Fine grains of snow would find their way through the smallest cracks around doors and windows or under the eaves. In the morning there would be drifts of snow, smoothly shaped into sharp crests or long loaves, lying against a wall or across a table or the foot of a bed. Cartwright patrolled the inside walls with his hands extended, feeling for blades of air. Where he felt them, he pounded scraps of discarded fur into the cracks the way a shipwright would caulk a hull. But even without draughts, the instant the fire died down the cold was there, rising up under their feet like the back of a whale. And six feet away from the fire the room was always cold, feet always numb, fingers clumsy.

Fire was something the body required more than food. To stop moving, without a fire nearby, was to start freezing to death. It was as though the house were a ship, and the land and everything else open sea. It was only strategy and vigilance that kept them alive. To step out the door absent-mindedly here, as he would in England, would mean dropping into a void.

And this was why the Inuit were so impressive. What was deliberate strategy for Cartwright was casual habit for them. He marvelled at them as people with gills who could live under water, or winged people who could flap along comfortably hundreds of feet in the air.

The jays, Cartwright noticed, were nearly tame. On a sunny day, he spread bird lime on some planks in front of the Lodge and scattered biscuit crumbs on top of them. It was similar to the porridge method he'd used to catch pigeons at the military academy years ago, only this time he took the creatures indoors and spared their lives. They ate from his hand at meals and perched on his shoulder when he dozed in front of the fire at night. The Lodge, the birds soon decided, belonged to them. They would fly out in the morning when they wanted exercise, and in again when they wanted warmth or an ear to peck.

Mrs. Selby called them messy creatures, but enjoyed their shrewd tactics and the festive air they gave the place. Cartwright made drawings of the jays in an effort to capture their cocky self-assurance. He sketched them eating grain from the rim of his hat on the dining table, but he was dissatisfied; he lacked the skill to show their quickness, their clever glances. For a few weeks, he repeated simple words to them, hoping to teach them to talk.

Cartwright was proud of his growing familiarity with the region's animals, and he sent descriptive accounts and specimens of them to his wealthy naturalist friend, Joseph Banks. Banks had had only a glimpse of Labrador in the late summer of 1766, and his collecting had been confined to the vicinity of Chateau. It was on his way home from that expedition that Banks had first met Cartwright in St. John's. The two had renewed their acquaintance later in London during the time when Cartwright was preparing to go into business in Labrador, and Banks, who was one of Cartwright's financial backers, had urged Cartwright to send him accounts of the flora and fauna he found in Labrador along with whatever specimens he could manage to ship back. Banks showed Cartwright the basic procedures for skinning, drying, pickling, and salting things and equipped him with plant presses and several cases of glass jars, none of which made the return journey intact.

He was pleased to act as a kind of colleague of Banks. Banks was an influential man, admired and doted on by a wide assortment of grandees, and the association was bound to serve Cartwright well. Scouting for Banks also added to Cartwright's business and sporting venture some of the dignity of a scientific expedition. It flattered him. It suited an image he had of himself: taking samples of this and that, making orderly notes. And it suited his cat-like instinct for studying anything with a motion of its own and trying to capture it.

Banks had also aroused Cartwright's competitive instincts. He gave him copies of the standard books and pamphlets on North American zoology – works by Nicolas Denys and Baron Arnaud Louis de Lahotan, for example – and asked Cartwright to see what he could add to them. Cartwright saw at once how laughably wrong and inadequate the books were. He filled their margins with scornful notes. The porcupine was *not* found on the island of Newfoundland. The polar bear did *not* change its colour to black in the summer.

The animal that most intrigued Cartwright was the beaver. Its furs had made fortunes for men trading in other parts of Canada, and although Lucas had told him beavers didn't exist in Labrador, Cartwright had been determined to find some. Cartwright had read and dreamed about beavers long before Banks loaned him his natural history books, and in his imagination they held the essence of the American North, something alien, secretive. He'd read of their industry, their skill as engineers, and the rational manner in which they divided their labours and governed themselves. He'd studied engravings giving interior views of their homes, which were constructed in suites of apartments several storeys tall. They had perfected the arch, it appeared, also the use of mortar and stucco, highway and bridge construction, and the art of felling giant trees. Their broad spatulate tails they used as trowels, and as sleds for dragging loads of mud-mortar to building sites. Their food, in the form of green willow sticks all of a regular length, was stacked in neat cords between stakes, sometimes beneath wicker canopies. Cartwright was eager to see these furry beings at work. He was sceptical of the accounts, but obsessed with their lore nonetheless. And their pelts were still worth a lot of money.

Within a week after landing on the bank of the Charles River, he had located a beaverhouse at the head of one of the brooks that flowed into the valley. The design of the house both disappointed and satisfied him. It looked, he wrote, like nothing more than a cartload of sticks. In a way he was sad that the fables of elegant beaver architecture were untrue. But, as a colleague of Banks, it pleased him to have disproved what his reason had told him all along were fanciful tales.

What followed were months of trying to trap the mysterious beasts. He opened their houses, studied their bedding and leftover food, their chambers and passageways. He placed traps in their underwater entrances and wrote optimistically in his journal that he had found a fresh house on Falcon Pond or Atkinson Pond. A week later he would write that he had decided the houses on Falcon and Atkinson Ponds were actually old ones, but that it didn't matter because he had found what was surely a new, inhabited beaverhouse on Island Brook.

The whole countryside was a maze of animal trails, flight-ways, feeding-grounds, breeding-grounds, nesting-grounds, burrows, and dens, like layers of interconnecting cities of animal cultures. Cartwright spent hours crouched among ferns or spruce, watching, making notes. And hours devising traps with nets, hooks, springs, levers, and weights.

✧

1770. November. Monday 19.
Wind N.W. moderate.

Arriving at the head of Long Pool, I met with the sliding of an otter which was so fresh that my greyhound challenged it, and I soon discovered the creature himself fishing in the disemboguing of the brook where it was yet open. I sat watching for an hour, in which time he caught plenty of small trout. He then got upon a small rock, which was at least one hundred yards from my station, and, while he was making room for more fish, I sent a ball through him, and killed him on the spot. I fixed him upon my back and hastened home, where I arrived at noon and found his weight to be thirty-three pounds.

✧

The sun would set at four in the afternoon, and although they made their own candles from animal fat, they couldn't make enough to light their house all the hours of darkness when they weren't asleep. At first Cartwright and Mrs. Selby tried to cut out the long evenings by going to bed shortly after dark, but then they'd wake up at one in the morning, still with eight hours of darkness to get through.

Eventually Cartwright learned from Attuiock how to make simple lamps that needed nothing more than a wick and a lump of fat, but while these lamps were more practical than candles, their light was never strong enough to read by for any length of time. Since the fireplace was the best source of light as well as heat, Cartwright and Mrs. Selby took to staying up as late as possible by the fireside, grilling pieces of meat, frying cakes of dough, making hot drinks, all the while chatting about their past experiences and their business in Labrador.

When they didn't have company, and had run out of things to talk about, they'd sometimes sing together, old well-known songs, and once in a while a hymn. Mrs. Selby, who claimed to be an agnostic, never proposed the hymns, but joined in when Cartwright began one. Cartwright himself wasn't a very religious man, but he enjoyed the occasional evening hymn, not for any devotional reason, but because of childhood associations and the sense of lonely fortitude he felt singing with Mrs. Selby in the dark in the wilderness.

Still there was often too much nigh' ̄ fill up, and Mrs. Selby, who couldn't even do needl   ᴜrk for very long by the light of an Inuit lamp without straining her eyes, bought a fiddle from one of the furriers and taught herself to play. She preferred holding the instrument upright between her thighs and bowing it like a cello. She began with familiar tunes, tried a few jigs and reels, since the fiddle seemed accustomed to that kind of music, then realized she could make it play anything she wanted and improvised long drifting pieces that she explained to Cartwright as journeys or stories. Cartwright accepted her playing as a kind of eccentric humming and would sit musing or writing in his journal by valuable candle-light, allowing his thoughts to mingle with hers, scarcely aware he was hearing her music at all.

✦

Attuiock: There was a young woman, and every night a young man would come into her house in the dark, get into bed with her, and make love with her. She had no idea who her lover was, so before going to sleep she took soot from the lamp and put it on her breasts. Her lover came to her as usual and slipped away again. The next morning, in the light of the lamp, she could see that her brother had soot on his forehead and hands. She was angry and horrified. She took a knife and cut off her breasts and said to him, "Since you find me so delicious, here, eat these too." And she flung her breasts at him, took up the lamp, and ran out of the house. Her brother took another lamp and chased after her. As they ran, they rose up into the sky. The sister's lamp burned brighter and brighter, and she became the sun. The brother's lamp burned paler and paler, and he became the moon. The moon is always following the sun, and sometimes he catches up with her and they lie together.

Cartwright: No. Listen. There is one God, who created the sun, the moon, and stars, and also the earth with everything on it. He created one man first, named Adam, and then He created the animals one by one in front of Adam, and Adam named them. And God said, "They're all yours to use for food and clothes, and to tame, and amuse yourself with. Just as I am God over you, you are god over the animals and the earth." And then God created a woman named Eve, and Adam and Eve did various things, and got into trouble with God. But that's another story. In any event, the sun and moon are not people. The sun is a huge fire, far away, and we are travelling around it, in the sky. The moon is a large ball of stone travelling around us. The earth is also a ball of stone. Because we know that, we can sail right around it. From England, over here, and all the way right around, past many other lands, if we want. There are tricks in the way things are put together – in the different types of rock in the earth – and if we figure them out, the tricks, we can change the way everything is done. To please ourselves. That's how we have iron, and ships, and guns. We have wheels pushed by water that do work for us. And engines now, iron animals with fire and water inside them, that are stronger than bears.

✦

In a box of earth near the kitchen stove Cartwright grew lettuce, mustard, and onions. In mid-December the plants were tall, although not as green as he'd hoped. He decided they must be ready to eat. He fried some slices of smoked ham until they were crisp, then crushed them into small pieces in their own drippings, added a dribble of olive oil (normally kept for medicinal uses), also some vinegar, and stirred the mixture together. When it was cool, he poured it over his greens in a wooden bowl.

He'd invited Attuiock and his family to share the meal. They came early in the day and joined the woodsmen and furriers in their usual Sunday pastimes, drinking rum, singing, and dancing. Several of Cartwright's men had musical instruments: fiddles, whistles, a small accordion. Charles had castanets that he'd carried with him ever since leaving Minorca. He played a single pair by rattling them between the palm of his left hand and his knee, like bones or a pair of spoons. The cooper had constructed a wide shallow drum. Attuiock tried it out, then kept it and played it himself the rest of the day.

Nan and Mrs. Selby had arranged platters of various roasted and boiled meats down the long communal table, along with plates of biscuits, pots of wild berry preserves, and jugs of spruce beer. At Cartwright's suggestion, they had lit more candles than usual. Supper was announced. Cartwright stood at the head of the table, the bowl of salad in front of him, waiting to serve a small portion to each of his people and guests as their plates were passed around.

His own people promptly set their instruments aside and took their seats, but the Inuit, who'd been snacking all afternoon on food they'd brought with them, were deeply involved in their songs and dances and weren't interested in sitting down at the table when the meal was served. They continued to circle the room, singing and stamping their feet, Attuiock in the lead, beating the drum.

Cartwright tried to get Attuiock to come to the table. Attuiock tried to get Cartwight to join the dance. Nan, who always sat to Cartwright's left, looked frightened, and Mrs. Selby, who always sat at his right, looked exhausted and annoyed.

Cartwright said grace in a loud voice and served salad to those who wanted it. His people helped themselves to biscuits and meat in the usual fashion, while the Inuit continued singing and jouncing around the table. Mrs. Selby took a few bites of food, then put down her fork, leaned her elbow on the table, and rested her forehead in her hand. A jay landed and began pecking at the biscuit on her plate. Wolves were howling in the hills, and that always got Cartwright's dogs worked up. They were howling and braying in the kennel outside. A greyhound with frostburnt toes that was convalescing by the hearth sat up and joined in with long wails. Mrs. Selby looked at Cartwright, who was eating his salad with studied nonchalance, leaf by leaf. She started to laugh, then took up a couple of spoons, clanged them together, and got up to join the Inuit's dance.

The sawyers at the far end of the table, who'd been furtively adding rum to their spruce beer, cheered and got up to join her. Charles and the rest of the people did the same, eating as they danced, reaching out and helping themselves to meat and biscuits as they went by. Cartwright stayed at the table, calmly taking small bites of food and small sips from his cup. He noticed how hot it was becoming and went outside to get his thermometer, which he propped against the salad bowl in front of his plate. It shot up to eighty degrees. Eighty-five. He continued to eat his salad, studying each leaf. The room was shaking under his people's feet. Ninety degrees! The fire in the hearth was actually dying out, but the room was growing unbearably hot, fuelled with rum and a bit of fat. He wondered if rum was cheaper than firewood. The labour required to cut the wood and drag it home constituted a considerable expense. Just give them rum and save on wood. They might even pay *him* to heat *his* house. But there was always the noise and the nuisance it caused. And however good a source of heat it might be, it eventually made people sick, sometimes dangerous. In contrast, cutting wood in the fresh air was actually good for them.

✧

1770. December. Monday 24.

At sunset the people ushered in Christmas, according to the Newfoundland custom. In the first place they built up a prodigious large fire in their house. All hands then assembled before their door, and one of them fired a gun, loaded with powder only. After that each of them drank a dram of rum, and together they concluded the ceremony with three cheers. These formalities being performed with great solemnity, they retired into their house, got drunk as fast as they could, and spent the whole night in drinking, quarrelling, and fighting. It is but natural to suppose that the noise which they made (their house being but six feet from the head of my bed) together with the apprehension of seeing my house in flames, prevented me from once closing my eyes. This is an intolerable custom, but as it has prevailed since time immemorial, it must be submitted to. By some accident my thermometer got broke.

7

The door of the Lodge faced east, away from the winter wind. Snow from the hills swirled over the roof and settled in front of the building in drifts to above the eaves. Cartwright woke up in darkness, lit a candle, opened the door to a wall of snow. He tunnelled his way to the top of the drift, then dug down in search of the windows, to let in the early light. Some of his mustard and onions were inside near the sill, still straining to live. The lettuce had died.

People were often sick now, some of them coughing from deep in their lungs. In the evening they came to Cartwright to be bled. He would take down the lancet and bowl from the shelf and perform the operation seated in his chair, his patient on a low stool before him holding a candle in his free hand. He bled his dogs when they were sick. He tried to bleed himself, sometimes piercing his arm a dozen times, but never with much success.

He also administered James's Powder and chamomile tea from his small pharmacopeia, and experimented with local plants. He looked for shrubs whose leaves remained attached to their twigs during the winter. Labrador tea was one. The drink made from its tough curled leaves seemed to reduce sweating. And willow bark was helpful against aches.

He thought of himself as his people's father, the rational governor to their chaotic moods. If order broke down in the business of getting food and fuel, they would all die. They were alone. For weeks at a time they could not travel even as far as Chateau, which itself was ice-bound until May. When some of his people refused to work unless they were served salt beef in place of their steady diet of otters and ptarmigans, Cartwright beat the most outspoken rebels with a stick. Their few barrels of salt beef would not sustain them for more than a month, he said, and had to be saved as a last resort.

But it was more than survival he was after. Furs were the point of their being there. And finally money. If Cartwright didn't lead them on with his own example, his people settled into doing the least that was needed to stay alive. And yet his own desire for work wasn't always strong. At least half the attraction of Labrador had been sport and novelty. He preferred investigating the habits of birds, or spending his time with Attuiock, learning from him how to harpoon seals, watching him make his tools. Cartwright expected his people to work on without him. But when he came back from trips with Attuiock, from sleeping in snowhouses and eating raw seal, he found his trap-lines neglected, the woodpile low, the stores of salt beef tampered with.

"You've got to drive them," Mrs. Selby said. "Charles does his best, but he's not well suited to the work. The rest, especially the Fogo Island crew, pretend to go off to work, then all they do is slip round behind the hill, build a tilt for themselves and spend the day in front of a fire drinking rum."

The traps were always being buried in fresh snow. Sometimes the furriers couldn't find them when they made their rounds.

"Build lean-tos or canopies over them," Mrs. Selby said.

Wolverines, wolves, foxes continually stole the bait from the traps and ate the animals captured there.

"Why don't you build a trap something like this," Mrs. Selby said. She sketched a cage-work box with bait at the inner end and a trip-line connected to a suspended door.

Cartwright looked at her drawing in silence for a moment. "Yes," he said. "I've thought of this myself." He had his men construct box-traps and immediately caught a number of wolves and wolverines.

His winter journeys took him across frozen ponds, rivers, ocean bays. Since there were sometimes thaws and winter rains, the ice could be treacherous. A number of times he fell through and barely escaped drowning. Then there was the problem of either having to quickly make a fire to dry himself or hurrying stiffly home in ice-covered clothes.

Once, trying to pole down the river on a pan of ice, he and Charles were carried out beyond the depth of their poles, and drifted into the open bay. Their ice floe, they discovered, consisted mostly of compressed slush. It became water-logged and transparent, and began dissolving under their feet. After hours of paddling with their futile poles, the small remaining cake crumbled between their legs, and they went down into the sea. But by then they were lucky enough to be close to shore, in water no deeper than three feet.

In the evening, with Mrs. Selby stitching a feather quilt in the flickering light, and Cartwright greasing a pair of sealskin boots, the loudest sounds were the burning logs snapping and scattering embers in the fireplace, and the wind throbbing above in the chimney.

"Nan's got huge this past month," Mrs. Selby said, after a long silence.

Cartwright had risen to wrestle a section of log into the fireplace. "Mm. Doesn't seem to be slowing her down though."

"A hard place here, for a child to begin its life."

"Oh I don't know. A good place in some ways, I'd say. No worse than most."

"Would you want your child to begin its life here?" Mrs. Selby asked.

"You mean our child?"

"Yes. If we were to have one."

"We've got to avoid that." Cartwright pried at the smouldering log with the poker. "It's different for Nan."

Nan's baby was due in February. Knowing this, a young surgeon named Jones set out from Chateau on snowshoes on the 26th of January to attend to her. No trail had been marked between Chateau and the Lodge. The journey was thirty miles through a maze of low lumpy mountains, identical-looking plateaus, and valleys matted with dense brush, the whole land waist-deep in snow. On snowshoes, the trip could take two days, although Cartwright often did it in one.

On the 28th, a man came to the Lodge asking if Mr. Jones had arrived. He was supposed to have been the surgeon's guide, but had been held up a day, and Jones, impatient to travel, had set out alone. It was a familiar pattern.

Cartwright sent out a search party which soon discovered Jones's trail, the scanty bed of spruce boughs on which he'd passed the night, and finally the man himself on Round Island in Niger Sound. He was sitting, his knees drawn up to his chest, and his head bowed. His black Newfoundland dog was beside him, wagging its tail as they drew near. At first they thought the surgeon might be asleep.

Jones had been following snowshoe tracks Cartwright had made only a day before, but he'd been following the tracks the wrong way, over the ice toward the mouth of the sound. Where he first met Cartwright's trail he had been only three miles from the Lodge. It had been sunny when Jones left Chateau, and he had not bothered to carry food, tinder, matches, or a hatchet. These were mistakes newcomers often made.

Not having a sled with them to transport his body, they emptied the dead man's pockets and buried him under heavy blocks of snow. But no amount of coaxing and calling could persuade his dog to leave the spot where they'd buried him. The dog was still there two days later when they returned with a sled to fetch its master's remains, and this time it willingly followed the small procession back to the Lodge.

This was familiar, too, Cartwright thought, looking

at Jones's frozen face. It was out of a mixture of songs he'd heard his Fogo Island furriers sing, out of stories they'd told of things they'd seen and been told themselves. Acting on people the land created a body of lore, a system of plots like a second geography. And like rivers and coasts the lore continued to shape people's fates.

✦

1771. February. Tuesday 12.

At six o'clock this evening my maid was taken in labour, and for want of better assistance I was obliged to officiate as midwife myself. She had a severe time, but at half after eleven I delivered her of a stout boy, and she did me the honour to say that, although she had been under the hands of three male and two female practitioners before she left England, she never met with a person who performed his part better. Fortunately for her, Brookes's *Practice of Physic*, which was found in Mr. Jones's pocket, gave me some idea of an art which never till then did I expect to be called upon to practise. Having taken proper care of the mother, I was obliged next to act as nurse and take the child to bed with me; neither of which offices do I wish ever to resume.

Mild weather all day, with snow first and rain afterwards.

1771. February. Wednesday 13.

Mr. Cartwright, you do well to congratulate yourself on your surgeon-like conduct during Nan's delivery.

Your kindness to Nan was a great comfort to her. Indeed, you played the midwife by the book. But is it not true that, while you were searching the pages of Brookes's *Practice of Physic* for instruction in what to do after the infant's head had emerged, I received the new-born child into my hands? And is it not true that when your faintness had come upon you again I tied and severed the cord and escorted the after-birth from the womb?

These matters, by some strange omission, do not appear in your journal.

Likewise, while it is true you were afterwards obliged to take the child to bed with you – poor Nan being too ill to care for it – you neglect to record that I was also in your bed, and that it was I who obliged you, against your inclination, to allow the child to nest between us to be kept warm.

I only make this intrusion in case your journal comes to serve as a substitute for you memory.

1771. February. Wednesday 13.

I received today a most unexpected and shocking affront. Mrs. Selby, as it now appears, has made a secret practice of reading my journal, and has had the audacity to take my pen and enter, by way of amending my notations, her own version of recent events here at the Lodge. The affront still lies before me on this very page.

I have reprimanded her, forbidding her further access to my personal writings; and I was satisfied by her show of contrition.

However, if you should disobey me, Mrs. Selby, and find yourself again reading these words, let me caution you that I shall not respond so lightly a second time to evidence of persistent meddling in this log. I make these entries, in large part, as a record of my commercial affairs; and I shall not allow them to be altered or treated frivolously.

I adjure you, Mrs. Selby, to remember your place.

I have been very ill all day, which I attribute chiefly to being up so late last night. Nan had a bad night, and her pains were very great today. I gave her chamomile, which soon relieved her; and myself took a dose of rhubarb.

Frequent showers of snow, with a free thaw.

1771. February. Thursday 14.

You must try to excuse me, Mr. Cartwright, for I do find myself writing here again with the purpose, once more, of attempting to bring greater balance and truth to your account of events.

My response to your show of ill temper the other day, which you termed my "show of contrition," was, I assure you, rather a mixture of boredom at your interminable sermonizing, and suppressed laughter at your facial expressions and tone of voice.

What, Mr. Cartwright, is that place of mine, which you adjure me to recollect?

I lot sun with continual showers of sleet.

Cartwright shut his journal with a bang that blew out his candle. Then he rose from the table and stared hard at Mrs. Selby, who was brushing her hair by the fire.

"Mrs. Selby, I want you to stop tampering with my journal!"

157

"Mr. Cartwright, I want you to stop tampering with the truth." She straightened to face him, picking loose hair from her brush.

"How *dare* you say that? What I write is no one's concern but my own. And I do *not* tamper with the truth."

"You omit all mention of me. That doesn't seem truthful. But very revealing nonetheless."

"*Very revealing*? You've studied my journal deeply it seems. Perhaps you've noticed then that there's a great deal I omit. My journal is mostly a record of business transactions here."

"That's not true! You record what's important to you."

"I avoid mention of you – and of other personal things – out of delicacy. Lest others read what I've written, and your reputation suffer thereby. I don't hold you in the same degree as my other people, whose doings I mention as I mention the weather, or shooting a squirrel. I hold you closer and dearer to me. You know that. Which is why your attack on my private writing is such a blow."

"And yet you *adjure* me to keep my place."

"I was angry when I wrote that."

"What is my place? You hired me as a housekeeper, yet I'm not paid. You call me your dear companion, but I enjoy none of the few, questionable benefits of being a wife."

"Your place . . . your place is the highest of all my people here at the Lodge. The success of our enterprise, our very survival this winter, depends on my leadership. And *you* keep my spirits up. You save all of us. The thought of you here at the fireside, the thought of you clothed in a silk gown in the midst of this wilderness fills me with pride, and a sense of victory – no matter how cold I am or how far away in the hills."

"When I'm too near, you tell me to keep my place, and when I'm distant you pet me and take me to bed. You think flattery's all I want. Your journal's a truer measure of how you value me. Even the slightest good thing Charles does is mentioned there. But although I do as much as any of them, and more, there's never a word about me. I'll tell you what my place is. It's the lowest here. You think because I share your bed you own me, and I can be overlooked."

"That's cruel and false. You're my partner."

"I haven't the freedom that a simple servant has. Nor any real partnership. What share do I have in the fruits of my work?"

"What do you mean?"

"Do you think I've come here for the food and climate?"

"I thought you came here partly because you care for me. And to share this venture. And the freedom here."

"I did. But shouldn't I also share the rewards?"

With a sigh, Cartwright sat down on the bench by the table. "What's got into you? Do you think I'm going to suddenly turn you out? Come here. Sit down. I'll take care of you."

"I'd rather be able to take care of myself, if I have to. What happens to me if you fall through the ice tomorrow? The others will take their pay and find new places. What happens if next year you fancy another housekeeper would please you more?"

"We're all very confined here just now, and bothered by various things – Nan's baby, Jones's death, the amount of illness we have. When this thaw ends, I'll get Attuiock to carry us down to Chateau on his sled. We'll have supper with Davyes. We'll shoot partridges on the way."

"I don't want to go to Chateau. . . . Look, if I'm not

merely your servant, as you yourself say I'm not, and I'm not quite your wife – and I'm not sure I want to be, though not for any lack of affection for you – then what am I? Your partner, you say. Not having made a financial investment in the affairs here, I can't expect a large share of the profits. Nevertheless I *am* investing myself in your business and your life – more than the others here, with less independence, and more to lose – and I require a reasonable return for my contribution. And acknowledgment that my *place* is well above that of housekeeper."

"You want money . . . what? After each fuck? Once a week? You'll willingly make yourself a whore?"

"If I'm not your wife, I'm either a whore or a fool. And fool is one title, here in America, that's kept its meaning. The others I don't care much about."

"It's marriage you're after, isn't it, in spite of what you say? There's no one else I'd rather marry than you. We *will* marry. When I'm out of debt. When my business has taken root. But we can't marry now. Next year I might be bankrupt, and back with my brother dining for free in the officers' mess on some man-of-war. What would I do with you then?"

"I'm not saying I refuse to marry you, Cartwright. I think it's right to wait. But meanwhile I want to be paid regularly each month, in private, not with the other people. And to be allowed to engage in private trade with the Eskimos."

"*What*? Where is the end of this? Have I brought with me, by mistake, one of those masquerade ladies from Covent Garden who favour men's dress?"

"I'm serious."

"I can't tolerate independent traffic here. All the work we do is done for the company. Otherwise each of my servants would be working for himself."

"I'm not one of your servants. We've cleared that up. I'm your partner, as you've said. Why should I not be allowed to amuse myself in collecting a few furs?"

"No. I refuse."

"Well, give me my salary then. There are ten months owing to me."

"What? Now? There's nothing to buy with it here but rum."

"I'd like it now."

"God! You are the oddest woman. I'll have to go and open the box. . . ."

He went into the bedroom while Mrs. Selby remained by the fireplace, then returned with his hands full of coins.

"There. That's for a year. What we agreed on. And a bit more."

"Thank you. Now, I'd like to buy some needles and thread. And beads and hatchets."

◆

The setting sun throws trembling peach-coloured spots across the wall in front of his desk. It is nearly too dark to read. He lights his candles. How many times has he done this, exactly this. He looks at Kaumalak, asleep. The soft ripe light striking her shoulder and head gives her a blue metallic sheen. Time never existed for her, he thinks. It means nothing now.

8

Cartwright and Mrs. Selby had no children together largely because of Cartwright's use of a sheath. When they left England he took with him two sheaths made from the visceral tissue of sheep. These were preserved in oil in a ceramic jar with a cork-lined stopper. He took scrupulous care of them, drying them on a piece of flannel before using them, washing them, inspecting them for holes afterwards.

The operation of extracting a sheath from its jar of preservative, drying it, and fitting it on was an interruption in the natural process of love-making that Cartwright overcame to an extent through the practised adroitness and the air of playful ceremony with

which he carried the actions out. "To your battle stations, men!" he'd exclaim, leaping out of bed when the time had come, imitating the sound of the drum or the bugle. "Powder! Wadding! Rammer! Shot! . . . Take aim! . . . Take better aim!" Or he'd pretend to be saddling a horse. While he stood by the bed, drying the sheath, Mrs. Selby would stroke his charger's neck lest he lose courage.

When the sheaths he'd brought with him to Labrador had worn out, Cartwright fashioned his own using the mesentery of the animals he killed. These devices were less satisfactory than the originals, being looser and bulkier. The design he settled on as the most practical had pleats and a drawstring, like a tobacco pouch. He softened his pouches with butter and preserved them in rum. Their odour was festive, but Mrs. Selby complained that they smarted, and ordered him to dilute the rum.

He experimented with tissue from various animals and would hesitate before the half-dozen jars that lined one of their bedroom shelves. "What about otter?" he'd say. "A tireless swimmer." Or he'd snort, tossing his head, "What about . . . caribou?"

"Stop it, Cartwright," Mrs. Selby finally said. "I don't like to think of those things inside me. Can't you let it go on my belly for a change?"

Cartwright preferred not to do this unless there was no alternative. "The souls of our children," he would say, "while they will not be given corporeal form, should at least have some fleeting taste of maternal warmth as they pass from our negligent custody back to God. To cast them directly into the cold air would be too cruel."

He persisted with his pouches and sheaths, and Mrs. Selby accepted them, in the same hardy spirit of self-reliance they brought to all their endeavours in Labrador. They enjoyed meeting obstacles, putting their modern ingenuity to work for them.

It wasn't only his penis that Cartwright decked in odd attire. By degrees he dressed the rest of his person as well in clothes of his own design and manufacture. Mrs. Selby did the same. While both she and Cartwright continued to wear English apparel at home in the evening, provided the house wasn't too cold, for camping and travelling they developed a wardrobe of fur and leather garments partly modelled on Inuit wear and partly the work of their own imaginations. Many stories about them and their odd appearance circulated among the people who sailed the Labrador coast in the late 1700s. Naval officers and the captains of merchant ships, when they passed Cartwright's station, would send a boat to invite the couple on board to dine in order to witness them firsthand and hear their tales. And Cartwright and Mrs. Selby, aware of their fame, played their parts proudly, boasting of blizzards, rough food, and encounters with bears.

There were times when Cartwright and Mrs. Selby were away from the Lodge, camping out in their tent or sleeping under the stars beside a fire, and had forgotten to bring one of the sheaths in its travelling jar. Then, if they made love, as they so much enjoyed, listening to loons or wolves, watching shooting stars or the aurora borealis, Cartwright had no choice but to withdraw in time and let his semen go in the cool air. It sometimes seemed to him, at those moments, that Mrs. Selby held him to her longer than was safe or reasonable, and he would have to whisper, "Let go! Let go!"

✦

1771. February. Tuesday 26.
W. little.

Seals now being plentiful off Lyon Head, my Eskimo friends moved there three days ago from their house near the Lodge. Today, after looking at my traps down the river, I went to visit them in their new snowhouse, with which I was greatly pleased. This curious habitation was hollowed out of a drift-bank of snow, in the form of an oven. The length was about twelve feet, the width ten, and the height seven. Across the farther end was raised a platform of snow. On this were laid some boards where the whole family slept upon bedding composed of a considerable number of deerskins, which are both soft and warm. In the roof, fronting the bed, there was a curious window which was nearly three feet square and made of a piece of transparent ice, shaved to a proper substance. It admitted a perfectly good light and was secured in its place by strewing the edges with snow and sprinkling that snow with water. On each side was a small pedestal of snow for the support of a couple of lamps, which gave a sufficient light by night and added so much heat to that occasioned by the breath of the occupants as to make the house entirely warm. I was even obliged to open my waistcoat for a while. This heat also thawed the roof and sides sufficiently to enable the external frost and natural coldness of the snow to form innumerable small icicles. These different concretions, from the reflection of the lamps, made the apartment glitter with the appearance of radiant diamonds or luminous crystalizations. The lamps were formed of stone, which they contrive to hollow out properly for this purpose; and the wicks (for each had several laid in a row on the edge of the lamp) were bits of a particular kind of moss, well dried. Having first poured some oil into the lamp, they spit a number of small pieces of fat upon sticks and place them horizontally at such a distance behind the wicks that their heat melts the fat equal to the consumption of oil. The dwelling as a whole, together with its furnishings and implements, was fashioned with an ingenious simplicity that was both highly practical and endlessly delightful to the eye.

✧

1771. April. Sunday 7.

Early this morning I put my provisions, bedding, and other baggage on Attuiock's sled; my gun and rackets upon my own, drawn by three dogs; and together with Haines and Mrs. Selby came here to the tilt on Eyre Island. I afterwards sent Attuiock to Seal Island with a plank.

Monday 8.
N. strong.

Two of the sealers called to inform me that they had killed a wolf which had got into one of their traps. I went with them to take a view of the beast, and a large old dog he was, but very poor, for he had been impelled by hunger to haunt about the sealers' house for some time past, to eat the seals' bones which had been left half picked by their dogs. Haines and I were employed all the rest of the day in cutting boughs to sewel the harbour in order to draw the caribou close to the point of Eyre Island where I intend to watch for them.

Tuesday 9.
N.W. moderate.

A man came from Seal Island and brought me a fore-quarter of wolf, a piece of which I asked Mrs. Selby to roast for my dinner; but it proved so hard, dry, and rank, that I could swallow but one mouthful. As I was, however, determined to get the better of my squeamish stomach, I set the remainder by for supper; but my success then was not much greater.

Mild and pleasant till noon, dark and raw afterwards.

Wednesday 10.
S.E. strong.

I was engaged in making some more harness for my dogs, and I added another bloodhound and the New-foundland dog to my coach. I ate part of the wolf today; but, as it was not altogether palatable, a little sufficed me, notwithstanding I tasted no other kind of food. For Haines and herself Mrs. Selby prepared bis-cuits and baked a fish which she caught through a hole in the ice.

Frequent showers of small rain all day.

Thursday 11.

The tilt has leaked very much through every part of the roof since the rain began. Mrs. Selby returned to the Lodge.

Sunday 14.
Wind S.E. fresh.

At daylight this morning I sent the furriers round the traps, and they brought me two brace of grouse. Whether my appetite or the taste of the wolf be better, I cannot tell, but I can now make a tolerable good meal of him.

Thick fog with rain most part of these last twenty-four hours.

Monday 15.

At daylight I sent the furriers to strike up the farthest traps, but the harbour being almost knee deep in water upon the ice, it was very unpleasant, laborious walking. The evening being clear, I walked to the top of the highest hill upon this island and had an extensive view out to sea, but could not discern a drop of open water. I finished my quarter of wolf today, and I believe that my stomach will not refuse such food again during my residence in this country.

✦

Of all his workers, Cartwright's Fogo Island sawyers gave him the most trouble. They regarded themselves as independent tradesmen and rarely worked more than a year for any one master. Like most of the men who circulated among the fishing and furring crews in Newfoundland, they were discontented and full of various vague plans for improving their lives. They hated the cold and isolation of Labrador, and were biding their time at the Lodge, waiting for spring and the chance to get out.

Their special skills, and the fact that they worked in areas removed from the trap-lines and fishing spots, set them apart from the rest of the people at the Lodge. While Cartwright worked alongside his fishing crews in the summer and his furriers in the winter, and was always discussing the business of trapping and fishing with them, he never took any direct part in the woods-men's work, nor spent much time chatting with them in the evenings. He'd give them their orders, so much fire-wood, planks, and beams, and send them out.

The leader of the woodsmen was a man named John Williams who kept his companions' spirits up with satirical antics, and mocked Cartwright's rules and orderly habits behind his back. To amuse his friends he'd play a game of making obscene or threatening gestures just up to the edge of Cartwright's vision, or of mutter-ing insults his master couldn't quite hear. While Cart-wright bent to assess the straightness and strength of a plank they'd sawed, Williams would stand behind him and stretch his hands out as though preparing to strangle him, or he'd line his index finger up with Cartwright's rump, then draw his arm and body back for a mighty thrust. The other woodsmen would snort and cough to cover their laughter. When Cartwright turned toward him or lifted his eyes, Williams's face would show noth-ing but bland attentiveness, his hands would be picking a callus, or removing spruce needles from a sleeve.

"Why don't you use your balls for bait?" he'd mutter, a safe distance away.

"I beg your pardon?"

"I said if we don't hurry we'll all be late."

"Late for what?"

"Um . . . supper?"

Cartwright pretended not to notice that Williams was mocking him. The bolder the sawyer became in his insults, the more reasonable and business-like Cartwright became in his treatment of him, but the more closely he examined the man's work. He wouldn't engage with Williams on Williams's terms, Cartwright told himself, but according to the letter of the law.

"This plank is crooked, Williams. You'll have to rip it down into laths and cut another log."

"The kitchen fuel supply is too low, Williams. If a storm struck now we'd run short. I want the shed filled by tomorrow evening."

But as the sawyer's insults grew more blatant, Cartwright's composure began to crack.

"What's that you said to me, Williams? I'll put *your* balls in a trap!"

Cartwright finally beat the woodsman with a stick, and Williams, although he was young and strong, accepted the punishment without striking back. He'd been born in poverty on Random Island, had been a sailor for a while, and was used to being ordered around and flogged. But he hated it, and wanted to change himself.

In late winter, when Cartwight prepared to discipline Williams a second time – for having spent the previous day drinking instead of fetching fuel – Williams challenged Cartwright to a wrestling match. Cartwright accepted the challenge, although he knew it was probably a mistake. It would mean lowering himself to Williams's level, or raising the woodsman up to his own. And if Cartwright lost, his pride and authority would be broken on the spot. But no one had ever defeated him at wrestling, and he was filled with the desire to crush his sawyer's insolence once and for all and enjoy a satisfying revenge.

But Cartwright had acted rashly. He was not in the peak of health; for several days fever had limited his trapping excursions. His headman, Milmouth, saw what the outcome would be and stepped in, saying, "I can't permit this to go forward."

It was as good as a victory for Williams. From then on he sang to himself loudly whenever Cartwright was near, drank openly during the day, toasting Cartwright with a flask he carried in his coat, and began coming in from the woods well before suppertime to pester Nan and Mrs. Selby at the Lodge. It was useless to threaten the man with a thrashing; Cartwright began to think he'd have to arrange a hunting accident or a mishap on the ice, when things took care of themselves.

Cartwright had been away looking for caribou with Attuiock. When he returned to the Lodge, Charles, Nan, and Milmouth ran toward him with shocking news. Williams had been fucking Cartwright's dogs, in open view, and had nearly strangled one in the process. Now he was threatening to do the same to Bettres, the carpenter's young helper.

Cartwright gathered his most loyal men – Charles, Milmouth, and Haines – and together they seized Williams, who was drunk and fairly passive, and chained him by his leg to a bed. There he stayed until they could take him down to Chateau to stand trial.

During the weeks he was held at the Lodge, Williams never made much effort to escape. At first he may have welcomed the chance to lie all day in bed. He had food and rum, and his friends still came and talked with him. But gradually he became silent and apathetic.

When the ice had broken up enough to allow careful passage, Cartwright sailed a skiff to Chateau accompanied by a group of his men. Williams lay chained in the stern watched over by Charles, who held a pistol.

Cartwright paid no more attention to Williams than to the rest of the baggage they took. He stood in the bow with Milmouth pointing out landmarks, scanning the coast for game.

At Chateau, Cartwright leapt onto the wharf to embrace his waiting friends, beginning with Lieutenant Davyes, the commander of the fort. Having escorted the group to his room in the blockhouse, Davyes poured glasses of rum, and Cartwright presented each of his Chateau friends with gifts – fur hats and mitts of his own design. Then, seemingly as an afterthought, Cartwright had Williams brought in and asked Davyes to record the charges against him: drunkenness, assault, breach of contract. Witnesses added their statements, and Williams was locked in a cell.

Later that day, after watching the woodsman receive his lashes, Cartwright entered against him the capital charge of bestiality. Cartwright then went rowing in the bay with his men and conducted an experiment whereby he measured the speed at which ducks could fly.

Since Davyes wasn't authorized to try capital crimes, Williams was held at Chateau until a ship could take him, with Bettres as witness, to St. John's for the trial. There, Williams confessed to his crimes, offered no defence, and was sentenced to be hanged.

Bettres waited nearly a month for a ship back to Labrador, then changed his mind, and took a job on a schooner bound for Boston.

✧

The flaking plaster on the ceiling of his room in The Turk's Head, boringly familiar as it is, is the earth Cartwright's eyes eagerly, prayerfully seek to rest on when he opens them. It was a dream. It was only a dream that Caubvick confronted him, under water, in a blackish green light, her hair longer than ever, floating out from her colourless face, her grin already devouring him before they had touched. Her hands, broken, her fingers lopped off and bleeding as she reached for him.

It was he who had condemned her to her watery jail. He had not just reduced her, made her pitiable, but had pushed her into another state, freed some monstrous power in her, that she now turned on him.

Cartwright looks at the stained ceiling, sees the head of the King, a vagina, an otter jumping through a hoop, the map of Italy, a bishop picking his nose. He swings his legs over the side of the bed, feels the familiar boards under his bare soles, and looks toward Kaumalak. The hawk opens her brilliant black eyes.

Hunger.

What nonsense has he been thinking about?

✧

"Cartwright, that man doesn't deserve to die for what he did." Mrs. Selby's words forced him to look up from the letter he was writing.

"What he did was monstrous," Cartwright answered. "I didn't create the law." He noted the colour rising in her cheeks, her intense eyes.

"What he did was disgraceful and mindless," Mrs. Selby said, "but in its effect it was no worse than what we do every day here – killing animals, maiming them in traps. And as for harming *himself*, Williams was *always* polluting himself with rum and filthy stunts, and you did nothing more than strike him or order him out of your sight."

"The law is clear in cases of bestiality. The man was a threat to us all. He'd lost his humanity."

"The law is a bugaboo. You use it to suit yourself. You said he was given twelve lashes in Chateau. Why didn't you leave it at that and send him away?"

"If we're not strict we'll lose control of ourselves and our people. We hang suspended here, in a gulf of savagery. It's only the law that holds us up."

"This is not true. You use the law as an instrument of your own savagery."

"I don't have to listen to this! What was Williams to you?"

"We don't have to drag the cruelties of England with us." Mrs. Selby placed her palms on the table in front of Cartwright and leaned toward him. "What does Davyes in Chateau, or the governor in St. John's know about what we're doing here? We can keep the good laws and forget the rest. This is a new place."

"This is England."

"England can't even imagine this."

"This is British territory."

"You're a hypocrite. You came here to escape England and so did I. But you bring with you the very things you wanted to flee."

"Those were things *you* wanted to flee. I don't think you understand the danger we're in. Our only strength is in our appeal to law, in presenting ourselves as representatives of our country. If we were only individuals, this land would devour us like a trout leaping and swallowing a fly."

"I say we've got nothing to fear but what we bring with us." She turned and went out of the Lodge.

The first leaf to appear that spring was a wild currant's.

Cartwright recorded this in his journal on the 21st of May and for the rest of the day carried the tiny half-opened bundle of green in the front of his mind like an amulet. He got out a spade and began to prepare a garden.

A boat from Perkins and Coghlan arrived with barrels of salt meat, flour, nails. There was mail from England. To Cartwright it felt as though he and his people were the ones who'd been on the ship, travelling for almost eight months, and had just now come ashore. He took his bundle of letters into the Lodge, cleared off the dining table, and spread them out. Some had been sent nearly a year before. From one scrawled piece of paper he learned that his partner, Lucas, had died the previous autumn when the *Enterprise* sank on its way to Portugal. Cartwright felt immediately smaller and more alone, his Labrador station seemed mean and mistaken somehow with Lucas gone. And although the *Enterprise* had been insured, the money Lucas had hoped to earn with his cargoes of wine and sugar wouldn't be there. Things would be harder than he thought.

News came also that Granby had died; deeply in debt, so rumour had it. At first this softened Cartwright's attitude to his old commander and patron. The man had been no better off than Cartwright himself in the end: borrowing money to keep up a front. But he'd died leaving his debts to others. His family would have to pay for his patriotic show, just as Cartwright had once had to help pay for it.

✦

On the bare gravel beach Attuiock constructed a new kayak. Cartwright watched the whole process from beginning to end. When he was finished, Attuiock gave his old kayak to Cartwright as a gift. Then gave him lessons in making it work. Cartwright wrote, via Chateau, asking Perkins and Coghlan to send him an extra shallop. When the boat eventually arrived – it was a slightly storm-damaged sloop called the *Indian Prince* – he presented it to Attuiock and showed him how to manage the sails.

"Watch," Attuiock said, "this is what happens when people die."

He had in his left hand a ball of some sort wrapped in blades of grass. He was trying to hide it from view in his sleeve, but Cartwright had noticed it.

Attuiock bent and chose a rock from the beach, showed it to Cartwright, then turned and cocked back his arm to throw it. The rock must have gone into his boot, because what he threw high over the sea was not the rock, but the ball he'd been trying to hide in his left hand.

As the ball reached the peak of its arc and began to drop toward the water, it split, unravelled, and a bird opened its wings and flew away.

Attuiock tilted his face up to Cartwright, his eyelids half lowered, his bristly lips closed in a proud smile.

"Wonderful," Cartwright said. "How is it done?"

One day the tents were there beside Attuiock's on Little Caribou Island. Friends of Attuiock's.

Cartwright often had the impression that Attuiock and his family were not as isolated as he and his workers at the Lodge. Before this point he had never seen any Inuit in the area aside from Attuiock's group, but Attuiock often had news from along the coast: a French or British boat having been sighted, a whale taken near

Chateau. Especially when spring approached, Attuiock and Tooklavinia were often away for several days at a time. Cartwright supposed they visited other Inuit settlements during their travels up the coast.

He approached the newcomers' camp, and Attuiock came out to meet him. There was the ruckus of many excited dogs, greasy smoke from the fires, the litter of bones and shit that always bothered him. The people greeted him happily. It was clear Attuiock had given a good report of him. He distributed beads. Surrounded by faces filled with wonder and pleasure, Cartwright allowed himself to imagine they might someday come to look on him as a kind of king.

Attuiock introduced him to Shuglawina, leader of the visiting group – a broad, powerful-looking man, someone apparently more important than Attuiock himself.

1771. July. Tuesday 9.

Early this morning I went to Cape Charles and there pitched my tent upon the continent directly opposite the Eskimo camp, having a tickle between us not more than eighty yards wide. The instant that I was ready to open shop I sent my people home with injunctions not to come near me until I sent them an order in writing for that purpose, or unless they had business with me which could not be deferred until my return. My tent was soon filled with Eskimos, and we carried on a very brisk trade till two o'clock in the afternoon. Shuglawina then came in, spoke a few words in a rough tone of voice, and all the rest instantly walked out. Taking me by the shoulder and speaking sternly, he made signs for me to go with him. As these people have hitherto plundered and murdered

Europeans whenever they had the opportunity, I must confess that I expected that was to be my fate now, and my suspicions were confirmed upon recollecting the apprehensions which they expressed at the sight of my firearms until I convinced them that they were not loaded. However, being well assured that if they were determined to kill me I could not prevent them, I put the best face possible on the unpleasant affair, locked up my goods, and followed him out. He led me to the top of an eminence at the back of my tent, and we were followed by all the men and boys. On observing a collection of brushwood and other dry fuel, I naturally concluded that I was to be sacrificed, but whether they intended to roast me alive or dead I could not determine. I did not, however, long remain in suspense, for Shuglawina soon dispelled my fears by telling me that we had done enough business for one day, and therefore he had brought me there to look out for whales and for vessels at sea, adding that the wood was to make signals to any ships passing nearby, to bring them ashore to visit with us. On discovering a whabby swimming in a small pond, I sent for my rifle, and broke both its thighs at the first shot. Shuglawina then fired and killed it. It was really surprising that he should kill a bird with a single ball, the first shot which he ever fired in his life, at the distance of a hundred yards at the least.

A very fine day.

Wednesday 10.

Not an Eskimo offered to cross the tickle this morning until they saw me up at five o'clock. Most of the men were gone out to kill seals and codfish, and those who were in camp then came to my tent, but as I had yesterday purchased the greatest part of their goods, my traffic with them was now trifling.

In the afternoon I went over to the island and visited the ladies. I found them variously employed, and observed that great attention was paid to the providing of belly-timber; for the kettle was either boiled or boiling in every tent. Some were busy in dressing green seal-skins, and others in jerking fish; some in making boots and jackets whilst others were sucking the fat from eider-duck skins, intended for winter garments, and engaged in a great variety of other employment. The most perfect good humour prevailed among them, and they took great pains to entertain me with singing and dancing. Although I did not admire their tunes, I could perceive that many of them had very soft and musical voices; but as to their dancing, one would have supposed that they had learned that art from the bears of the country.

As visiting was not my sole object, I took with me a box of beads and other trifles with which I picked up several skins and a little whalebone. In the evening, Shuglawina made me a present of a very fine silver fox-skin, but he insisted on having the same price for the tail of it as I had just paid for another entire skin. However, as he only demanded a small ivory comb which cost me no more than twopence halfpenny, and the skin and tail were worth four guineas, I made no scruple in completing the purchase.

✦

In late July, tallying his goods, Cartwright discovered an extra bundle of furs in a corner of the storehouse. They were Mrs. Selby's, he suddenly realized. There was a keg, too, with whalebone and whalebone carvings packed in moss. He felt an impulse to untie her furs and stack them and bind them more neatly, the way he did his own, but he restrained himself. It was her business. And there was nothing the matter with the way she'd done it herself.

He never saw her making her trades, but he was often away during the summer, and Inuit women were frequently at the Lodge. She had done well, multiplied her earnings many times.

"Determined," he said to himself. He poked around in the keg and drew out a whole unchipped walrus tusk. It wasn't for the love of the goods or her trading partners that she was doing this. She always argued they should keep to themselves, employ fewer people, leave the Inuit alone. Yet here was the stash of her Inuit goods. Part of some scheme of hers.

West of the Lodge, above the valley of the Charles River, the treeless plateaus were littered with boulders, many larger than the blockhouse at Chateau. The highest parts of the plateaus were bare rock. The dips and level stretches had gathered a covering of moss – decomposed peat, topped with green tufts – as absorbent as sponge, holding decades of rain in ponds without any outlets or springs.

The way the peat grew, spreading over the rock in successive layers, and the way the frost worked, splitting the bogs, heaving the peat in wide circular ridges, rings of ponds were created, thin crescent-shaped pools spiralling out from a centre. Cartwright followed the deep-worn caribou trails among the ponds, thinking a French landscape-gardener might have laid them out. In the heat, the air rippled in quick rivers across the top of the land. Water and hills, water and hills, rising in tiers. Mirage. It was like being at sea again. Every small leaf in the shadowless landscape shook with excessive clarity under his eyes. The weave in the cloth of his trousers was the same, the thread-hairs gleaming prismatically, the pores and beaded seams in his hands. His head seemed to ride by itself, his body dissolved in the visual crackle, the equivalent texture of what lay around.

Long days of sun had dried the high paths to black powder, still springy from the moisture underneath. At the edge of a spruce clump there were butterflies in the grass tuffets, and there was the smell, the mysterious smell of ripe strawberries that often came to him along trails on hot sunny days. Cartwright parted the grasses and flower stalks, sniffing like a hound. It was no specific thing that he could locate. Certainly not strawberries. But the smell was luscious, thick and red and heart-shaped, heavy, overripe. He crawled to the tree roots where the sun fell strongest, his knees wet in the moss, smelling the bark, the lichen, the tiny white berries he knew tasted of wintergreen, not straw-berries. But the smell was there, somehow, huge, enveloping. All he could do was breathe it. Breathe it and sleep in it.

Attuiock and Shuglawina waded into the Charles River and showed Cartwright the best location for a salmon pound. They helped him shift boulders, drive in stakes, and position the nets.

Later, when the pound was full of salmon, the Inuit returned with their spears to help themselves to some fish. Cartwright stopped them. He tried to explain that the King had granted the river to him, that the salmon pound and the fish in it were his, and other people were not allowed to take his catch.

Attuiock and Shuglawina rested the butts of their spears on the ground and looked searchingly into Cartwright's eyes. "These salmon are for everyone," Shuglawina said.

Cartwright had the sudden thought that he might be re-enacting a scene his predecessor, Darby, had played out four years earlier, which had ended with the Inuit killing three of Darby's men. "Fine," Cartwright said, "help yourselves."

After all, there were hundreds of salmon in the pound, and the Inuit only wanted a couple each.

9

By the end of the summer of 1771 it was clear to Cartwright that Perkins and Coghlan were serving him badly. Their ships were slow in coming, and he was always short of supplies. Because of a lack of nets and salt, he took less than half the salmon the river could have yielded him.

A shipment of food, traps, and tools arrived just before freeze-up, and they were into the winter again. Summer had been unbelievably short.

This time Cartwright had more furriers working for him, some stationed in small outposts several days' journey from the Lodge. He also had better sawyers. There would be no repetition of the Williams affair.

Because he and his people were now used to the climate, they knew when to stay indoors, avoiding the worst weather, yet they still accomplished more than they had the previous year. Cartwright stored his kayak over the dining table in the rafters of the Lodge, got out his sled, and hitched up his team of dogs.

Attuiock and his family stayed with their own people farther up the coast. Cartwright would drive his sled out on the ice near where Attuiock used to camp, find a seal's breathing hole, and wait with his harpoon the way Attuiock had taught him to. But there was no pleasure in doing it alone. He preferred roaming the hills and valleys, following animal tracks. There was a sense of the chase in that, of reading the quarry's mind. Under the ice there was no telling what was going on, although Attuiock always seemed to know.

Not long after Christmas (which his people celebrated as they had before) Nan's baby, Lewis, began to walk, and Cartwright's old servant Charles began to die. Cartwright moved Charles into the Lodge, and for weeks in his journal he charted the ups and downs of his servant's health. He sat by his bed for a while every day feeding him Labrador tea or James's Powder. Sometimes, when Charles was feeling especially sick, he'd sit by him all night, keeping the fire high. The wind was so cold outside and Charles's pulse was so weak that his fingers and toes froze while he lay near the fire under an eiderdown cover.

"I never imagined I'd end my life in a place like this," he said to Cartwright one night when an icy wind was shaking the Lodge.

"It's better than Minorca, Charles."

"Yes. . . . But it's so godforsaken bloody cold. . . . When I'm done, could you put me in a barrel with salt, and see that I get back to England? To my sister. Or anywhere nearby. You could pour me out in a ditch or meadow, so long as it's in Kent. . . . I'll pay for it. There's my watch and musket. And last year's pay."

"You're going to get better, Charles. You'll see your sister again next fall. Try to sleep."

Charles died on the 6th of February 1772. Cartwright had the cooper make a barrel-shaped coffin for him and buried him in the snow under a north-facing cliff near the sea.

✦

Cartwright hears something behind him and turns in his chair. Kaumalak's eyes are open. She's doing her morning routine. First she ruffles her feathers out, then she shakes them down smooth in a brisk rustle and leans forward, gripping the perch, rowing the air with her wings. But the window beside her is still black. It's unusual for her to stir at night. "Have you been dreaming?" he asks gently. "I'll take you out. I'll take you out when it's light."

✦

It was a more productive winter as far as the business of getting furs was concerned – Cartwright had learned the terrain, the animals' habits, and how to assign routines – but there were few adventures or discoveries. Mrs. Selby and Cartwright spoke together less. They even argued less. And he had little to write in his journal aside from listing the numbers of birds he shot. The days, crowded with work, blended together. After supper, Mrs. Selby would play her violin for a while, then make yet another batch of candles, and Cartwright would mend his traps by the fire until he began to nod. As they'd get into bed she would hesitate, heavy-eyed, before blowing the candle out and say, "Weren't we just going to bed five minutes ago?"

In the middle of March, Cartwright was out on a camping trip with a friend from Chateau named Bullock. Each took a dog sled, and Cartwright brought with him a man named Fogarty to mind the teams and cut firewood while Bullock and he went out shooting on snowshoes.

The weather was fiendish. Vicious southwest and north winds wrestled each other directly on top of them. One wind would prevail for a few hours, then the other would enter the contest again and dominate for a similar length of time. The temperature rose and fell with each change in the wind, the southwest gales bringing broadsides of wet snow, huge flakes like water-logged gun-wadding aimed at their mouths and eyes, the north winds freezing it in a stucco cast on the fronts of their bodies.

Between Temple Bay and St. Modeste they took shelter for the night in a stand of short fir trees. Fogarty, a noted axe-man, assembled a pile of trunks and limbs and worked throughout the night trimming and splitting them for fuel. Cartwright and Bullock tended the fire, trying to keep themselves warm.

The wind continued to pounce from above, driving the flames of their fire downwards and sideways, filling their eyes with smoke. There was no chance of sleep. All their clothes and bedding were wet. They had to huddle as near to the fire as possible for warmth, and if they had left it untended for more than a couple of minutes it would have gone out. It burned poorly not only because of the wind and pelting snow, but because it was built on a snowbank. As it burned, it melted its way down and came apart, its embers falling away and fizzling out. Cartwright and Bullock trampled and dug the snow from under themselves to stay on a level with the descending blaze. Fogarty, swinging his axe, sank along with his woodpile beside them.

At three in the morning they reached solid ground and the fire composed itself and began to throw more substantial heat. They heaped on more wood, and the snowbank drew back from the fire's edge to a radius of five or six feet. At last they stretched themselves out on the fir boughs, exhausted, and fell into sleep.

With the coming of dawn the blizzard died and the fire burned itself out. Feeling the cold, Cartwright opened his eyes. The first thing he saw was the other two men, watching for his reaction. He looked around. They were all at the bottom of a pit in the snow over ten feet deep. The sides of the pit, which tapered inward toward the top, had frozen in glassy walls, streaked with soot. They were much too slippery to climb.

Fogarty went to work with his axe, hacking out niches for foot-holds. He uncovered the tips of the branches of a nearby fir tree frozen into the wall. By hanging on to the sprigs of fir and driving their toes into the niches, they were finally able to drag themselves up out of the pit.

Then they began digging around for their dogs and sleds.

1819. May. Wednesday 19.
Wind S.W. light.

Rescue devices, portable things for emergencies in the

woods, that's what most of my inventions were. Hot air balloons with signal lamps attached, folding ladders, tin stoves, grappling hooks to be fired from a bow. Tools to help the solitary man get out of holes, cross rivers, escape starvation or freezing to death.

My brother Edmund's inventions were different. He understood society as a whole, it seems – what people wanted, how they could be changed. And yet he started out as a preacher and poet, and it was only a bet that got him inventing things. He always said machinery was simple compared to poetry. I think he could see moving parts in his mind, wheels and cranks and arms, pushing and turning one another.

Once, while visiting Matlock, he fell into conversation with some Manchester cotton manufacturers about the troubles in the textile industry. Hargreaves's spinning jenny was having the paradoxical effect of putting English hand-loom weavers out of work. Machine-spun yarn had become so abundant that the weavers couldn't use it all. So the spinning mills were selling their yarn to weavers in Belgium and Germany who were turning it into cloth that sold in England for less than what the English weavers could afford to sell their own cloth for. Cheap English yarn was making English cloth too expensive to sell.

Edmund said the obvious solution was to invent a power-loom that could use all the yarn the spinning jenny produced. The cotton manufacturers laughed and said that would never be done, the process was too complicated. So Edmund went home and, without ever having seen a hand-loom, invented a basic power-loom that would work from a turning shaft.

After that it was one thing after another, rope-making machines, combing machines, alcohol engines, plunging boats, interlocking bricks. It never made him rich.

But every time I slip into the present I seem to be caught in the teeth of some engine or process he first set in motion.

✦

In the late spring Mrs. Selby's forehead and nose were sunburnt. There were blackfly bites at her temples – small red marks and tiny cinders of dried blood near the roots of her hair. Leaning toward her across the table, Cartwright raised his hand and slowly removed the dried blood, taking each particle like a bead between his thumbnail and finger and sliding it to the end of the hair around which it had formed.

She had been fishing without a hat. Her hair and eyes, which were the same dark brown, both had a new lustre since the winter had passed. Cartwright had often remarked to himself on the sameness of browns in her countenance. Even her eyebrows, which were broad and thick, were the same rich brown. This consistency, the air of deliberate beauty that nature had given her, seemed to him a sign of her self-possession, her inner composure.

Her cheeks were fuller, too, her lips more relaxed since the ice and most of the snow had gone. The graceful curves at the corners of her mouth were coming back again. Ships had arrived with supplies, flour and butter, even cheese. She was rarely indoors now as long as the sun was out.

"Not a single deer did I see," Cartwright was saying. "Plenty of tracks. Always ahead of me." He'd been away for three nights.

Mrs. Selby looked into his eyes. Haines had finished the garden, she said. And Milmouth had got some salmon. She seemed reluctant to divulge all of her news. At last she added that Attuiock had returned with a lot of his people. They were on Great Caribou Island . . . waiting for Cartwright to visit them.

Cartwright leapt up and began searching for his boxes of needles, his beads and thread.

For a ball they used the inflated bladder of a seal. Everyone played. The oldest men and women, the youngest children, even the dogs were on one team or the other. The playing field was the whole mossy broken top of the island above where their tents were pitched. Shallow gullies and small scattered spruce gave variety to the game. The goal lines were vaguely represented by boulders and trees. Aside from the special field it was like football anywhere. Most of the play consisted of tussling and falling down. Those who were not kicking the bladder, colliding and sprawling, were collapsing with laughter. Pairs of dogs were snarling, rolling together under the players' legs. Cartwright was on Attuiock's team. They shunted the bladder back and forth to one another, dodging opponents. Cartwright flipped the bladder up with his toe, bounced it from knee to knee, then sent it high and headed it neatly right to Attuiock's feet. There were squeals of amazement, and Cartwright found himself flying head-first into a patch of the island's low, juniper-like spruce. The Inuit were short, but surprisingly solid. He braced himself more carefully for the checks and tackles. Elderly women like kegs of butter bounced off him and lay laughing in the Labrador tea.

After football, Cartwright assembled the whole community in a long, snaking line – each person one pace from the next, bent forward with hands on knees – and then showed them how to play leapfrog, explaining that the one left last in the row should immediately follow by vaulting those in front. The line moved like a giant inchworm down through the tents, along the beach, over the island's summit, and around again. Cartwright dropped out and lay panting. The rest continued above him – a loud, bouncing chain – across the island's horizon line, against the blue sky.

Then it was archery. Again two teams, although only the men and the older boys shot at the target. The women encouraged their men by putting on pairs of clean white mitts and gesturing with them elegantly while they danced and sang. When their opponents took up their bows, the women called out comical insults, so that the archers found it difficult to concentrate.

Cartwright found concentration easier than the others. He surprised himself by hitting the centre of the target from over a hundred yards away.

The sun was intense, even late in the afternoon, and he was sweating in his fur clothes. He had rowed out to the Inuit's island at dawn, pitched his tent among theirs, and spent the morning trading with them. To show how glad he was to see them again, he'd worn his Inuit-style clothing that he'd made himself. Attuiock and the other men had admired his costume and joked with him. The women had examined it closely, criticizing the stitches.

Overdressed, flushed with the exercise and sun, Cartwright began to feel sick. He excused himself from the games and crept into his tent to rest.

At sunset Attuiock and his wife, Ickcongoque, brought Cartwright food. They saw at once that he was ill and, after clucking sadly and feeling his hands and face, they quietly withdrew.

Then they burst in again at the head of a small group. Attuiock and another man each had a drum. Attuiock reached into his parka and lifted a pouch on a thong over his head. He helped Cartwright sit up, and hung it around his neck. From another bag he extracted what looked like a bird's foot and touched it to Cartwright's mouth, stomach, and groin. Then he and the other man took up their drums, knelt near Cartwright's head, and began drumming and chanting in high nasal voices.

Cartwright watched with interest at first, but after a few minutes he sat up, waving his arms and calling for silence. It was sleep he needed more than anything, he explained. If he could only sleep he would likely be better by morning. He thanked them for coming, but asked them to please go outside.

The Inuit nodded gravely and left. Cartwright dozed and woke again. The wall of his tent was glowing orange from the light of a nearby fire. The whole of the Inuit camp seemed to be out there shouting and banging on drums.

This lasted all night. Cartwright saw their voices as a range of jagged mountains through which he slowly flew. There would be deep shadowy chasms, throaty and vibrant, then high soaring spires, scratchy with brambles and dead trees. At times his stomach seemed to be sucked out, drawn into the gulfs that opened beneath him. At times, rising, his face seemed to inflate, wobbling vastly, out of control.

Through it all, groups of dogs were fighting outside, tumbling together onto the sagging wall of his tent. For a moment the snarling bodies rolled heavily over his chest and face, with only the thin canvas between him and their raking claws, the sharp vertebrae of their backs.

Amazingly, the next day he was better. He sat on the beach watching the women drying thin fillets of fish on a line.

That evening he joined Attuiock and his family in their tent for supper. "You are Inuit," Attuiock told him. "You are human." Cartwright had the impression of pairs of eyes around him reflecting the light from the stone lamp, supporting him somehow, holding him as though in a hand. He dozed, and when the others took off their clothing to sleep, he did the same.

Spread over so many people, the heavy caribou robe was weightless. It touched only his shoulder and hip. It was warm air, not fur that surrounded him. Caubvick was at his back, her hand on his waist. Her husband, Tooklavinia, lay behind her, already snoring. Cartwright rolled over to face her.

Her fingers danced slowly along his eyelids, his cheeks and lips. He reached under her hair, cupping the nape of her neck, her smooth shoulder blades, running his palm down her strong spine; then, with his hand on the small of her back, he pulled her toward him, felt her breasts lightly touching his chest, her legs against his. She slid her knee and thigh up over his hip.

After moving slowly within her for a minute or two, he withdrew and rubbed his penis against her clitoris. He thought it a friendly gesture. It was what Mrs. Selby liked him to do.

Caubvick chuckled in his ear, reached down and reinserted his penis inside her. "Silly *kablunet*," she whispered, "no wonder you are so few."

When Cartwright returned to his own tent a man was there. One of their great hunters, nearly Attuiock's equal. He had opened a satchel. He was stealing a skein of green thread.

Others were looking into the tent from behind him, so Cartwright made a great show of his disapproval.

Taking a stick he struck the man on the shoulder, but before he could strike him again the man snatched the stick, hurled it down, and leapt toward Cartwright. Cartwright grabbed his opponent's arm and, using a throw called a cross-buttock, sent him flying outside where he landed heavily on some stones. The man got to his feet, baffled by what had happened, and walked quickly away.

Cartwright stood in front of his tent and made a long speech. He would not steal from them if they would not steal from him, he told them. They were his friends, but if they stole from him he would punish them. They listened patiently. Instead of turning against him, they seemed to admire what he had done.

When he told Mrs. Selby how he'd won their respect and obedience by standing up for himself and being impeccably fair, she said, "Oh, let's stop bullying them, Cartwright, and fooling ourselves. I'm sure you've won their admiration. You do take tremendous risks, humiliating their leaders in front of their families. Probably, as you say, it will make them more tractable and useful for bringing you furs. But you don't have to pretend to yourself or me that you think it's fair, or that you're serving the cause of civilization here. What you give them isn't worth one fiftieth part of what you get from them. You know that better than I. So who's stealing from whom? And how does your trade improve them, or your lessons in honesty? I think you'll weaken them, make them dependent and tame."

"But you trade with them yourself when you get the chance! You've got your basket of buttons ready right now."

"I do. But I don't pretend it's brave or virtuous. Or that it's for anyone's good but my own. I have plans for the future."

What plans, Cartwright wanted to know.

She explained her idea of staying there in America, cutting their ties with England, with investors and estates. They could live very well, she said, if they didn't need to make so much money, if their business were smaller. Perkins and Coghlan were more of a hindrance than a help. Cartwright was having to pay for equipment he never saw. If they were on their own they could hire a crew of furriers, trade with the natives for a year, save their money, and start a plantation in Canada or the other American colonies. Or they could live in St. John's in the winter and take a salmon crew to Labrador in the spring. They'd make money enough on that alone if they owned their own ship and nets. "The Eskimos don't begrudge us their land," she said. "If we were independent, we could live here and leave them alone."

"I haven't come here to merely scrape by."

"But that's all you're doing now. You could do it with less work, and less trouble from partners and crews."

"Leave that to me. We'll see how I've done at the end of the summer. And we can't live here and leave them alone, as you say. They wouldn't let us. We've invaded their land. All we can do is retreat . . . or involve ourselves with them."

"You mean conquer them."

"That's not what I said."

✦

The second time Cartwright slept with Caubvick he touched her face very gently in the dark, her eyebrows and cheeks, her fine nose and wide, muscular jaw. Even her skull seemed muscular. Her hair was a denser darkness within the dark. Its thickness. Her body's stream.

195

He had never imagined a person could be so strong yet so human and tender. Encompassing. Calling his manhood out.

✧

Noble and Pinson, Perkins and Coghlan, Noble and Pinson. These pairs of names were tattooed on Cartwright's brain.

When he started his business in Labrador the Board of Trade, the First Lord of the Admiralty, the Governor of Newfoundland had lavished favours upon him. Other men with plans similar to Cartwright's had come along after him and received the same generous treatment.

In the summer of 1772, men from the firm of Noble and Pinson showed up on the Charles River with boatloads of nets and supplies and a document stating that the Board of Trade in London had granted the river to them. They tramped through Cartwright's garden, strung their nets from bank to bank in the river, and took most of the fish.

Attuiock and his relatives saw what was happening. "Are these men your friends?" Attuiock asked.

"No," Cartwright said.

"Nor do we like them," Attuiock stated. "We will kill them for you. It will be our pleasure."

For a few seconds Cartwright toyed with the idea of making himself king of the independent nation of Labrador. With his Inuit army he could easily take the blockhouse at Chateau, capture its guns and the naval ships in the harbour, and drive the Nobles and Pinsons off the coast. But the British navy and army would be relentless. And his men were too few and too primitive. It would be stupid glorious suicide, nothing more.

"No," he said. "Leave them alone."

His decision was made – he would have to return to England that fall to clear the matter up with the Board of Trade. To the members of the board, Labrador was a mythic land; they divided it up for whoever asked for a piece. Most likely they'd never seen an accurate map of the place.

He'd been wanting to visit home anyway, to see his parents again, his sisters and brothers, to put his new self in old settings, for the pleasure of feeling transformed. He wanted to boast a little, show his family what he'd made of himself, shock them with his tales. And he'd have two years' worth of furs to take back and the summer's dry fish. He might as well go along and see that the selling was carried out properly. And he wanted to see a city for a change, just for a change. He could take Attuiock and his family along to show them the things he'd been trying to tell them about. Show them his home. He'd been two years in theirs, it was time for him to play host. The trip would be fine sport with Attuiock sharing it. The attention he'd win with the Inuit's company would make him the leading figure in Labrador trade.

"There's no need to hurt these strangers," he told Attuiock. "The King and the King's captains will help me. I am going to talk to them. Why don't you come with me? You and your family. We'll visit the King. We'll go to my home."

"I would like to," Attuiock said. His calm smile showed he couldn't imagine what was in store for him.

Cartwright wrote to his parents and sent the letter to Chateau, hoping it would find a ship to England ahead of him. He'd be coming to Marnham with Eskimo friends, he wrote, dear, gentle people, the most sincere and honest of any he'd met on earth.

Milmouth agreed to oversee operations in Labrador while Cartwright and Mrs. Selby were gone. Cartwright would pay the men's wages when he returned the following summer, provided they could show they'd done their work.

Seated on rocks on the shore of Cape Charles, looking over the water, Cartwright and Attuiock discussed the trip, using their usual mixture of English and Inuktitut words.

"I would like Caubvick and Tooklavinia to come also, along with you and your wife, Ickcongoque," Cartwright said.

Attuiock nodded. "If they wish."

"And bring your children, of course."

"Only my young daughter, Ickeuna," Attuiock said. He and Ickongoque would miss her too much, he explained; but his son, being older, would be safe with his nephew's family at home.

✦

There was too much smoke coming out of the chimney of the Lodge, also smoke from the far side of the roof. Cartwright was running up the path from the river, his rifle in hand. Haines was running behind him. Noble and Pinson's men had come to the Lodge that morning en route to their salmon nets, and Cartwright and Haines were just now returning after escorting them part of the way to make sure they didn't damage or steal anything. Cartwright shouted, *"Milmouth! Mrs. Selby!"* They must have been fishing, picking berries.

He reached the door of the Lodge and swung it open

into a wall of smoke smelling of burnt cloth, burnt leather. He watched the smoke curl inward away from him, then glow greenish-yellow and flash into solid flame. The flames sucked backward into a tall blaze next to the fireplace under a hole in the roof, and the air became nearly clear. Rags of fire were flapping along the rafters, the backs of the chairs. Cartwright yanked a key on a thong out from the neck of his shirt and over his head, then, taking a breath, lunged past the table into the bedroom, opened the chest that was bolted onto the floor, heaved a satchel of money out through the parchment window, swept his hand down a shelf, over a table, sending his journal, ledgers, books onto the bed, plucked up the blanket's corners, swinging the bundle across his back, looked around once, grabbed Mrs. Selby's violin, and in four blind strides was outside gulping the air, checking his clothes and hair for flames.

The Lodge was already lost. Cartwright and Haines draped wet sails over the nearby roofs of the servants' house and the salmon house, but the heat of the fire dried the sails faster than they could wet them with buckets from the spring. They gave those buildings up too and concentrated on saving the storehouse where the winter's furs and half the summer's fish were kept. They used wet sacks like flails. Cartwright stood on the storehouse roof swatting the burning bits of the Lodge that were falling around him. Haines scrambled back and forth at the edge of the clearing beating at flames that had caught in the trees.

By late afternoon there was nothing left of the Lodge and the two other buildings but fireplaces and smouldering beams. Sixteen tierces of salmon were gone and all of the goods for the Inuit trade, most of Mrs. Selby's books, all their clothes.

Cartwright and Haines stood coughing, exhausted,

staring at the large rectangular patches of ash. There was a quarter of fresh caribou in the storehouse. Cartwright sent Haines to cut some steaks, then he wetted his boots in a bucket and picked his way into the remains of the Lodge, to about where the gun-rack used to be. Under the ashes he found four musket barrels, still nearly red-hot, their stocks burnt away. Using a stick, he levered them up and propped them over some charred beams with embers underneath. When Haines returned, Cartwright wetted his smoking boots again and spread the steaks over the musket barrels to grill.

At the smell of the sizzling meat he started to hum. He was already planning how to get timber, how to get new buildings up and fresh supplies before sailing to England in two months' time.

✦

The westerly autumn winds generally made the homeward crossing of the Atlantic much quicker than the trip out. It might take two months for the fishing crews to come over to Newfoundland in the spring and two weeks to get back to Ireland and England in the fall. With the wind behind them and a valuable cargo below, their spirits were usually high as they started home. The biggest problem waited near the end. The wind that drove them east so efficiently often didn't give them a choice about where to land. They might see the coast in time and aim for a sheltered bay. They might just as easily end up on Irish or Cornish rocks. Sailing out was like climbing a long zig-zag mountain trail, coming home was like jumping off a cliff.

Luck was with Cartwright's group in November 1772. Apart from one incident when the *Mary* got side-on to the wind and lost part of her rigging, the crossing, at least as far as Ireland, was quick and relatively easy. The Inuit ventured briefly on deck from time to time to scan the horizon, but otherwise preferred to stay in their cabin. They didn't dislike sailing, but hated being so far from land.

Only Ickongoque with her recurrent headaches suffered physically to any extent. Attuiock was often occupied in administering his remedy, the sound of which Cartwright could hear through the cabin wall. With few books to read, and little desire to stay long on the spray-drenched deck, Mrs. Selby was restless and moody returning home, a puzzle to Cartwright.

During rough weather on the 22nd, their fifteenth day out, Attuiock approached Cartwright and told him they were all going to die, that they had sailed beyond the end of the earth. Cartwright showed him a chart. "Here's where we are," he said. "Late tomorrow we'll see Ireland. Here."

On the morning of the 23rd, the wind abated, the clouds and mist cleared, and they discovered themselves less than four miles from the Irish coast near Bantry Bay. They had been travelling faster than they realized and had mistaken their location on the chart. If they had not been slowed down earlier, while fixing their rigging, they would have been driven on shore during the night. Always optimistically biased in his view of accidents, Cartwright attributed their escape to Divine Providence.

A day later, they anchored near the Irish town of Waterford where they planned to refresh themselves before sailing on to England – a part of the voyage that could be most dangerous of all. Immediately word went out that Eskimos were on board, and, as Cartwright and his companions travelled by cart into town, crowds began to gather, people lining the streets, faces filling each window overhead.

They cast off from Waterford on the 29th of November, but spent another two weeks dodging storms in the Scilly Isles and in various small ports on the south coast of England before they finally reached London. In every village and harbour on the way, gangs of curious spectators followed them. "This is nothing," Cartwright told his silent Inuit friends at each stop. "Wait till you see London."

10

In the morning light, the Thames was opaque grey. It seemed thicker and slower than he remembered it. A completely different species of river from the Charles in Labrador. But the bustle of shipping, the traffic on shore were exciting. It was what he'd hoped for, everything operating full tilt. He turned to Caubvick and Ickcongoque beside him at the rail of the barge, Ickcongoque holding little Ickeuna tightly by the hand. It was their faces he wanted to watch. "How do you like it?" he asked in Inuktitut, and glanced again at what they were looking at, the north bank near the Tower, and saw what they saw without their having to tell him – angular rocks, cliffs with countless caves, a jumble of scree.

"So many boats," Caubvick was saying, "I've never seen so many before."

"Look," Cartwright pointed, "those are all *houses*. Not cliffs and rocks. All houses that people built up stone by stone." The women's eyes widened, but it seemed to be more in response to his tone of voice than to what they were seeing.

They weren't looking at things the way he wanted them to. Instead of admiring the steepled sky-line, they would stare down at bits of rubbish floating by in the water, or study the clouds, or look at the caged eagle, the dog, the trunks and bundles they had with them on the barge.

Attuiock and Tooklavinia had been worse. On the previous day, Cartwright had left the women on board the ship at Gravesend and had gone ahead with the men in a post-chaise to find lodgings in London. The streets had been crowded and hectic, but the men had slept most of the way, or pretended to. Even when he shook them to point out sights such as the Tower of London or St. Paul's Cathedral, they only opened their eyes a crack, nodded, smiled, and closed them again.

He wanted Ickcongoque's and Caubvick's first encounter with London to be more satisfactory. This was why he had chosen to bring them into the city by boat. The approach would be more spectacular. It would be slow and relaxed, there would be time to marvel at things. Mrs. Selby, at least, was enjoying the ride, seated alone at the prow of the barge.

Now they passed under London Bridge, fighting the current, without his Inuit friends noticing what was overhead.

"What do you think that is?" Cartwright asked, pointing back.

"Rock," Caubvick said.

"Ice," said Ickcongoque. "Water has carved it out. It will fall down in the summer."

Cartwright tried to convince them that men had made it, carved the individual stones and stacked them up, but the women laughed and covered their faces. They thought he was teasing them.

When they went under Blackfriars Bridge, he insisted they focus their eyes as he did. He showed them the joints in the stone-work piers, the marks of the masons' chisels on the massive blocks. He lifted his arm and face toward the arch overhead, the hundreds of fitted stones. His companions followed his gaze, and he turned and looked at them. What their faces revealed was a kind of revulsion, a kind of fear.

They landed beside Westminster Bridge. Cartwright stepped ashore carrying the eagle in its cage and leading his Eskimo dog, which was three-quarters wolf. The crowd at the fish market alongside had seen them coming, and by the time Cartwright got to the top of the stairs that ran up from the river he was surrounded. He turned and beckoned to Mrs. Selby to hurry. She was coming behind, escorting the Inuit women. Ickeuna, holding her mother's hand, was finding it difficult to lift her feet high enough to get up the steps.

"C'm'ere an' look! A wolf! A man's got a wolf! And Africans, look! Are you from Russia, sir? Those aren't Africans, they're Chinee! GIVE YOU A QUID FOR THE BIRD! Are they cannibals, those? Red shank slamkins, they are. Are they men or women? ARE YOU FRENCH? Are you actors? 'Ere, does yer dog like fish?"

Cartwright waved his arm, bidding the crowd make way – without effect – but the people fell back conveniently from in front of his dog when he roused it by shaking its leash and crying, "Up, boy, up!"

It took time to get coaches in through the mob along Bridge Street and to make arrangements for the servants to follow with the trunks. And when they had finally managed to wrestle themselves into a vehicle, along with the dog and eagle, and had pulled the doors shut and were on their way, they discovered the eagle was missing a number of feathers, and Ickeuna's small whale-bone doll had been stolen out of her hand.

All afternoon and evening Cartwright's friends and acquaintances came to the second-floor rooms he had rented in Leicester Street to look at the Inuit. The five of them sat in their sealskin clothing on the settee and upholstered chairs shyly smiling while dozens of strangers stared at them and endless questions were asked. In the midst of the goings-on Mrs. Selby and a couple of servants tried to proceed with unpacking the trunks. Mrs. Selby's temper was short. She would take out a jacket or dress, shake it sharply in the faces of the milling visitors, push her way wordlessly through to one of the adjoining bedrooms, and stride briskly into the parlour again straight to the trunks.

"Are they cannibals?"

"No. They are gentle if treated gently, and respectful of human life."

"Have they discovered fire?"

"Yes."

"Do they understand English?"

"A little."

"Get them to say something in their language."

"They're rather shy right now. Um . . . Attuiock, tell them where you are from."

"Netcetumiut."

"What did he say?"

"Netcetumiut."

"Oh."

"Have they invented the wheel?"

"No."

"Are their sexual parts the same as ours?"

"Yes."

"Do they worship idols?"

"No."

"Do they play a version of cricket?"

"Don't be daft," another says. "They probably haven't invented the ball."

"Or the wicket."

"Do they eat raw meat?"

"Sometimes."

"All bloody?"

"Mm."

"What do they use for napkins?"

On their third day at the lodgings the landlord made his way through the ever-present crush of visitors, looking distressed. He drew Cartwright aside. He was sorry. It couldn't go on, he said. Complaints were coming from every quarter. The street outside was obstructed night and day by chairs and carriages; the continual concourse was disturbing the other tenants. Even the neighbours across the street and next door were protesting, threatening legal action. His lodgings were not for the use of freak shows and charlatans. They would have to go.

Cartwright rented a furnished house in Oxford Market, and Mrs. Selby packed their trunks again, violently, surrounded by many observers. The number of people wanting to see the Inuit continued to grow. The street in front of their new residence became blocked as before. There were fights between carriage drivers.

Attuiock and Ickcongoque began refusing to come out of their room. Mrs. Selby and Cartwright rarely spoke except to shout over the heads of their guests about ordering food.

In the bedroom, Attuiock looked out the window. Cartwright stood beside him, sharing the view – a tangle of horses and carriages. "It is hard to travel in London," Attuiock said. "Why do your people go everywhere with those animals dragging those things? They are always caught on one another. If people got rid of them, they would be free to walk."

At Mrs. Selby's insistence, Cartwright posted a notice restricting visits to Tuesdays and Fridays, and everyone relaxed. For two days they did nothing but eat and rest. They set a washtub up in the parlour and all took turns bathing. The Inuit combed one another's hair for most of one afternoon. Cartwright brought in a tailor and had them measured for English attire so they could go out in public undisturbed. He also bought bolts of woollen and flannel cloth, beads and embroidery thread, and brought some furs from the warehouse where his own supplies were stored. Ickcongoque and Caubvick studied the cloth, considering colours and weights, then set about cutting and stitching new clothes for the family, garments they trimmed with beads and furs in exquisite style. Their old sealskin clothes, which they'd worn all through the crossing, they cut up and burned in the fireplace when there was a good draft.

With the Inuit settled in and equipped for their stay in England, Cartwright turned to his other affairs. Carrying gifts of fur mitts and walrus tusk carvings, he went to the Board of Trade. The board's director, the Earl of Dartmouth, studied Cartwright's letters and permits, looked at a map, ordered a clerk to bring him a bundle of files. Of course, the Charles River was Cartwright's territory, the Earl confirmed. He couldn't imagine how the mistake had occurred. He would see that Cartwright was issued a new licence. Noble and Pinson would be confined to the coast south of Cape Charles, and Cartwright could have what was north of it, all the way to Hamilton Inlet, if he liked. The Earl wanted to know when he could visit the Eskimo-Indians, of whom he'd heard so much talk.

Perkins and Coghlan's agent would arrange the sale of Cartwright's cargo. After that, the term of his partnership with the firm would expire. With his profits, and with loans, he planned to continue his business by himself. Cartwright visited the vast, chilly auction houses to see that his goods were intact and that they received a fair price when they were sold. Mrs. Selby went with him to arrange to have her portion of the cargo auctioned separately. Then there were banks for him to visit, creditors to pay, preparations to make for the return to Labrador in the spring, five months away. Mrs. Selby went off on business of her own.

1772. December. Wednesday 30.

Among those who have come to observe the Eskimos during the past week and a half was a young artist who asked permision to draw their portraits. He was first here a week ago Tuesday, when he worked assiduously with his chalks and pencils while all around the usual questions were asked and comments were made. On Friday he returned, presented his subjects with miniature portraits of themselves, and delighted Ickeuna with the additional gift of a small copper bell. He then sketched the group in watercolour the whole of that afternoon. He was here again yesterday.

An engraver's apprentice was how he described himself, and confessed that his master believed him to be drawing effigies in Westminster Abbey rather than here making portraits of Eskimos. His interest, he said, is in innocent people uncorrupted by civilization. When I attempted to inform him that crime is not unknown among the Eskimos, he asked if they had churches and armies, and when I said no, he nodded as though his point had been confirmed. He also asked if I intended to make slaves of them, and when I answered that I did not, he said he hoped I would abide by that intention. He then shook my hand, as well as those of the Eskimos, and took his leave.

✧

The King and Queen attended the opera on the same night Cartwright was there with his Labrador entourage. When the royal couple entered their box, the house rose and broke into applause. The Inuit's eyes shone at the sight of this spectacle. Whatever they thought of London's traffic and buildings, its social glitter clearly appealed to them. In the same way, although it exhausted them, the attention they drew in high society, the gifts and invitations that flowed their way, pleased them immensely. It suited the way they preferred to think of themselves: not as curiosities or captives, but as dignitaries, representatives of their people.

Caubvick especially took to the new way of life. She wanted dresses like those of the ladies she saw at the theatre. She got Mrs. Selby to take her to a hairdresser and came back with her glossy hair swept up in an impressive chignon. She was remarkably beautiful, Cartwright saw.

They made a striking group at Covent Garden where they went to to see a performance of *Cymbeline*. Caubvick's hair was gathered in braids and ringlets behind her ears, and her white sequined gown was cut low to show off her smooth shapely shoulders. The rest of her family were wearing their newly made parkas and boots. When they entered their box, the audience greeted them with enormous applause. Attuiock and Tooklavinia sat proudly erect during the tribute, then remarked to their wives that they had been welcomed with as much respect as the King.

Ickeuna watched the play's action open-mouthed, never taking her eyes from the stage. When the sword-fight between Posthumus and Iachimo began, she let out a scream that brought the performance to a stop for over a minute. Then she buried her face in Mrs. Selby's breast and went to sleep.

They were invited to dine at the home of John Hunter, a famous surgeon and anatomist. Joseph Banks and his friend, Doctor Solander, were there asking eager questions across the table. "What vegetables play a part in their diet in Labrador?"

"To what extent and by what means do they heat their houses in winter?"

"Do they have legends of early encounters with Europeans?"

"Do any of them alter their bodies surgically through tattooing, circumcision, that sort of thing?"

"Where do the souls of their dead resort to at death?"

Attuiock left the table to visit the privy, then almost

immediately rushed back into the room, his face rigid with fear. Ignoring the company, he rounded the table to where Cartwright was rising to meet him, gripped Cartwright's arm, and spoke close to his ear. "They plan to eat us here! I have seen the bones! Inuit bones. I know whose they are."

He tugged Cartwright into the hall, into Hunter's study. There were human skeletons in glass cases on two of the walls.

The attendant was there at his elbow. "You may approach His Majesty." Then being led through the reception hall's multitude, the high murmur pierced by laughter echoing from the frescoed dome, around groups in close conversation, the blur of marble floor, backs of satin jackets, movement of lace, into a circle of courtiers – the King raising his hand in generous greeting.

Cartwright bowed deeply.

"So these are the Eskimo-Indians everyone's talking about.... Do they speak English? No? Tell them, then, that I give them my personal welcome to England . . . that I am pleased to accept them and their countrymen as subjects . . . and that as such they shall enjoy the full protection and . . . elevating benefits . . . of English law.

"What curious people. Bright and good-looking, wouldn't you say?" He drew a murmur of assent from his courtiers. "Tell me," he looked at Cartwright, "are they physically constructed like a European, in all particulars?"

Cartwright bowed. "They are, Your Majesty, except they seem to have a greater tolerance of cold, and a more sanguine complexion."

"Are they a numerous people?"

"No, Your Majesty. Their exact number is unknown, but I would estimate no more than three or four thousand."

"Good. How are they governed?"

"Only by heads of families and village leaders."

"Do they use money and value precious metals and gems?"

"No, Your Majesty. They value steel because it is useful to them."

"Have they a form of writing?"

"No."

"May I hear their language spoken?"

Cartwright turned to Attuiock, Caubvick, Ickeuna. "The King wishes to hear you speak," he said in Inuktitut.

"We could sing," Attuiock said.

"What's that?" The King tilted his face inquiringly. Attuiock looked at the floor while the rest of his family giggled amongst themselves.

"Well then ask one of them to count." The King sounded slightly impatient.

Caubvick counted to twenty-one in her language.

"Why did she stop?" he asked.

"Their numbers only go to twenty-one," Cartwright explained.

The King pondered this information a while. "What was their number for twenty?"

"*Awatit*," Cartwright said.

The King repeated the word.

"What was their number for two?"

"*Malrok*."

The King repeated it to himself, then gestured significantly to the Inuit, collecting their full attention. "*Awatit-malrok*," he announced. He showed them his outstretched fingers once, twice, and held up the first two fingers of his right hand while casting a pleased grin to the courtiers on either side. He dropped his hand, signalling that the interview was about to end. "There. I have advanced the cause of knowledge in their civilization. I trust I'll be remembered as the Eskimo Euclid."

The courtiers laughed with vehement appreciation.

"You're doing good work, I'm told." The King let his last words drop as he turned away. Someone or something else drew his attention. "Whatever assistance you need shall be given. Arrange Lord Dartmouth Board of Trade."

"Excuse me, Your Majesty, I have a . . ."

The King turned to Cartwright again.

"I have a gift for the Queen." He reached behind him and lifted the wicker cage containing the eagle. "Also, I hoped, I wondered . . . you do collect guns, I understand."

A dog had begun barking in shrill bursts somewhere nearby.

In the midst of the racket the Queen, who had been chatting with another group to the rear of the King, was sought out.

The King slipped away as a servant accepted the cage from Cartwright and held it for her inspection. "My, what a remarkably . . . cross-looking bird." The Queen glanced about, trying to guess from whom the gift had come. The dog continued to bark. "Thank you Mr. . . ."

"Cartwright," someone said.

She nodded, smiling. "I shall have him placed on a mantel somewhere. . . . Or mounted on a wall."

✦

It can't be what he's eating before bed, Cartwright thinks, since he never eats anything at all. He who was such an addict of fresh meat. He remembers the time in Labrador that he nearly made bow-wow pie with two of his young dogs because he hadn't killed any game for over a week. One of his Inuit friends happened to come by with a recently caught seal on that occasion and saved the dogs. What is his stomach like now inside? Shrunk and dissolved? Calcified? Full of some kind of bile? It doesn't feel any different from the outside, except it never feels hungry. Strange that his animals eat and he can't. In any case it can't be his diet that causes these dreams. The shame and ugliness hanging like rags on his body when he wakes up.

He looks at Kaumalak on her perch without the usual lifting of spirit. Instead he feels a painful reminder of what he dreamt, which was all about hawks. He dreamt he had broken into the chemistry of hawks.

He had a menagerie of eagles, peregrines, gyrfalcons, goshawks, kestrels, lanners, and ospreys. Some he adored for their speed, some for their ability to wait on and stoop, some for their size and strength, some for their ability to hunt in forests, some for their ability to take fish from rivers, some for their dignity, some for their fixed ferocity.

He wanted to produce a hawk that combined the various features he favoured in each of his different birds. He constructed a tall white felt hat with deeply fluted sides and elaborate puffs and indentations on the top of the crown, with a silver medal in front, and a wide brim with a turned-up edge. Somehow he knew it embodied what male hawks love. He put it on, and a male goshawk immediately left his perch and landed on the hat, curling his talons in through the base of the crown, into Cartwright's scalp. The bird pushed against the back of the hat with sharp jerks, then extracted his talons and flapped away, knocking the hat slightly askew. Cartwright caught the hat, kept it level and lifted it off. In the trough-shaped brim was a pool of nearly clear goshawk semen. He took a straw and drew the semen up into the front of his mouth. Then, keeping the straw between his teeth he went to his female peregrine, stroked her, turned her gently head-down, leaned close enough to insert the straw into her, and discharged the goshawk semen from his mouth.

The offspring of this union was immediately there, and, using the same technique, Cartwright crossbred it with an eagle, and its offspring with a lanner, and that with an osprey.

The combinations finally produced a hawk-faced boy with red eyes, dressed in a blue frock coat, stockings, and breeches, wearing a tricorn hat and a silver sword.

Cartwright leans against the wall by the side of his window in The Turk's Head, looking out. There is no defence, he thinks, in this region, against what his mind will do.

He would like to go riding without his hawk for a change.

✦

With the window open cold air poured into the study, but the moon was full and the night was perfect for using the telescope. Banks aimed the instrument and adjusted its focus, then invited his guests to have a look. Cartwright was there with his Inuit friends and his brother John. Solander peered through the telescope and began talking with Banks about the Mare Imbrium.

John took a look. Cartwright beckoned to Attuiock. "A close look at the moon," he said.

Attuiock put his eye to the viewing piece, then straightened and nodded. "The moon's *house*," he said, correcting what Cartwright had told him. "I have been there. I have gone inside and met the moon."

Everyone gave them gifts. Clothing and combs for the women; mostly tools for the men. Banks gave Attuiock a set of saws, chisels, and hammers that fitted into removable trays inside a chest. Cartwright's brother John gave Attuiock a heavy knife and an Irish Ordnance Department medal. He'd won the medal years before in a bet, and although he didn't value it much – it was only silver – he thought Attuiock would be glad to have it.

Attuiock and Cartwright looked at the medal together. On the back was a shield with field guns, a harp, a crown above palm and laurels. On the front, the royal arms, and the motto "DIEU ET MON DROIT." "It means 'God and my right,'" Cartwright explained. "It's the King's power. The power he gives the British."

In the small house in London they were all more confined than they were used to.

Mrs. Selby went to stay for a few days with her brother. When she was gone, Cartwright announced he was taking Caubvick to the theatre so she could show off her dress. None of her family seemed to mind being left behind.

The two of them dined at an inn, polishing off a platter of beefsteaks and roast potatoes. This was the food Cartwright dreamed of during the winter in

Labrador, what he most often boasted of eating in vast quantity. It was clearly a passion he shared with Caubvick. She matched him steak for steak, squinting and giggling as her jaws worked, catching the juice from her chin with the back of her hand.

"Do you miss Labrador?" he asked.

"No." She showed her graceful mastery of knife and fork. "It's better here."

In the room upstairs she didn't resist his caresses, but insisted on taking her dress off to keep it from being mussed. He wanted her to keep it on so he could run his hands over her shoulders and breasts under its white sheen, so he could lift it over her hips and take her on his lap. Instead she hung it over a chair and pulled him down on the bed on top of her.

"Come on, hurry," she told him. "I want to go the theatre like you said."

Leading the Inuit along Piccadilly, all of them dressed in cloaks with the hoods up to avoid attention, Cartwright ushered them into a shop that sold exotic animals. He fixed his eyes on his companions' faces, watched them discover the parrot, the gawdy comic sidling up, the black-tongued yawning, saying "Hello, Doll." The Inuit jumped, their eyes large, fear flickering through their faces, which immediately opened in laughter. They were like children, he thought, the way their naked emotions instantly showed themselves. For them, everything here was new. It was what he had wanted, to relive through them his own first experience of things.

At the sight of the chained monkey, Attuiock froze. He muttered something quickly to the rest, and they stepped back. There was real fear in Attuiock's eyes, and distrust. "Is that an Inuit?" he asked.

Cartwright nearly laughed and felt himself blushing all at once. "No, it's an animal, it's. . . ." He wasn't sure whether by "Inuit" Attuiock had meant human in general, or Eskimo. Surely they couldn't suppose such a thing, even if the monkey's coat did look something like sealskin or caribou clothing. Even if it was smaller than Englishmen. The Inuit weren't *that* much inferior in size. And certainly no one proposed to lead them around on a chain.

✧

Attuiock's hunched back bounced and swung in the saddle in time with his horse's long stride. Cartwright, his own horse galloping flat out, watched him from well behind. Attuiock with Tooklavinia slightly ahead of him disappeared into a shallow glen following the hounds whose ragged braying echoed up from beyond the trees. Cartwright, too, plunged into the glen, lurching precariously over his mount's neck, raked by branches of hawthorn and wild pear.

The Inuit's riding style was far from graceful or orthodox, but it did the job. They managed to get their horses to go wherever the fox and the hounds went, and just as fast, down no matter what kind of embankments, through every thicket and hedge. They didn't know it wasn't normally done.

At the top of the next rise he could see them again, clumps of turf flying behind their horses' hoofs. Sometimes a foot of sky showed under Attuiock's rump. He seemed to be flying parallel with his horse, only holding on to the reins. Cartwright had argued with him about the length of his stirrups, but Attuiock had wanted them long, saying he needed to grip the horse with his legs.

Tooklavinia's style was different again. He rode like an overweight jockey, bent over his horse's neck, his stirrups short, the reins bunched up with a handful of mane.

Cartwright ducked a branch, reined sharply around a stand of trees, laughing to himself. Remarkable talent, he thought. This was only their third time on a horse. And their commands were all in Inuktitut.

What splendid light cavalry they'd make! He watched them gaining on the hounds across a meadow, the fox clearly in view and losing ground. He pictured a squadron of Inuit men in their boots and parkas, their long hair streaming, armed with sabres and carabines, himself at their head, thundering down on the French or the Austrians. Even the pandours, the hussars would have been put to flight. *Ayeeee-ya-ya-ya-ya*! Swinging their sabres overhead. Unmatchable savagery!

The fox was already dead when Cartwright came up and dismounted beside the stone wall at the edge of the field. Tooklavinia was holding the slight red body up by its tail. His eyes and Attuiock's eyes were beaming, their faces flushed and bright. Since they'd all left London and come up to Marnham, the change in the Inuit was remarkable. The size of the fish in the brooks and the fact that they couldn't hunt deer were disappointing to them, but just being able to roam through the fields and woods every day had lifted their spirits. And they'd fallen in love with horses and hounds.

Attuiock was scratching one of the hounds behind the ears, the dog grinning and panting, gazing up at him adoringly.

"They are skinny dogs," Attuiock said, his breath making long clouds in the damp February air, "but they can see with their noses better than any dogs I've known. As well as a hawk can see with its eyes."

Other men who were part of the hunting party

arrived. John Lilly and his son, from the neighbouring village of Skegby, dismounted heavily and were followed soon after by Edward Wright and John Popple.

"Didn't come down through Handley's forest, did you?" Lilly asked.

"Yes." Cartwright lifted his horse's left front hoof to see if a stone was lodged there. She had been limping slightly. "Easy country," he said, "compared to Labrador."

"Bloody madness," Lilly snorted. "Break your neck. . . . Were your Indian chaps in at the death along with you then?"

Cartwright let go of the horse's hoof and straightened to watch Lilly's face. "Actually, Tooklavinia and Attuiock were the only ones in at the death. I couldn't keep up with them."

Offended, Lilly turned to meet more of the party as they arrived. Servants ran up, collecting dogs for their masters, putting their leashes on.

Lilly had moved a few paces off with his friends. "Yes, very poor outing," Cartwright could hear them saying, "bit of a run for the dogs is all . . . no, couldn't call it a hunt . . . ." Their hounds gathered, the men mounted their horses and began heading home. Lilly paused and turned in his saddle. "Oh, George, refreshments at my house. Do join us, won't you?"

Cartwright declined.

Tooklavinia carried the fox draped over the front of his saddle as they rode back to Marnham Hall. The dogs, tired and satisfied, were content to lope alongside, close to the horses. Attuiock looked at the dull yellow stain in the clouds where the sun was hidden. Fields and groves sloped away to their left toward the Trent. "It is all *made* here," Attuiock said with a slow sweep of his arm. "The land is all made by hand."

It was what Cartwright had tried to tell him about St. Paul's.

Tooklavinia was leaning over his horse's neck, stroking her shoulder as he rode. "My beauty, my beauty," he was saying in Inuktitut. He caught Cartwright's eye. "I would like to bring her with me to Labrador," he said. "And four of those good-nosed dogs."

"It would be possible," Cartwright said. "But you would have to live differently for the sake of the horse. You would have to build her a house to live in, and feed her grass and grain. . . . I could show you how to grow grass and cut it. And you could buy grain by trading furs."

"I'll be the man, Caubvick." It was Dorothy speaking, the youngest of Cartwright's sisters. "We face one another and bow. Good. Then we hold hands, like this. Now listen to Lizzie while she plays. Slowly Lizzie. *One* two three, one two three. Little steps Caubvick, very little steps, that's good, always the right foot first, bending step forward, left bending step gliding, right straight, left straight, good. Do you understand?"

Caubvick smiled, holding Dorothy's hand at arm's length. Could anyone else ever send such a warm embrace with her eyes as Caubvick could?

"And *I've* eaten it, too!" Cartwright was saying to a group including Lady Tyrconnel, Mrs. Selby, and his father. "Fresh and raw! Best thing for you! Look, have you seen a woman's knife? *Ooloo*, it's called. Bit like a cabbage-chopper. Watch." He held up a piece of ham in his left hand and took one end in his teeth. "Shlice 'rom 'elow. . . . Swallow. . . . 'ite again, shlice 'rom 'elow. . . . No need for a plate, fork, or any of that. Only mind your nose."

"Here, let me try," John said, setting his wine aside.

"Mary!" his father called. "Bring more toasted

cheeses around if they've got some ready! And wake up Attuiock here, offer him wine!"

Mary headed out of the room, grumbling about gypsy savages, ignoring Attuiock who was sleeping in a chair.

"Commodore Throsbey, back from the Spice Islands," Lady Tyrconnel said, "spoke of the cannibals using a similar knife, on the more elastic portions of their cuisine. Only, the knife was made of shell in that case, I believe. And I think it lacked a handle."

"I use one for scraping frost off the window," Mrs. Selby said. "George never eats with an *ooloo* at home – only for show."

"Come on, Edmund!" This was Cartwright's youngest brother, Charles. "Grace the occasion with verse!" Charles was going around with a bottle of wine in each hand, topping the glasses up.

"Oh, don't get him started, please." This was Edmund's wife, Alice. Edmund threw a scone at her. They'd been married for less than a year.

"I let it effervesce in the form of a fermenting wort," Edmund was saying, "and then I gave it to a fellow suffering from putrid fever, and it . . . what? . . . No, it cured him in one day. What? . . . Yes, *baker's yeast*. What? . . . No, the fellow who keeps sheep for Mr. Stenwick. . . . Yes, now he's completely well."

Ickcongoque was examining glass figurines on the mantelpiece. One disappeared into her parka.

"Have I told you about my letter to Lord North?" John asked generally.

"Oh, he's a lewd man," William said. "Roll him in a carpet and smoke him for a cigar." He smiled to himself, brushing his arms and thighs. He never expected responses to his remarks.

The fowling pieces and inlaid muskets in the rack on

the wall held Tooklavinia's interest. Lifting each gun, he sighted at pictures, vases, candles.

Ickeuna was spinning, spinning herself around on the carpet and falling down.

"Do you know what the navy *pays* for its oak? And how it comes by it?" John's voice was loud, eager to disabuse.

Lizzie lifted her hands from the clavichord. "Oh, I *wish* this were louder," she said, turning to Dorothy and Caubvick who approached hand in hand at the end of their minuet. "Can you hear me at all? I *said* we should get a harpsichord *years* ago. Now a pianoforte's what I want, I heard one in London. So loud and resonant."

"Not for the minuet though," Cartwright said, laying his arms across both of his sisters' backs, his right hand nesting in Caubvick's hair. "I heard them in Germany. German-made instruments. Excellent craftsmanship. Like my rifle from Hanover. I've yet to see an English gun that can match it. Saved my life many times. Even saved me from drowning."

"Oh? *How?*"

"And so I sent my scheme directly to Lord North," John was saying. "Perhaps he'll think it impertinent, but I believe we ought to correspond with Prime Ministers much as with other men. It's our obligation. The government has got to be made more . . ."

"But we can't all be wasting the government's time," George put in.

"What's their time *for?*" John exclaimed. "They're out of touch with the people they're meant to serve. Look at this Wilkes affair. They ignore or honour election results as it pleases them. And their treatment of the American colonies is disgraceful. Given their freedom they'd be our strongest ally on earth. As it is, we're making them allies of France."

"I agree with John," Mrs. Selby said.

Cartwright ignored her. Since arriving in England, she'd been off on her own much of the time, first visiting friends in London, then with her brother in Bedford, where Cartwright had picked her up on the way to Marnham. She and Cartwright had not discussed Caubvick openly, but Caubvick's changed appearance and manner and Cartwright's attention to her were obvious. Mrs. Selby was more dignified, more short-tempered than usual.

"How can you say that?" Cartwright demanded of John. "Can we in Nottinghamshire declare ourselves a separate nation if we choose? No more can the colonies! They owe a debt of . . ."

"I agree with George," their father said. "Of course we need to improve conditions for all men, but order must be maintained. Take for example this business of giving tips. You can't get a servant to do anything for you anymore without a tip. I've started a campaign, I have. To abolish tipping! Now Mary here, she doesn't mind not being tipped. Do you? That's right."

"*Papa*, make him stop pointing that at me!"

"Look here, Tookla . . ." his father broke off. "George, you speak to him."

"Tooklavinia, the gun isn't loaded, is it? Well don't point it at my sister anyway."

"*Mary!* Bring in the ham! And see if there's more toasted cheese!"

"And you, Mrs. . . . . Mrs. Selby, how do you like Labrador?"

"It agrees with me, Mrs. Cartwright . . . although I often curse the place. It agrees with me better than England."

"Really? And will you be finding a husband out there do you think, among the wild Eskimo? A woman like you must find herself the centre of a great deal of attention."

"Indeed, I do. . . . Actually, I plan to take *several* husbands there, and enjoy them all at the same time."

"Oh!"

"It's when the frost comes *out* that it really hurts." Cartwright grinned.

"Oh? Why is that?"

"You hardly feel it going in. That's the danger, see, and your flesh is as brittle as that china cup. I've seen men come in, their hair and moustaches all hanging in icicles, sit in front of the fire, take off their mitts and socks, and watched their fingers and toes all drop off in rows, plink-plink-plink-plink-plink, like pieces of chalk."

"How does William seem to be faring? Should we have Mary take him upstairs?" Mr. Cartwright posed these familiar questions close to his wife's ear. Together they turned and peered across the room at their eldest son. Fat, white-faced, he was seated playing with Ickeuna who was standing at his knee. He was making figs and sugared nuts disappear into a handkerchief spread over his lap, and the child was burrowing with her hand to find them and popping them into either her mouth or his.

"Well, he's kept his breeches on so far," Mrs. Cartwright said. "Let him stay."

"Come on, come on! Everyone up and move back the chairs!" It was his sister Catherine. "We'll have a contre with everyone joining in. George, you dance with Caubvick. And Charles, where is Charles? You dance with Ickcongoque, don't make a fuss."

From the side of the room Attuiock and Tooklavinia watched the elaborate revolutions, people pivoting, passing under each other's arms.

When it ended, Cartwright called for attention and announced they would have an Eskimo dance. He located his father's militia drum and handed it to Attuiock who surprised the Carwright family by stepping calmly to the centre of the floor and beginning to drum and chant. Cartwright and Tooklavinia joined him, shuffling and dancing rhythmically. John took Mrs. Selby's hand, and they joined in. Then Charles and Lady Tyrconnel followed, and eventually everyone but Caubvick and the servant, Mary, who stood on opposite sides of the room making faces of extravagant disgust.

Caubvick ran outside, and Cartwright, who had noticed, left the dance and followed her. On the terrace outside the salon's bright windows, he caught her by the arm. The night was wet and cold. For a minute they watched their families inside jouncing and stomping. The beat of the drum and the chanting came through the glass in a heavy muffled vibration.

"I hate them," Caubvick said. "They are spoiling everything here."

Cartwright held her, fondling her breasts.

"I am done with my husband," she said. "He is too ignorant. Why do we have to go back to Labrador?"

Cartwright was lifting the sides of her dress.

"Because we'll soon be out of money," he said. "We need to catch fish and furs."

"There are forests in England. Aren't there deer in them?" Fine specks of drizzle glistened in her hair, on her cheeks and arms.

"Yes." Reaching under her dress, he caressed the tops of her hips.

"Why can't we move to a house in the woods and kill deer for a while?"

"Kill deer in England? I'd be hanged for that." He laughed close to her ear, then took its whole curled shape in his mouth.

While they were speaking she had unbuttoned his breeches. Now he slid his hands under her buttocks and drew her up on his body, her legs closing around him as he leaned his shoulders back, crackling the leafless ivy against the wall.

11

1819. May. Wednesday 19.
Wind S.W. light.

Only Caubvick, among all of us, was sad to leave
England. Attuiock was almost merry again at the prospect of seeing his home. And although I had done
everything in my power to show my country in a favourable light to the Eskimos, to impress them with its
wealth and superiority, I myself was happy to be quit-
ting it. I had a new brig, new servants, and new dogs. I
was in business on my own for the first time, and eager
to resume my life in Labrador.

We boarded ship in the Thames on the 8th of May,

1773, and toasted London as it slipped away. Then we toasted Labrador and sang and danced a variety of jigs and Eskimo dances on deck. I sent for Caubvick to perform a minuet with me, but she stayed below, refusing to celebrate our departure with the rest of us.

She had changed since coming to England. Whereas before she had been a normal sweet-tempered Eskimo woman, different from the rest only in her exceptional neatness and charm, now she was openly at odds with her family in everything. Eskimo clothes were ugly, she said, Eskimo food was unclean. She wanted to stay and live in a tall house and learn to read, and live like my sisters.

Just before sailing, she told me she had repudiated her husband, Tooklavinia, and asked me to allow her to share the cabin which Mrs. Selby and I were to occupy. I denied her request, urging her to accept her position among her people and, instead of shunning them, to attempt to influence their conceptions and manners in order to make them more closely conform to her own. My intention had been, after all, not to transform a few Eskimos into Englishmen, but to create a core of Eskimo allies and interpreters who could mediate on my behalf with their countrymen for the purpose of trade and exploration.

In spite of my refusal, Caubvick renewed her complaints and requests at every opportunity, and Mrs. Selby of course was angered by this affair and blamed me for toying with Caubvick and leading her on. She was right, I suppose. Caubvick was more to me than an interpreter; and I would have gladly allowed her to live with us at the Lodge on our return had Mrs. Selby not objected so strenuously. But I had come to rely on Mrs. Selby in many ways, and however much I enjoyed Caubvick's company, I was not prepared to lose Mrs.

Selby on her account. Perhaps this was cowardice or stupidity.

After numerous delays on the river, on the 11th of May we discharged the pilot and went to sea. Almost immediately, Caubvick began complaining of sickness in her stomach. I assumed it was merely a symptom of her reluctance to go home, or a device to force me to take her into my care.

The following day she was vomiting, and delirious with fever. I looked in her mouth and found red spots, and was terrified. It occurred to me then that my influence, my country's influence on her, and on all of them, was likely to be much greater than I had imagined, and more terrible.

✦

On the 13th of May, they called in at Lymington to load salt, and a surgeon there confirmed that Caubvick's sickness was smallpox. He ordered Cartwright to send for a bolt of red flannel, and when it arrived they removed Caubvick's clothes and wrapped her in flannel from chin to foot while she shivered and struggled with them. Then the surgeon made her drink red-coloured medicines and red wine.

On their second day in port, a rash had begun to appear on her forehead and wrists. Her breath had a strange stench like a mixture of fruit and decaying meat. Part of the time she lay panting, turning her sweat-beaded face from side to side, part of the time she strained against her coverings and cried hysterically. She looked at Cartwright with gleaming recognition and screamed at him to lift the stones off her and pull her out. Cartwright calmed her delirium. He dried her eyes and forehead, untangled her soaking hair and spread it back from her face. With his fingertips he could feel the small pustules forming everywhere on her scalp.

He asked the surgeon to give medicines to all of the Inuit. He knew it couldn't prevent the disease from striking them, but hoped it would help them survive its attack.

Attuiock looked closely at Caubvick's face, touched her forehead and eyes, and quietly wept. It was as though the disease was foreign and beyond his knowledge, as though he had no authority anymore.

When the crew learned what was happening, some deserted. Those who remained did their work silently and kept out of sight as much as they could. For the next month it seemed to Cartwright that the only sailor he saw was the captain. He would glance up and discover the man in the doorway watching him, his heavy eyes full of a kind of ironic knowledge, and Cartwright would give him his orders and send him away. It was as though the ship had begun mysteriously sailing itself.

They left Lymington on the 18th and cruised the coast slowly, lingering at Weymouth where they loaded nets, waiting for the disease to either subside or fully reveal itself. Cartwright was desperate, seeing his voyage delayed, time running out for the summer's projects in Labrador. He was equally desperate at the thought of the Inuit dying, his having to return to face their relatives alone.

Caubvick's rash spread over her whole body and rose in a mass of blisters. Then her fever subsided, and Cartwright assumed the crisis had passed, but that same day, the 22nd of May, Ickcongoque became sick.

The next day, Tooklavinia was vomiting, unable to control his bowels. "I'm sorry for this," Cartwright said. He put his hands on Tooklavinia's to stop him from scratching the pimples that had appeared on his wrists. Anxious, haggard, Tooklavinia muttered and twisted constantly in his bed.

"I'm sorry," Cartwright said, bending over Ickcongoque who was in the next bunk. "Most English people get this. I had it when I was young. You'll all be well again soon."

"Horses," he said to Tooklavinia. "Horses in Labrador. We'll do it together, my friend."

Frantic at losing time, unable to foresee how long the disease might take to run its course, angry at his misfortune, Cartwright decided to embark on the crossing in spite of the illness which had struck his friends. He bought more medicine and more flannel, intending to nurse them at sea, and on the 29th they set out from Weymouth. Within a day, Attuiock and Ickeuna were struck with the fever, and a cloying stench had begun to pervade the ship. The captain appeared, wearing a handkerchief over his nose and mouth. Mrs. Selby did the same, using a silk scarf dampened with gin.

She came up the companionway carrying a bundle of sheets and a bucket, the sweet putrid stink billowing around her from below. The sun was bright, the breeze perfect, but the ship seemed to have gone rotten under their feet. The ropes in the rigging were strained and sick, the sails filling and snapping were inflamed, as if about to break out in boils. "This is out of control," she said. "Little Ickeuna's bleeding from the mouth, and three of the sailors are down with it now. Even if we survive, we'll likely find ourselves at mid-Atlantic without a crew."

Defeated, Cartwright ordered his ship into Plymouth. As they entered the harbour he felt certain that people on shore would be able to smell them coming, would be able tell by the look of the ship that it was swarming with pestilence, and would try to drive them away. He went to the mayor, to Earl Cornwallis, to the admiral in charge of the naval facilities there. None of them would lend or rent him a building or part of a building where the Inuit could rest and receive treatment for their disease. The mayor spoke through a bunched handkerchief. There were no houses for rent in his city. There were laws about plague ships. He would not arouse his citizens' fear and hostility if Cartwright would take his ship elsewhere immediately.

That night on the ship Ickeuna died. There were only a few red spots on her skin, but for a day she had bled continually from the mouth and anus. Convulsions had caused her eyes to roll up so that only their whites showed. Since Attuiock and Ickcongoque were too sick to understand that their daughter had died, and since he thought it best to dispose of her body as soon as possible, Cartwright himself wrapped the weightless child in a sheet and carried her to the cemetery outside Plymouth. He knew there was no point trying to buy her a churchyard grave.

The cemetery-keeper came out of his hut, and Cartwright, dizzy with sleeplessness, gave him some coins and passed him Ickeuna's stiff body. The keeper tucked her under one arm, on top of his hip. The sun-warmed air was thick with the odour of corpses; the old smell of Germany. Beyond was the edge of an open pit. Cartwright gagged as he spoke, stating the cause of death for the register. He explained his predicament. Yes, the keeper said, he knew of a house for rent in a neighbouring village. A family had died there not long ago.

Cartwright found the house, paid the owner twice what it was worth, then moved his ship along the coast near the village and had the Inuit carried ashore into the empty building, its floors littered with chicken dirt,

234

straw, pieces of broken chairs. Most of the rest of his crew packed their belongings and disappeared. Only the captain and a handful of sailors remained on board.

On their first night there Ickcongoque died. She looked as if she'd been roasted over coals. The skin on her face and arms had lifted up in broad black-crusted bubbles that had burst and peeled off when she'd scratched at them.

Cartwright and Mrs. Selby knelt with Attuiock stretched between them on a mattress of straw. While Mrs. Selby helped Attuiock to drink water, Cartwright quietly told him that his wife and daughter had died. Attuiock spoke to neither of them, looked at neither of them. He rocked his head slowly from side to side on the mattress, moaning with open mouth. His eyes, focussed on nothing, brimmed over with tears.

The disease in Caubvick entered a new phase. Her fever increased again and the sores on her body enlarged and began to leak. It looked like hundreds of bluish mushrooms were trying to break out from beneath her skin. The stench in the house was unbearable. On the recommendation of a doctor from Plymouth, Cartwright placed Attuiock and Tooklavinia in separate red flannel tents outside the house. This was to remove them from the noxious miasma that filled the place. Caubvick, he said, was past help and might as well lie where she was.

The doctor also urged Cartwright to surround the patients with as many red objects as possible, to give them red beverages – even, if possible, to approach them in red clothes. That colour, with its natural heat, had always proved effective in drawing out the disease. In Plymouth, for a shilling, Cartwright bought a scarlet foot-soldier's coat, like the kind he used to wear. He wore it as he crouched and entered the red light of the tent where Attuiock lay. The smallpox had changed him beyond recognition, given him the face of a lizard, a red toad. Attuiock looked at Cartwright, then closed his eyes. "So," he said, "you were a soldier all along."

"This is just for the colour," Cartwright said. He persuaded Attuiock to drink wine and water, although the sores in his throat made drinking an agony. "Do you remember that stone you threw? The one that turned into a bird?"

Attuiock's eyes filled for a moment with some retort. But he didn't answer.

At last he said, "You were right. . . . Your people are many more than mine."

Attuiock and Tooklavinia died on the same night in their separate tents, and in the morning Cartwright hired a cart to carry their bodies along with Ickcongoque's to the burying field. He had gone so long without sleep that whenever he took a step or made a turn the earth slid past farther than he expected it to. He watched the cart carrying the three wrapped bodies climb sideways up the road to the left of his vision, then he went into the house. Mrs. Selby was sitting by Caubvick. "I never loved a man more than him," Cartwright said. His face felt wooden, knotted inside. He crawled over a blanket thrown across straw and pieces of chairs, and was asleep.

When he woke up, Caubvick was still alive. Mrs. Selby was kneeling beside her fanning her face to keep off the flies.

"This is the second time I've come back from death," Caubvick said, her head motionless on the pillow, speaking as though to the empty bunk above. "I've used up two of my souls. . . . The next time I won't escape."

It was the most she'd said for over a month. She had lain, through the whole of June, on a cot in the house near Plymouth, too weak to lift an arm, too close to death for Cartwright to risk moving her to the ship. Once she had asked where Tooklavinia and the others were, and when she learned they had died, she said nothing, and did not refer to them again.

In early July, when she appeared to be out of danger, Cartwright had Caubvick lifted on her cot and carried to the ship. With a new crew, hired in Plymouth, they resumed the voyage. He was almost two months late, but had resolved to save her life at any cost. She was his permit to return to Labrador, his only witness, his only protection, the only proof he could offer her people that he had not abandoned or murdered those whom he'd taken away. His honour, his credibility, his friendship with the place, all hinged on bringing Caubvick back safely.

"How did you die the first time?" Cartwright asked. In one hand he held soup in a pewter tankard, in the other a piece of dry bread. Caubvick drew herself up in the ship's bed to be able to handle them. Her face was still pale and thin and dotted with scabs.

She drank, and Cartwright broke off a piece of bread which she slowly chewed.

"The first time was in my husband's family's home. I was very sick, and Attuiock couldn't make my soul come back. They dressed me in my grave clothes while I was still alive because they knew I wouldn't get well and they did not want to touch me when I was dead in case my death passed into them. They bent my knees up to my chest, and my head down, and tied me with sealskin thongs. Then they opened a hole in the roof of the house to take me out.

"I died when I felt the outside air on my face. They buried me on the beach under rocks and went away. But

I came back to life there. Perhaps it was Attuiock's torngak doing his work, bringing my soul back into my body.

"The dogs were rolling the stones off of me, biting my clothes. I freed my arms from the thongs and rolled the stones away and sat up like I am now. I had to shout at the dogs and hit them to stop them from eating me. It was lucky I had so many stones piled beside me to throw at them."

The ship creaked and rolled in the open Atlantic. She drank more soup, and Cartwright handed her more bread.

"I walked back to the village followed by dogs. My grave clothes had been torn by their teeth. I was very cold. When Tooklavinia and his family saw me, they ran inside and blocked the doorway with sticks. I sat outside and called to them that I was not dead, that I brought no evil or harm to them.

"At last Tooklavinia came out and saw that I really was alive. He held the door-skin open for me, but I would not go in that way. They had taken me out through the roof, the way a corpse is removed, and that was the only way I would go back in. I waited while they dug the stones and earth away from the roof."

They bathed Caubvick with chamomile tea. Most of her pox had healed and their scabs come off. Her hair was the final problem. It was bunched in a kerchief on top of her head. Cartwright undid the kerchief and spread out her hair. It looked and smelled like a dead animal. From her forehead and temples back, the mass of scabs and dead skin had come loose in a parchment-like layer that contained the roots of her hair. He lifted it gently. New pink skin had formed underneath. Caubvick flinched and pulled his hands away. Above her ears and at the back of her head, hair was still firmly attached and growing. He would have to separate the dead scalp from that part with scissors. When Caubvick saw what he had in mind she struggled and refused to let him proceed, and he had to tie her hair up in its kerchief again and leave it alone.

Only after several days of coaxing and promises would she let it be done. The disease was still in her hair, Cartwright explained. It couldn't be washed, it had to come off. It would grow back again, he said. Although he knew most of it never would.

Caubvick held her hair in her lap, crying quietly, as Cartwright shaved a mixture of scabs and stubble above her ears. He paused with the ship's roll, wiped the razor, and gently massaged more oil into the patch he was working on.

When he was done, he asked Caubvick to give him her hair so he could throw it into the sea. She sprang to her feet, bald, skeletal, dropping her blanket, the bright pink scars of the smallpox dotting her body. She raved through the cabin with frightening energy, clutching her hair in her hands. It was hers, she said, hers, she would lock it in her trunk. And she did, while Cartwright looked on. Shaking, falling with the ship's gentle roll, she found the key in her clothes under the bed, opened her trunk, and folded her hair inside.

He couldn't have stopped her.

He knew that for some reason, if he had thrown her hair into the sea, she would have thrown herself in after it.

"I know that's what she wants," Mrs. Selby said, closing her book, "but I think she'd be better off with *her* people."

"But the way they live is very hard," Cartwright said. "Don't you care about her? You helped save her life."

"Just because I didn't want her to die doesn't mean I want her to live with me."

"She could stay with Nan or the other servants."

"No. She won't be content until she's in your bed. . . . She'll get used to her old way of life. It suited her before."

"Well Caubvick! You'll soon be the fattest woman in Labrador, just like before! And the most beautiful. . . . Are you ready to give me your hair?"

Every day through most of August, as they tacked westward across the ocean, he approached her with this request, and every day she flared up in rage and grief at the mention of it.

"What good is it in your trunk?"

"*Stop chewing at me!*"

"Caubvick, listen, it's full of disease. It will kill your people."

Within sight of Labrador, he appealed to her one last time to give up her hair. All her old clothes, her old blankets and bedding, had been burned or thrown away.

"What would you like in exchange for it?" he asked. "I'll give you whatever you want."

A bitter look came into her eyes. "Can I stay with you? Will Selby come and promise I can stay with you?"

"No," he said. "I think it's better if you find a new husband."

She turned and spoke facing away from him. "Then there is no trade."

✦

They approached in a fleet of more than twenty old English and French boats, unpainted boats, crowded and cluttered, with untidy sails, unmistakably Inuit boats. All of the three southern communities were there, almost five hundred people. They had heard of Cartwright's return and were coming to greet Attuiock and their relatives.

Cartwright stood on the rocky shore. Only Caubvick was with him, seated behind him on her trunk, a scarf wound on her head like a turban. He looked back at her. She was watching the boats come in, her face blank, a thin, strangely vacated thing. The trunks that had belonged to Ickcongoque, Tooklavinia, and Attuiock were beside her on the rocks waiting to be taken away. It was the last day of August. The weather, the colours, were pure Labrador. Lucid darkness. The sky heavily overcast, the clouds high, a ribbed vault in opal and slate-blue spanning the whole earth, the air beneath clear to the rim of the black, flattened hills, the black, flattened sea.

The water near shore was shallow and rocky. When the Inuit had brought their boats in as near as possible, they anchored them and came ashore in kayaks, one man paddling and two other people lying face down, one fore and one aft, on the skin-covered surface of each craft.

In a minute the crowd gathered, closed around Cartwright and Caubvick, laughing at first, shaking the water out of their clothes, then silent at what they saw. Where were the others? Cartwright shook his head, spread his hands. Dead. The howl that immediately seized them, contorted their faces, twisted them on the ground, startled him, made the hair on his scalp stir. Some took up rocks and beat their faces until they were swollen and streaming with blood. Some stabbed and tore at their clothes. Attuiock's sister broke open her cheek and put out one of her eyes. Cartwright found himself sobbing, pleading with them to stop. He was shocked and astonished by this wild show of grief, this intense objection to loss on the part of people who seemed to possess so little, to whom death was such a common thing.

When they saw Cartwright crying and appealing to them, they assumed he thought their violent emotions were directed against him, that he was afraid of their revenge. They gathered around him, some holding his hands, some patting his back, telling him that they didn't blame him for the deaths, they would do him no harm.

Turning to Caubvick he explained the disease to them. She was still seated on her trunk, her face as devoid of expression as before. No one had touched her, no one had spoken to her. He unwound the scarf from her hairless head, pointed to the pock-marks on her skin. She gave no resistance.

After that, Shuglawina, the head of her family's group, spoke to Caubvick, and she followed him to one of the kayaks. She did not look back.

Two women with bloody faces picked up Caubvick's trunk and took it away.

12

Having persuaded the Board of Trade to restore his title
to the salmon posts that Noble and Pinson had stolen,
Cartwright foresaw for himself a long period of peaceful prosperity harvesting fish and furs in the watershed
of the Charles River.

He was wrong about this. The Board of Trade went
on doing its work, hearing proposals and petitions from
a series of men, furnishing them with titles and permits
for territories and activities that overlapped with his
own. Noble and Pinson came back with new documents
in their hands, and, in the course of the following years,
men representing firms he'd never heard of appeared and
proposed putting nets across streams where his salmon

pounds stood. And a new type of settler arrived. In St. Lewis Inlet he discovered a badly built cabin and in it a run-away sailor with his Indian wife and their barefoot child. Cartwright gave them supplies to help them survive the winter. Then to the south of Cape Charles he found another even more ragged family of settlers. And another group came right to the rebuilt Lodge and asked if the hunting was good nearby.

Even Cartwright's former partner, Coghlan, was back in the area, now as a rival, putting gill-nets off every likely headland and cove. It was time to look for fresh country. In June of 1775, he sailed north from Cape Charles, following a channel of water between the pack ice that covered the sea to the east and the shore ice that was mounded along the coast. The region was unbearably dismal. The islands protruding above the ice were steep-sided, made of bare stone. The mainland was mountainous, the dark headlands were high treeless rock. There were no landing places, no open coves. The few low spots where beaches or meadows might have been were buried in drifts of snow, guarded by ten-foot ramparts of ice. There seemed no point in continuing north.

Then the channel opened out to the west in a large bay, and they followed the open water behind an island, behind a wooded headland, and that night, in a state of amazed elation, Cartwright wrote in his journal it was as if they had shot into the tropics.

The bay was embraced by mountains with gentle forested slopes and valleys at their feet. And the forest was not only spruce and fir. Birch and aspen hung on the hills like puffy green clouds caught in the spires of the dark evergreens. There were grassy meadows along the shore, and beneath their boat the water was clear over a white sand bottom, and the light wobbled and shimmered up in their faces with incredible heat. Fish flowed in schools so thick under their keel that Cartwright filled the dip-net with one stroke.

He knew from his sketchy charts that the bay had been glanced into some years earlier by naval surveyors and named after the Earl of Sandwich, but no Englishmen had yet made it their home. It was arriving in Labrador all over again. Where they anchored was Cartwright Harbour. The first river was Dykes River, for Captain Dykes. The widest river entering the bay was Paradise River. They built a salmon post on Paradise Point and found that two nets gave them more salmon than they could process in a day.

Cartwright chose a site for a house on the shore of Cartwright Harbour and set his men to work cutting trees. On the meadow nearby he laid out a garden, sowed radish and turnip seeds, and amongst the long grass discovered a caribou skull with antlers of seventy-two points. He decided at once to send it to the Earl of Dartmouth, head of the Board of Trade.

A thunderstorm rolled in, a rare occurrence for Labra-dor, with deep vibrating echoes from the surrounding mountains, and warm gouts of rain. The turnips and radishes sprouted immediately, eager green.

At the western end of the bay a river came down a gorge between mountains and plunged over a fourteen-foot ledge before entering the bay. Salmon roiled in the pool at the foot of the falls and scores were continually in the air, leaping, falling back, thrashing their way up the vertical torrent. On the banks and surrounding rocks were old bones and fresh pieces of thousands of salmon, left there by bears. And from every direction, along the coast, down the steep hillsides through trees, well-used bear trails converged on the site. Cartwright examined the claw marks, the tracks. White bears, they were.

White Bear River and White Bear Falls were the words he said.

By late August of that year the house was nearly finished, and he sailed with a couple of men back down to the Lodge. The ice had cleared from the sea and the shore, and the whole coast was less dismal than he remembered it. When he saw the Charles River he couldn't believe he'd been willing to stay there as long as he had. The place was so undistinguished, so random, so lacking a centre compared to Sandwich Bay. He told Mrs. Selby to start packing her things, all their belongings were going into the boat. She was annoyed at first, in the middle of drying two hundred trout and making jam. But she felt the change, the excitement in him, and was amused finally, curious to see what kind of place had made him dismiss, so lightly, his carefully guarded home.

✦

1819. May. Wednesday 19.
Wind S.W. light.

It's strange that God allows us to make mistakes and go on living for years in situations created by our mistakes, situations very different from what would have been had our lives taken another course.

In effect we become strangers to our real selves, which perhaps continue their lives parallel to us, invisibly, in a separate world.

I wonder if I'm actually somewhere else, doing something completely different?

1819. May. Wednesday 19.
Wind S.W. light.

It's well known that people do not contract smallpox
more than once. The disease either kills them or leaves
them scarred but immune to its influence.

The thought of what Caubvick endured on that
island, with everyone dying around her, has become
more terrifying the longer I've dwelt on it.

✦

Daubeny, Cartwright's new headman, was the best he'd
ever had. Cartwright named a lookout-hill after him,
and a brook, and a cove that was excellent for cod.
Daubeny, who was twenty-nine years old in the fall of
1775, was not only hard-working, he was intelligent, he
had a grasp of what he was doing, and constantly
thought of ways of getting more done. He was more like
a partner than a servant. In the evening he would often
sit with Cartwright and Mrs. Selby in their new house –
which Cartwright named Caribou Castle, and Mrs.
Selby shortened to Caribou. Daubeny played a wooden
flute and a copper whistle, and while Cartwright wrote
in his journal or cleaned his guns, Daubeny and Mrs.
Selby would sit in the flickering light, take up their
instruments, nod to each other, and either play an assortment of Daubeny's favourite jigs and reels, in which his
whistle would weave a shrill ecstatic line around her
fiddle, or else join together in the slow improvised melodies that Mrs. Selby loved.

Daubeny was an expert cobbler. He made Cartwright
and Mrs. Selby sealskin boots. He made Mrs. Selby a
pair of warm elegant caribou slippers in exchange for an

embroidered linen shirt that she'd made. He kept an exact count of how many furs and how many fish were taken, and by whom, and recommended that Cartwright dismiss certain men and encourage others by raising their pay. He suggested new places for trap-lines and fish pounds. Mrs. Selby baked blueberry tarts because Daubeny loved them so much. At the end of the day she would sit with him on the bench by the south wall of the house while he smoked his pipe, discussing the season's business, the day's events.

For Cartwright, Sandwich Bay with its white-bottomed coves, its mountains and gathering of rivers, became an obsession, a newly discovered extension of himself he needed to get to know. He would rise before dawn, record the temperature, check on his livestock, his garden, whatever structure his men were working on, then head for a valley he hadn't yet entered, a brook he hadn't followed or tasted, an island he'd not yet felt underfoot. He remembered every detail that he saw. He made maps of the coast and interior, charts of the channels and reefs; he drew plans for farms, for sheds and extensive wharfs, dams, waterwheels, mills for timber, tram-roads for ore. He listed the birds, the fish, the berries, the flowers, the rocks, the trees, shrubs, and plants he found. He measured the rainfall, the wind, the amount of snow. Like a captain preparing his troops for battle, he'd march from where one of his crews was caulking a boat to where another was salting and packing fish. He'd slap shoulders and laugh and promise rum, he'd sing a few encouraging verses of "Britons, Strike Home," he'd lift men off their feet by their shirt-fronts, shake them, cuff them, strike them with sticks. Then his dogs would smell animals and start braying, or he'd notice a new trail or a flock of ducks, and be gone for a night, three nights, a week.

However long he was gone, he would alwa
home with his game-bag full of birds and small
"We don't need these right now," Mrs. Selby wo
"They're more trouble than they're worth. Daube
we should send a boat to Chateau with an order fo
supplies, or we're going to run short this winter. F
we need salt, nets, nails, and another cooper at o1
one's to be had." Daubeny, as she often said, ad
doing fewer things at once and making each of them

Cartwright would dash his orders off, then sit up
the night writing letters to Joseph Banks and Do
Solander. "I have ascertained," he would write, "that
porcupine cannot dart his quills at pleasure into a dist.
object, as most believe, but rather implants them
striking his assailant with a sharp stroke of his tail, o1
sudden jerk of his back."

"I *do* love it here," Mrs. Selby said. She was pickin
leaves and twigs out of a basket of berries. "This is a
splendid place to try our luck for a few years. . . . But
how long do you think we'll have it to ourselves? The
same thing will happen here as happened down at the
Lodge. . . . That's why we've got to make the best of it
while we can. . . . That's why we've got to make it pay."

In Sandwich Bay, Cartwright's business flourished. His
workers tripled in number in four years. He maintained
his old station at the Lodge; and, between 1776 and
1778, he built new stations with storehouses, wharves,
and quarters for workers on Great Island in Sandwich
Bay and on the Paradise River as well as on Cartwright
Harbour near his main residence. In the winters he sent
pairs of furriers to stay at isolated outposts on Hamilton
Inlet to the north, and to the west in the valleys of the
White Bear and the Eagle River. A couple of times, in

going to visit these lonely trappers in the spring, to bring them supplies and tally their furs, he discovered their cabins empty, and knew at once they had not survived the winter. The tracks of people were much easier to read than those of animals. A glance at the meagre wood-pile, the dull axe left behind, the few furs, the soiled, empty flour barrel, the unused powder and shot, the unrepaired traps, showed him clearly what had happened. The last six months of the vanished men's lives sped before his eyes, a pantomime of losing control, starving, wandering off in the snow. Once, he found the men frozen in their beds, eight months of provisions squandered in less than five. He blamed the victims for mismanaging their supplies and their health, for failing to balance food and fuel against weather and game. He knew this juggling act, enjoyed it like sport, and, although he pitied the men who died, he felt in a way that those who came to Labrador and lacked this skill didn't deserve to survive.

Cartwright travelled almost all the time. He would live at Cartwright Harbour with Mrs. Selby for a while, and then with his crew on Great Island, and then on one of his ships, cruising the coast, and then in a tilt or tent beside some river. He claimed to be keeping control of his growing enterprise, but in the summers especially, when people came and went freely by way of Chateau and the coastal fishing boats, he often didn't know half of his workers by name. Daubeny did most of the hiring, and had devised a system of submanagers in each of his company's operations, patterned on the structure of command on a ship. Cartwright approved of the system, and the business ran well, almost by itself. He would show up at a camp of his salmoniers, ask the names of the strangers, give a few orders, and move on. Except for Daubeny and a

couple of others, he had few friends among his people now, but it didn't matter. He was in love with the land, and was getting rich.

✧

1819. May. Wednesday 19.
Wind S.W. light.

Today Kaumalak struck a pigeon that fell into a thicket of thorns. I tethered Thoroton and attempted to force my way through the thicket to where the fallen bird hung. At one point, while ducking and fending off branches, I closed my eyes. When I opened them I was in a bar in the Broad Marsh Shopping centre in Nottingham. The air was scratchy with smoke, and music was thumping out of the jukebox.

A putty-faced young couple was sitting almost directly under where I found myself standing. The man kept saying it was no fucking use, there was nothing to do in the place. The woman agreed, but tried to cheer him up by suggesting a motorcoach trip to Spain. "With what?" the man asked. The woman said the men were coming to take the telly away. "Not if we're not home," the man said. He suggested hanging themselves. The woman didn't hear at first. She was paying attention to the television across the room, and then she said, "Not a bad idea," and started talking about someone having her ovaries removed.

I wanted to hang them both. These creatures who don't know whether they want to live or die. Edmund's bastard offspring, I thought; John's too. Boredom. The last big problem left. In *my* time, anyone who doubted for more than a moment whether he really wanted to live was already done for – had already chosen death. You had to be up early in every kind of weather to hold your life together. And if you had others dependent on you, you had to fight that much harder – none of this lazy self-pity in a world that makes death something hard to attain.

People now are still coasting on the physical stamina bred into their bodies by all their courageous and passionate ancestors. The weak ones, the doubters, quickly died off, and the strong ones passed their love and determination on into the future. Now these bland dumplings coast along on that old fuel wondering why they're travelling forward in time at all. But they're slowing down. Not even Edmund's machines could keep them alive.

Men got the better of me – Captain John Grimes got the better of me – but nothing ever made me give up.

✦

The white bear with her cub came out of the trees on the opposite side of the pool. Cartwright had been following them, scrambling from boulder to boulder up the river's edge, since mid-morning when he and his men, Jack and Kettle, had left their boat at the rapids several miles below. This was the Eagle River, the largest that entered Sandwich Bay at its northwest end. He had never climbed this high up its valley before. The other two men had fallen behind, out of sight. Cartwright's legs were shaking partly from hunger, partly from eagerness.

The female bear turned, thick-legged and rhythmical in the steep shafts of sun, and lightly mounted the bank into the trees again, the fat swaying loosely under the fur on her sides, but the cub lingered on a rock, looking into the water. Cartwright fired his rifle, trying a long shot while the chance was there. The cub jerked, was down on its side, then crawled into the woods. It had had it, though; over the sound of the river Cartwright could hear its cries and knew it would soon die.

At the head of the pool, where the black water came down a chute between points of rock, he now noticed more bears swimming. More white backs lifted up in the sun among boulders, white snouts pointed his way. Another female and her nearly adult cub had dived and were gliding toward him, leaving a strong V-shaped wake. He swung his pouch to the front of his hip, lowered his rifle to load it, worked his arms like a man whose clothes are on fire – cursing himself for having brought so little powder, so few balls, no shot at all to reload the small double-barrelled gun on his back – and broke the ramrod, angling it roughly out of his rifle, the loose piece falling into the river as he aimed; the female rose just at his feet, an amber sheet of water falling from her, and he placed a bullet in her head, her fur and the water immediately swirling with blood. The cub paused by its mother, was not at all baffled by what had happened to her, looked at him on the bank and came forward furiously, roaring, showing its teeth. It was what he loved about these animals, that they didn't retreat when they heard a shot, that they knew who you were, that they gave you a contest. He pulled the double-barrelled gun over his shoulder just as the cub bounded onto the rocks in front of him, and fired one of the barrels into its right eye. It spun around pawing its face where its eye had been, blind with its own blood, then, when it could see, came on again, blasting him with noise from its black mouth, and he fired the second barrel into its other eye. He could hear the creature crashing into trees after it passed him, flailing up the

253

bank. Its voice had been shrill like a horse's, like a loud saw.

More bears were approaching his side of the pool. He looked down the valley. Jack and Kettle were still not in view. He ducked into the woods, loaded his rifle again, shaking the short ramrod up and down in the barrel until it had done its job, then loaded the double-barrel with powder only, thinking to blind them for a minute at least if they had him trapped.

He headed back to the pool knowing he should keep away from it until help arrived. A large female was in the shallows, sniffing the air, swinging her head from side to side. He shot her through the ear, and she floundered for a moment, then loped sideways into the woods where he found her at the end of a short trail of blood. He heard Kettle's voice then, calling over the river's noise from the mouth of the pool, and he ran through branches and bushes to meet him and Jack, told them, breathless, where they would find the bears he'd shot, told them to skin them, quarter them, save the meat. Then he ran back to the head of the pool, pausing to load as he went. He had only five balls left.

On a platform of rock by the top of the falls he sat down, calmed himself, filling himself with the scene. He wished he could draw it, record it, keep it somehow. At the foot of the falls, the round basin was three hundred yards across, its rocky shore exposed under the forested bank because the river was low in the dry summer weather. The salmon were jumping, skittering up the current beside him, within arm's reach. At the cascade's brink, the water curved like the glassy back of a huge whale diving. He counted thirty-two bears in the water at once. They were plunging from rocks, coming up with fish in their mouths, tossing them in the air and diving to catch them again. The motion was constant.

While some sauntered into the woods, others appeared and slipped into the pool.

The abrupt hills encircling the spot were like islands capped in dark spruce. Surrounding them, like a delicate green sea, a forest of larch, birch, and aspen flowed down to the pool's edge. In the silvery clear sky the afternoon sun vibrated bluish, giving glitter instead of colour to all it touched. One of the bears he'd killed was a patch of white in the violet shade near the right-hand shore. The plummeting river's crash sent mist, fragments of rainbow, twisting up in the deafened air. An explosion that didn't end. The rock on which he was seated quivered as though alive.

A movement caught his eye. An old male bear was padding out on the ledge toward him, its head down, sniffing his trail like a dog. He quietly shifted to face it, lifting his gun level, propping his elbows on his knees. This shaggy fellow, he thought, has never doubted the woods. He wanted to let it come as close as possible. If his rifle misfired, he knew, the bear would take him. The gamble filled him with freedom. Over the foresight of his gun he watched the bear breathe deeply, mulling the thought of him over. When it was four yards away, it saw him – it stopped, its eyes filled with decision. It moved forward again, and he squeezed the trigger. The bear rolled, as though still pondering what it had found, down off the ledge into the pool, where it drifted in a slowly widening circle until it touched the shore.

He shot one more bear, another large male that approached through the water, its legs wobbling fish-like and golden under the surface, memorized where his bullet entered and left its skull, watched it fight its death angrily for a long time, and then tore himself away, feeling weak and light-headed, and went to find Kettle and Jack. He had only three balls left, and the sun was low.

His two men had managed to skin only one bear, the youngest cub. The others were too heavy to turn. He joined them now in their efforts. The bears had dispersed as the sun went down, so it was safe to approach the pool, but even the ones that were dead in the water couldn't be moved. They tried levers, tried floating them up on logs. The animals' great bodies were stubborn and expressionless, as though held to the place by chains.

They couldn't stay longer, the spaces between trees and rocks were filling with darkness, becoming unjudgeable. They clambered back down the boulder stairway toward the boat, pausing often to listen, taking turns carrying the wet skin on their backs. Cartwright was now shaking more than ever, needing to use his hands to get from one rock to the next. It was from too much sun, he told himself, from not having eaten for nearly a day.

✦

"Here's one of the things Phippard found there," Daubeny said. He patted his waistcoat pockets, took out a piece of candle, a tinder-box, a pipe, a ball of fishing line, a tobacco pouch, a ship's biscuit, a clasp knife. But these small supplies from his trip were not what he was looking for. He laid them one by one on the table and rummaged his pockets again. He'd been gone over a week, visiting a crew of their furriers at a new post in Hamilton Inlet. "I know it's here," he said, "not in my pack." He glanced at his sailcloth satchel leaning beside the door. He had come straight in with the news as soon as he got back. "Here." He drew his left hand out, opening it. A large silver coin lay on his palm, no, not a coin, a medal.

The object pulled Cartwright's understanding into a hard factual node about the size of the thing itself.

It had come back on one of the inevitable cogs of causality. There was no final forgetting. Things set in motion by will or whim went on pursuing their course out of sight. Their turning paths always eventually crossed with yours. Sometimes with the force of an avalanche.

"I gave him a fox skin for it," Daubeny said. "Do you think it's worth anything?"

Cartwright had taken the deeply stamped disk in his fingers. DIEU ET MON DROIT. The heroic profiles and ornaments.

"Phippard had with him a small chest of tools that he found there too. But I couldn't persuade him to part with it."

"And where was the place?" Cartwright asked.

"Near the mouth of Hamilton Inlet, he said. An island, not very large, he said. He found whalebone too, and some carvings, but all of the furs were spoiled."

"And their belongings were all still there?"

"That's what he said. Old kayaks, cooking pots. Old tents fallen down. He said it had been that way at least for the winter, maybe more than a year."

"And their bodies?"

"Mostly just bones he said, scattered around. And their clothes. He said he counted more than sixty skulls."

There was no question. So many unburied. No one had left the island alive. They had camped there for the seals, and the disease had taken them like the fulfilment of one of their terrible myths. It had lain coiled in her trunk like a vicious animal. Did she take it out and put it on like a wig? Did she dance with it on? Wave it over their heads? He pictured it bobbing through the air like a

257

torch trailing black fire and smoke. He should have thrown it into the sea, trunk and all. And her with it. And as for himself . . .

"It was Attuiock's," Cartwright said, closing his hand on the medal and putting it into his pocket. "My brother gave it to him."

13

On the 25th of August, 1778, the temperature soared
out of control. Air thick with the smell of parched rock
and lichen poured out of the hills southwest of
Cartwright Harbour. The sun's bite grew sharper by the
hour. Watching for his fishing boats to return, Cartwright winced and shielded his face, glancing up at the
white glare. The fish piled in salt on the end of the wharf
had begun to melt. The shallops came in empty, the men
looking for water and shade. The nets held nothing,
they said, the rivers were without fish. And then the
clouds, purple and soapstone green, mounted up over
the hills in a standing wave that seemed twenty miles
high, making the whole land's surface flat and small, and

the smothered flashes began, the thunder over Separation Point, the air going yellow. Cartwright ordered his men to row quickly out and move his two large ships, the *Reconciliation* and the *Countess of Effingham*, farther off shore where they'd be safe. Then the harbour darkened from brown to black, and a wind, cold, smelling of mud and sap, struck them just ahead of the rain. The first volley, mixed with bullets of ice, stopped at a stroke, then came again with a crash, a load of water hitting them like a falling lake.

The next day was cold, more like November. Chalky pellets of snow swirled down in gusts. The sun would briefly appear, melting them. All his vessels were safe.

Kettle said a strange boat had been seen off Horse Chops Island trying to come in. Cartwright's salmon crews and baitskiffs had gone out without their complete orders. Where were Mrs. Selby and Daubeny? Exasperated by the confusion, he climbed to the top of the hill with his telescope. A ship was tacking and turning behind Round Island. The sea was passable in the strait. Why didn't she enter the bay? He made a fire to signal her in, but saw no reply, no change in her movements.

When he returned, Mrs. Selby and Daubeny were back at the house with some of his people and supper in progress. No one knew what was happening exactly. The wind seemed to have blown through everyone, snatching their understanding away.

On the 27th of August, at one in the morning, a banging on the door woke him up. Whatever had been coming had arrived.

Men shouldered their way into the room with peculiar energy, with guns in their hands that were pointed at him. Two of the men he recognized: one was fox-eyed John Downing, who was supposed to be catching salmon for him down on the Charles River, the other a beaver-toothed furrier of Noble and Pinson's.

"We belong to the *Minerva*, privateer of Boston," one of the group said. He asked for Cartwright's keys.

All of his ships, his goods and stores, Cartwright heard, were now the property of John Grimes, captain of the *Minerva*.

Cartwright spat invective and ordered them out of his house. But then, seeing their smiles, he knew his commands were useless, and fell silent. He saw that the privateers must have had help from his own men in Cartwright Harbour. The disappearances, the confusion of the past days were now explained. There was no point making himself look foolish, or getting shot. He would wait to see what kind of resistance he and those still loyal to him could organize.

Mrs. Selby, holding a candle, her long hair loose, went close to the one who had spoken, an American-voiced man with wide-set eyes. "We're not representatives of the British Crown," she said. "We're free individuals the same as you. Do you steal from your fellow colonists as well as from us?"

Cartwright pulled her back by her nightgown's sleeve, shaking his head to silence her.

Daubeny came in under guard. Then more of his servants appeared, their faces different – frightened, but eager, with something released in them. They were all invited to join with the privateers, the American said, to sail to Boston, beyond British law, and to have an equal share in the goods captured here and at every post they chose to visit along the coast. Some of them, bright-eyed, grinned at Cartwright and immediately went to the other side. Some glanced at him sheepishly but stood with the privateers all the same. Daubeny approached Mrs. Selby, opened his mouth to speak, but the privateers pulled him back and said he would have to stay on their ship as a hostage, while they loaded their cargo.

Cartwright did what he could with words. He shouted the privateers down and appealed to his men by name, those whose names he was certain of. He urged them not to assist the privateers in any way. The ones who showed signs of turning against him, he threatened with English law, and his personal curses. He warned them not to be fooled by the privateers. "They'll cut your throats as soon as you're out at sea. Why would they want to share their plunder with you?" But the privateers laughed, and most of his men, seeming unconvinced by his words, slipped out of the room without showing any support for him.

When daylight had fully come, a couple of privateers rowed Cartwright out to the *Minerva*. Captain Grimes, who dressed and spoke like a gentleman, offered him wine in the state-room of his ship. Grimes's light brown hair was drawn smoothly back from his narrow sloping forehead, his shirt was perfectly white. He regretted the rough intrusion, he said, pursing his large lips between sentences, but owing to the unfortunate war, the people of Boston were in need of just such supplies as Cartwright happened to have an abundance of. He had no desire to ruin him, only to take a share of his assets, if he'd co-operate. He could think of it as a tax of the colony on the motherland for a change. He gazed at Cartwright placidly over his glass, his lips in a loose O. "For security, we have Mr. Daubeny with us," he added. "And our cannon are trained on your house. With your co-operation, it won't be necessary to knock it flat."

Later that morning Cartwright attempted to send messengers to his other posts to have his goods there concealed from the privateers, but informers revealed his scheme, and then, using his own skiffs, they openly guided the privateers to his buildings on Great Island and Paradise River, and returned with barrels of salmon, bales of furs, which they lined up on the wharf in front of his house. The privateers and their new recruits went through his storehouse and kitchen, taking his flour, his salt beef, butter, rum, bags of dry peas, gunpowder, nails, bolts of fabric, washtubs, feather pillows, nets, sails, grindstones, buttons, bottles of ink, even the sundial from the garden behind his house.

For most of the day Cartwright wandered among the traitors, as they carried his things away, and berated them or urged them to be decent and fair, but then he drew back. It was beneath him to grovel. And more than anything he wanted the ordeal finished, the enemies and traitors out of his sight. Let them take his things if he couldn't stop them. He would survive, he and whoever was with him. They had done it before. The weather now was lovely. What he really wanted was to take his rifle and go tramping in the hills. To fill his senses only with hills and sky.

By noon on the second day of the raid, Cartwright's own two ships had been loaded with goods; and the mutineers sailed them away. His man, Kettle, sailed the *Reconciliation*. A mate from the *Minerva* took charge of the *Countess of Effingham*.

For another day the privateers continued to load the *Minerva* and win defectors to their side. One privateer attempted to embrace Mrs. Selby, inviting her to Boston as his companion, but the blow she gave him, and her verbal reply, made him retreat looking horrified. After that, apart from taunts and threats, she was left alone.

By the following morning the wharf and beach were clear of all but a few empty barrels. Cartwright stood on the shore, together with Mrs. Selby and his remaining people, and watched as a couple of privateers brought Daubeny back to shore in a small boat. The *Minerva* was about to depart. A few more of Cartwright's people, terrified of the winter without supplies, seized the last chance to join the deserters and leapt in the privateers' boat as Daubeny got out. Cartwright waited until they were gone and then took a punt and rowed himself out below the *Minerva*'s stern, and called up for Grimes, who had kept out of sight on his ship since speaking with Cartwright the first morning. Grimes appeared at the rail along with his first mate.

"Your tax has been higher than I expected," Cartwright said. "I ask you to spare me at least a few nails to help us survive the winter."

Grimes nodded and disappeared again, but the mate leaned over the rail, wrinkling his nose and showing his teeth. "You shit-lord. Fine British gentleman on his estate, his little kingdom with all his servants and ceremonies. They all hated you. See how loyal they were? If I was commander of this ship I wouldn't leave you a rag to cover your arse, by God. I'd carry off all I could, and what I couldn't, I'd burn. Then you and those stupid enough to stay with you could either eat the rocks on your fine estate or starve and be damned."

Grimes returned on deck with two of Cartwright's men, who lowered a keg of nails to him. Then the *Minerva* weighed anchor and sailed away. Cartwright rowed ashore to where Mrs. Selby and Daubeny, haggard and speechless, were waiting for him. He walked past them without saying a word, dug his rifle out from under the heap of birch bark where he'd hidden it, and went shooting curlews for the rest of the day.

At night, writing in his journal, he calculated his losses at £14,000. There was no way now he could pay back his debts. From his payroll, he copied the names of the thirty-seven who'd joined the privateers. Half of his people had gone. Each of their faces was clear in his mind. "May the devil go with them," he wrote at the end, and drew a double-lined box around the column of names.

14

By December, Mrs. Selby's dresses didn't fit her any-more. She ripped some of them up the sides and spliced in pieces of sheeting. She made a robe from a couple of blankets and wore that indoors during the day. She stopped denying that she was pregnant.

Week by week as they sat by the fire, Cartwright watched her belly grow, an odd mixture of feelings tum-bling inside him. Here they were in the naked rib-bones of winter, his business in ruins, and everyone wasting away, everything shrinking except Mrs. Selby's belly, which was waxing with a purpose of its own. He watched her reading, her cheeks flushed in the candle-light, her lips slightly apart. She was business, fortune, family, estate, all in herself, all in her swelling middle. Her self-containment annoyed him; what she was harbouring filled him with dread. It was another defeat for him, another loss added to all his losses, his debts, his entrapments and obligations, the ways his future would now be hedged and prescribed for him. True, no healthy gentleman had ever allowed responsibility for a child to hamper him, but it was different here, confined in a small cube of warmth in Labrador. There was no way of sending the child out of sight, nor the mother.

And, in truth, he did not want to. She was his wife after all. He had begun to think of her as such, after what they'd been through. There was not much difference between them anymore. An acceptance, a relenting flowed through him, even a pride. Life was having its way with him in spite of himself. They would *have* a child, would live somehow, somewhere, who could say how.

Mrs. Selby rarely went out, rarely spoke to anyone.

It was all right, Cartwright tried to tell her, in spite of what he'd said before about not wanting children. But she shook her head and looked at him with a kind of wider knowledge and said it was all wrong, it was too late.

She never played the violin anymore when she was by herself. And when Daubeny came with his flute, it seemed the two played sadly together, always the same slow melodies with no inventions or games.

This winter was worse than their first on the Charles River had been. Cartwright's hunting was mostly for food, rarely for furs. Whole portions of daylight he spent hunched on the wind-swept ice, remembering Attuiock's lessons, trying to pull seals up to their breathing holes with his prayers, with the blankness of his mind.

267

There was more sickness, more darkness, more cold, more grumbling about food than ever before.

Cartwright listened to himself lecturing his people, threatening them, making new rules, new penalties, driving them out before dawn to visit their traps. The phrases, the shrill tones he heard himself using, belonged to the kind of lieutenant he'd always despised.

1819. May. Wednesday 19.
Wind S.W. light.

Who, if not God, is to blame for making monsters like me?

But I can't think why He would.

Even Kaumalak tires of killing before I do. And I've made her specialize in the business of slaughter, taken away every other pursuit from her. In the wild she would kill only enough to feed herself and her young.

Either I've broken God's restraints, or my appetites and my ingenuity are a kind of stupidity, the infancy of intelligence, perhaps.

Adam and Eve ate their fruit and divided themselves from the animals only a short time ago. Mentally, I have barely learned to toddle and talk. I am still at the stage of trying to break whatever I pick up, or of putting it in my mouth.

✧

At dawn on the 21st of April, 1779, Mrs. Selby went into labour, and at ten o'clock Cartwright delivered her of a daughter. As soon as he had caught the infant and lifted it up, he realized it was not his. It was partly Mrs. Selby's behaviour that told him this. She didn't deliver the child to *him*. She fought against her labour, she endured it alone. His hovering above her seemed to exasperate and worry her. The instant the child was wiped and the cord cut, she took it on her breast and covered it with a sheet. But Cartwright had seen enough newborn humans and animals to be able to predict the form their small wrinkled features would take. In two years the child would look like Daubeny. She had his temples and forehead, his coarse dark hair.

Cartwright walked to the top of Lookout Hill. On the face of the frozen sea, a single dark vein of water meandered southeast as far as he could see, parting the ice. Toward the horizon it was a sparkling thread of light.

Later, he spoke to Nan. "Are they lovers? What have you seen?" Nan was behind the pantry chopping frozen salmon out of a block of ice. She paused, her eyes round with surprise and misgivings.

"That's not for me to say, sir . . . I . . . they do walk out together. We all thought you knew and didn't mind."

Cartwright put on the old red coat he'd bought in Plymouth. He dug out a wig, gave it a dusting of flour, and set it on top of his hair, which he'd grown long for the winter and wore gathered behind his neck with a thong. He pulled on his polished boots, strapped on a sword, and ordered all of his people to assemble in the dining room of his house. He had arranged the room like a meeting hall, with the table in front of the fireplace, his large chair behind the table, its back to the fire, and the rest of the room filled with chairs, stools, and make-shift benches.

Mrs. Selby came in from the bedroom with her child bundled up in her arms. She had named her Maria. The child was fretful and sickly, and Mrs. Selby, too, had been unwell since giving birth. From behind the table, Cartwright pointed her to a chair by the wall to his right. When Daubeny entered, Cartwright directed him to the chair beside her. Nan and the other domestic servants he directed to a bench by the wall to his left between the two windows. The furriers and sawyers took their own places in the centre of the room.

When everyone was seated and quiet, he strode out from behind the table and paced the room.

"It is necessary to conduct a court of law here, at which you are all present, in order that justice be served and that you all see and agree that justice is served, according to the law.

"It would appear that disloyalty, dishonour, and infidelity have been committed here. But this needs to be proved, or admitted, and, if it is, appropriate measures need to be taken according to the process of law.

"First of all we need witnesses."

He passed in front of the windows, the panes of shaved and oiled caribou skin admitting a pale buttery glow. He turned and passed before them again, looking at his domestic servants' sealskin boots as he spoke, then at their upturned faces, pale and translucent as wax, at their hands folded in their laps.

"We need witnesses because, as we all know, confined in a place like this in the winter, on short rations, enduring the hardships we have all had to endure since our misfortune last autumn, a man's mind is apt to conceive false notions, dangerous to himself and others. Notions and suspicions are dangerous. We need to seize on the truth."

He spun, facing his household servants on the bench. "Nan! To your knowledge have Mr. Daubeny and Mrs. Selby been having secret, illicit commerce?"

"I can't say for certain. . . . But they have walked out

together." She looked across at Mrs. Selby and Daubeny and began to cry.

Others spoke of seeing them arm in arm on Lookout Hill, of Daubeny staying late at the house on the nights Mr. Cartwright was away – whether he stayed all night or not no one could say.

"Is it your opinion, Nan, that everyone knew they were lovers?"

Nan nodded.

Cartwright turned and strode to the table, his sword swinging, striking the end of a bench as he passed. He took up a sheet of paper. "Mr. Daubeny, I have a deposition to read to you." He glanced at Daubeny, who was sitting upright, expectant, without fear in his face.

"Whereas Mr. George Cartwright of Cartwright, Labrador, has employed Mr. Richard Daubeny as his headman for a period of more than three years and eight months – I've dated it at the bottom – and whereas Mr. Cartwright paid Mr. Daubeny generously and bestowed on him special benefits – such as the right to do some personal trade in furs – and whereas he admitted Mr. Daubeny to his house as a friend and entrusted him with obligations of a personal nature, Mr. Daubeny has betrayed Mr. Cartwright's trust, both as a friend and employer, by secretly having unchaste relations with Mr. Cartwright's *de facto* wife."

"I never was your wife *de facto*, *de jure*, or in any form," Mrs. Selby broke in. "I am your housekeeper."

Cartwright ignored her. "Do you agree with the substance of what I've read?"

"I do," Daubeny said. Cartwright handed him the paper, then brought him pen and ink to sign his name.

He read a similar deposition to Mrs. Selby, full of whereases and mentions of loyalty, bonds of natural intimacy, infidelity, and broken trust. He asked if she agreed with the charges, and she answered, "I do." He noticed she had to disengage her hand from Daubeny's to accept the paper when he held it out to her.

She signed it, and then she and Daubeny leaned toward one another and kissed.

Cartwright looked at his people. They were staring at him, a strange look of satisfaction, almost amusement in their eyes, as though he had been conducting a wedding instead of a trial.

"On the basis of what has been stated and confirmed, this is what I pronounce: As for Mr. Daubeny, at the end of this season he shall be paid according to our agreement and afterwards shall never be in my employment again. As for Mrs. Selby, I divorce her and disown her child. Let its natural father provide for it. The lady shall house with the servants henceforth."

She was looking at him with thorough, merciless understanding, her eyes seeming to see right back to his boyhood.

She and Daubeny still held hands.

In the servants' communal kitchen the salmoniers shared their meals with Mrs. Selby, thick fish soups with dough fried in fat. Daubeny made her salads of fresh greens, and teas from tansy and kelp, and her health slowly improved, but her daughter's didn't. Late in the summer the child died. The cooper made her a coffin of planed boards, and Mrs. Selby chose to have her buried on Lookout Hill, coincidentally on the very spot where Cartwright had stood when he'd seen the first vein of open water in the spring. The soil was shallow there, and it was necessary to build a cairn of stones over the grave.

As master, Cartwright insisted on reading prayers.

With no particular expression in his face he looked across the mound of stones at Mrs. Selby and Daubeny, who were standing side by side. And with no easily described expression they looked back at him.

On the way to his house, where he stayed alone now, he would pass the servants' building. At night its oilskin windows glowed like old coach lamps. Sometimes there would be music, a whistle and violin. Sometimes dancing, blurred shadows and silhouettes. The whistle and violin, he noticed, were slightly more light-hearted again. They were trying tunes he hadn't heard before.

✦

With his reduced crew, Cartwright worked furiously through the summer of 1779, trying to accumulate as much cargo as he could in the short time left to him. He saw that he had no choice but to return to England in the fall to attempt to renew his loans and either find a financial partner or borrow more money to revive his business and recover the losses caused by the privateers. The harvest of furs and fish gathered over the winter and summer would barely cover the cost of the ship and crew to take it across the Atlantic. And he had his workers to pay. Those who were staying in Newfoundland agreed to be paid in equipment and goods – boats, traps, furs. Those who wanted cash would have to wait for their wages until they reached home. Mrs. Selby said she would take her earnings in cash. Because she was still frail, she thought it best to return with Cartwright to England, where she had family and savings, in order to rest and fully recover her health.

When the season ended, Daubeny took an open skiff and a share of the year's furs, and embarked for Newfoundland with a couple of other men. As far as Cartwright could gather, Daubeny's intention was to sell his goods and make his way to the American colonies where he hoped to find work and prepare a new home for Mrs. Selby and himself. Or perhaps Daubeny would return to England on another ship and meet Mrs. Selby there.

In late October, when he sailed for England, Cartwright's Labrador business came to a halt. He had dismissed all of his people but the few who would accompany him on the ship. He nailed planks across the doors and windows of his buildings, even though they were empty. He was determined to return with new crews, new supplies, the following spring.

15

This crossing to England was the slowest and most dangerous of any Cartwright had made. He had delayed his departure longer than usual in order to gather as much cargo as he could. When he finally sailed, the small ship, hired in Fogo, was over-loaded, and the season of freezing storms had begun. Towering waves rolled over their low deck, and, while they were still within Newfoundland waters, spray froze in the rigging, threatening to capsize them. The buffeting and constant submersion weakened their ship's joints; its hull let in the sea through countless cracks, and required continuous pumping. Mrs. Selby lay alone in her damp bunk, reading when it was calm and light enough, rarely speaking with anyone. Because England was at war with the American colonies and France, the seas were doubly unsafe; so in St. John's harbour they waited to join a convoy of merchant vessels under British naval protection. When the convoy sailed, Cartwright's ship couldn't keep up with it and made the crossing alone after all, floundering helplessly in gales and darkness. Once more they were nearly wrecked on the Irish coast, then found shelter in the harbour at Kinsale, where Cartwright left his ship to be repaired. He and Mrs. Selby went on ahead to England as passengers on a British privateer, but off the coast of Wales storms again threatened their lives. Then, within sight of Bristol, a press-gang tried to board the privateer, and the privateer's crew and passengers – Cartwright included – had to fire guns at the press-gang to drive them away.

When he finally reached England, in mid-December, 1779, the first thing Cartwright did was take Mrs. Selby by coach to the home of her brother in Bedford and deposit her there with her earnings and luggage, with his polite regards to her brother. Then he returned to London to meet with his creditors. They'd given him chances enough, those grave men said. They ignored his new proposals and schemes, his stories of secret rivers, untapped wealth. They couldn't extend or renew his loans. He sold what was left of his Labrador holdings, paid what he could, and declared himself penniless.

Cartwright made his way to his father's in Marnham in late December. There he prowled through the house like a ghost, fingering the coin-like medal he kept in his waistcoat pocket. He stood with moonlight on his legs in the drawing room where he'd once watched Caubvick dance; paced the pantry and the hallway where they'd hastily, recklessly pushed their bodies together, the terrace where he'd lifted her up in the rain.

Of his sisters, only Catherine was still at home, keeping her scrapbook, playing the clavichord in the afternoon. His father trembled and talked to himself in his greenhouse. His mother wrote letters, embroidered, made sure her servant, Mary, had work to do. Cartwright avoided them all, sitting alone in rooms, walking the dull country lanes, the land that was all made.

Twice he'd been wrong about what he was capable of, and come home again. He felt it was too late now to start anything new.

In the spring his father mentioned that the Nottinghamshire militia, which he had helped to create, was in need of a barracks master. The work would be decent and comfortable. Why not apply? Without much enthusiasm, Cartwright followed his father's advice and went to be interviewed by the elderly gentleman in charge of local defence. Discussing what his duties as barracks master would be – his role in various parades and festivals – Cartwright felt foolish and out-of-place, like a tamed bear in a village, but when the position was offered to him he accepted it.

From that point on, his life became retrospective. But he had volunteers to give orders to and admirers and a fine blue coat with epaulets. He had a room of his own in the barracks, which he decorated with pelts and antlers, remnants of Labrador. His Hanoverian rifle, oiled and polished, hung on the wall. His journal lay under his bed in a trunk.

Every day there was billiards or hawking, and a few young men always begged him for stories. He demonstrated how to kill a bear with a knife – the same as a boar, only the bear fought harder and its blood would spurt up inside one's sleeve as far as the elbow. Some of the stories he told about India and Germany were not true. All of the stories he told about Labrador were, though he left things out. He never told about how he lashed men until they fainted. He never talked about Williams the sawyer, or Mrs. Selby's child, or Caubvick's hair. He boasted about how much he could eat, and at banquets and dinner parties would demonstrate, holding the knife and fork poised and announcing: "With me a leg of mutton is but an affair of two slices, the first slice taking one side away, and the other clearing the bone." His friends would chant this well-known boast in unison with him, then clap and cheer as he performed the stunt and devoured the slabs of meat, gripping them whole in his teeth and sawing off morsels Inuit-style.

"Old Labrador," they called him. He was famous, around Nottingham.

In the first few years after he joined the militia, Cartwright would ride out to Marnham every couple of weeks to call on his parents. He helped Catherine attend to their father during his final illness, and was at his mother's bedside when she died shortly after. Then, briefly, the Marnham estate became Cartwright's; and he sold it to John, and John rented it out, and Catherine moved down to London. Thereafter Cartwright never rode out to his old family home. It was Edmund, with his family and farm in Kent, whom Cartwright began to visit. Edmund's children were now having children of their own, all of them wild for their great-uncle's stories of Labrador. And Edmund's passionate campaign to improve life through science and labour-saving machines was appealing, and inspired Cartwright to tinker with simple inventions of his own. Every few months he would journey to Kent to dine at his brother's large, lively table, join the games of the children racing from room to room, and then walk through the orchards or barns discussing with Edmund their various projects: Edmund's fertilizers or alcohol engines, Cartwright's bear-traps and folding stoves – equipment designed for a country he no longer lived in.

More than anything, Cartwright had continued to think about Labrador, about his disloyal people, about John Grimes, deft plunderer of a lifetime's work, with the towering freight of Cartwright's curses on his head. But what tormented him more than his injuries, more than his hunger for revenge, was all the work he had left unfinished, all that had gone to waste. He had so much practical knowledge of the place, its landscape, its seasons, the habits of its game, he had so many new ideas for making a business work. If only he could get money and backers to do it again. But then he began to think he was probably too old anyway to be sleeping in snowbanks. He was past forty, and sciatica troubled him. The winters in Labrador had taken their toll.

So that his hard-won knowledge wouldn't be lost completely, he started to put it into a manuscript. "The Labrador Companion" was what he called it, and thought of it as advice to an ideal younger version of himself. He made headings with notes underneath that he enlarged as ideas occurred to him. "To fix a net around a beaverhouse by men standing on shore." "To cure the bite of mosquitoes." "Cheap stoves for servants and storehouses." "A sailing sled." "To preserve bladders that they may be ready when wanted": *Blow them up when green, to prove their goodness, then press all the wind out, put them into a keg or wide-mouthed jar and fill it up with a strong solution of salt in water.*

But the task began to seem hopeless. The times were changing so fast that most of his methods would be antiquated by the time he'd gathered them all and published his book. And there was so much advice, it was hard to divide it piecemeal and put it in words. And his recollection of certain procedures and problems was fading.

He dug out his journal to get back a sense of his real experience, the real place. At first he was frustrated by what he read. Why hadn't he written more often about the important things? Why hadn't he written *more*? It gave such a false, shallow impression of what he'd done.

But then, the more he read of it, the more pleasure it gave him – and the more adequate it seemed. Though it conveyed only a slim version of the truth, only a faint portrait of himself, it had grown naturally, day by day, parallel to his life, and presented at last a rough approximation, a kind of a memorial for what he had done. The journal was his book. It was already there.

He began to correct the grammar and spelling with the thought of making it fit to print. But then, with his journal open before him and his pen in hand, a new idea occurred to him. He turned to the last entry, which was dated 1779, December 17. Why not continue his journal, making entries for subsequent years in Labrador as he imagined they would have been?

On a fresh page he wrote *1780, February 23* – that had been his fortieth birthday – and for that date he briefly described how he'd succeeded in negotiating a generous bank loan, and hired a new brig and crew. In the pages that followed, he put up new buildings in Cartwright Harbour, enjoyed victory over commercial rivals, prospected for gold near Sandwich Bay with the help of a Derbyshire miner, suffered various accidents and misfortunes, surrounded himself with Indian mistresses, and continually trekked the hills with his rifle. He made no substantial changes to what he had actually written in Labrador. He was scrupulous about that. And he was careful to hold his imagination in check and to make his new entries conform in style with the original ones. He did not allow himself a written revenge upon Grimes (although he *did* recover his ship, the *Countess of Effingham*). Nor did he bring Caubvick back. It was not fantasy he wanted, but the future as it could have been.

When, after several years of writing, his journal entries had reached 1786, he felt his imaginary self was due to retire from Labrador; so he wrote of selling his debt-burdened business and returning to England in December of that year, not rich, but satisfied, and of taking up the occupation he had in reality – barracks master in Nottingham. He was content with the story he'd made for himself – for the time being at least.

Although he made no new entries after that, he went on polishing the journal for several more years, making it one seamless whole. Then in 1792 he published the work himself – "sins and all," as he often boasted – under the title *A Journal of Transactions and Events, During a Residence of Nearly Sixteen Years on the Coast of Labrador*. It ran to three volumes and cost him £38 and a penny to print 350 copies. As he had arranged in advance to sell most of the copies by subscription, at two guineas each, to old patrons, friends, and curious booksellers, he made more money from his journal than he had made from his business in Labrador, which had left him with nothing but debts. But it was the reputation it earned him, more than the money, that Cartwright was proud of. Let them count how many birds, how many foxes he'd bagged in one year at Cape Charles – he'd recorded the numbers every day, and had never exceeded them in his later fabrications. Not even the finest sporting gentlemen in all England could come close to him.

Ladies would shudder at the thought of the slaughter, and he would beam at them and offer his recipe for bear stew.

When his family and close acquaintances questioned him about the dates in his journal, he showed his crooked grin and said they would find as much truth in his book, and as much instruction and entertainment, as in anything else they were likely to read.

✦

1819. May. Wednesday 19.
Wind S.W. light.

When I set Mrs. Selby down at her brother's on my final return to England, she left the door of the carriage open and walked straight to the house without saying a word. I didn't expect her to say goodbye, we had hardly spoken during the whole crossing, and not at all on the way up from Bristol. My feelings at the time were mainly relief at being rid of her, and satisfaction at having honoured my word: I had paid her salary and brought her home without allowing the slightest return to friendship or intimacy. Still it was odd. Her back moving quickly away was the last I saw of her.

Her brother came out, and I explained that Mrs. Selby and I had agreed to end our association. I said my solicitor would send her an annual allowance of £15. It was money I could ill afford to be promising, but it felt like a final victory for me. The brother shook my hand and thanked me, glancing fretfully at her baggage on the walk.

A year later a letter came by way of my solicitor saying that as Mrs. Selby had left the country and made new arrangements, the allowance would not be expected in future.

Through men in the navy and in the Newfoundland trade with whom I kept in touch I heard that Daubeny had gone down to the American States and had sent for Mrs. Selby to join him. I heard they were living in Pennsylvania, that they owned a farm.

Eventually I learned – through the brother of my former servant, Bettres – that they had two children, a prosperous farm-implement business, and that Mrs. Selby was running a school.

1819. May. Wednesday 19.
Wind S.W. light.

During my thirty-seven years as barracks master I became almost florid, almost theatrical, with my uniform and my fine voice. I had made my life into a cycle of dramatic legends, and I was their sole custodian and performer.

Yet there was still a side to me I never shared with anyone. Sometimes in the morning or at night when I looked in the mirror, I would see myself inside my costume, my eyes inside my mask of a face, and I would admit to myself that my life had been all selfishness and vanity. I was a piece of human regalia, a mascot, a ceremonial mace. At times I felt I should give what little I had away, take a vow of silence and pass the remainder of my life in some work of charity. Serving orphans is what came to mind.

I would imagine going to the charity hospital in Manchester, dressed in my plainest clothes, offering to work in the kitchen serving soup. They would give me a cot in a loft with the other servants, who would be mostly paupers working there for their keep.

I would imagine what followed. When the soup was not to their liking, the young urchins would spill it down my legs. I'd want to shake them until their rotten teeth rattled in their heads, but I would tell myself a truly unselfish man would ignore their insults and serve them without complaint.

Meek forbearance, however, would only make things worse. Everyone, even the other servants, would laugh and call me "the humble gentleman." They'd recognize that what I was doing sprang not from material need, or a desire to proselytize, or even from real compassion, but from an impulse to atone for something and satisfy a complex private vanity.

I would imagine myself, after a week, going back to the barracks and pretending I'd been in London on a spree.

And so I did nothing.

I continued to live in my Labrador journal. I returned there every night before sleep like a pigeon flying back to its cote.

1819. May. Wednesday 19.
Wind S.W. light.

I think now that I should have learned to worship instead of slaughter.

The things we most love to kill we ought to worship most passionately.

The pleasure, I think, must be as great and as ancient. And the consequences less limited.

Less predictable.

16

1819. May. Wednesday 19.
Wind S.W. light.

Time is of such variable density. A decade may hold
sufficient experience to fill up a life; even several lives.
Thirty-seven years might not contain enough to satisfy
a vigorous person for one month.

When I think of Labrador, my remembrance shoots
into those ten years like a bird diving into a forest. It
swoops on and on through turnings and changes, seasons and episodes. People appear, speak, act; their stories
unfold. Labrador is limitless and never the same.

When I call to mind events from my years as barracks

master they all seem to have taken place on a single day. The weather, the grey light, is always the same. My ageing body inhabits its uniform in unchanging settings and routines. The only memories not caught in the monotony of that time are of being with Edmund in the midst of his whirling gadgets and family.

✦

"Skin-a-bear! Skin-a-bear!" The children's shrill voices bubbled and jingled toward him in the sun-filled air. Edmund, Annie, and Lizzie, Edmund's grandchildren, were running ahead of their parents to greet their great-uncle George where he stood under a tree at the mouth of the laneway to Edmund's farm. John and his family also were waiting with Cartwright where the coach had stopped and the coachman had helped them down with their bags and parcels. They were all waving to their approaching relatives. John's wife was at John's right side, his adopted daughter, Frances-Dorothy, was at his left, her arm linked with his. At Cartwright's urging they had joined him in London and come along to visit with Edmund and witness the testing of Cartwright's latest invention. As he waved and called to the children, part of the apparatus swung from his shoulder in a canvas sack.

"Look at these gypsies," John said. The children were nearly there, their hair flying, their knees and elbows a colourful blur.

"Skin-a-bear! Skin-a-bear!" The children were circling Cartwright, leaping and growling ferociously. Forgetting his stiff back, his painful hips – he was seventy-three now – he let his sack fall from his shoulder, brought little Edmund up in the crook of his left arm, roaring theatrically, sawed with his right index finger up the writhing boy's belly to his collar-bone, then dug elaborately under each of his arms. The way the boy shrieked with laughter, Cartwright thought, he could have afforded to be deafer than he was. The girls sprang on his arms and back, snarling, biting his coat. Cartwright toppled sideways under their weight, laughing, gasping for breath, the three now on top of him, their surprisingly strong little hands gnawing under his waistcoat.

"Children! Children!" Their parents were pulling them off.

"Hello, Edmund," Cartwright said, squinting up at his nephew, father of the attacking bears. "Thank you for saving my life." He stretched up his hand and his nephew pulled it to help him up. Where were his hat then, his fallen wig? Cartwright turned, scanning the ground.

The children, of course, were wearing them, running back up the lane.

His brother Edmund had arrived in his famous centaur carriage with his wife, Susannah (second wife, young wife, Cartwright couldn't help thinking), the pair of them sun-tanned and smiling, pedalling slowly side by side on the front seat. So good was the system of gears, Edmund had said, a child could make it go.

"Here, put your luggage aboard, and save your arms!" Edmund said. "You get in, too, if you'd care to ride."

"Oh, I wouldn't want to break your centaur's back. Or *your* legs, trying to haul *me* along." Cartwright patted the vehicle's slender steel frame.

"I rode it all the way up to London last week," Edmund protested, "and brought back a plough and the iron block for my gunpowder engine. And I think they weighed more than you. I've almost got the engine running by itself. I'll show you after we've had something to eat."

"Well I'm feeling better now," John was saying to Susannah, as he climbed into the vehicle from the other side. "I'd resigned from the Hampden Club, you know, because I'd heard it noised about that some were reluctant to join an organization that counted among its members a dangerous radical such as myself. But my resignation did nothing to boost its membership, as it turned out, and so they've made me assistant secretary again, and I'm run off my feet writing letters this last while. You're looking well, my dear."

The invention which Cartwright had come to demonstrate was a device to make small boats unsinkable. It consisted of a series of bladders and cork blocks connected by ropes.

"Here, everyone blow up a bladder!" he called, stretching the tangled harness out on the grass beside the pond. "There will be a prize – a partridge-whistle of my own making – for the first one inflated! And make sure they're tight!"

The family gathered around and took up the contraption. What followed looked like a group game of cat's cradle combined with a bagpipe competition. Everyone large-cheeked, red in the face, the children tangled in the ropes, the adults laughing and trying to shoo them away, losing the air from their bladders and having to start again.

Frances-Dorothy got hers blown up first and won the partridge-whistle.

Cartwright was pleased with the crowd that had turned out. All Edmund's servants and farm-hands, the blacksmith he worked with, the carpenter, people from the neighbouring farms were there. Cartwright lowered the apparatus under the bow of Edmund's paddle-wheel boat – a machine he'd worked on with Robert Fulton –

and drew it under the hull of the craft toward the stern. Bladders and corks rose to encircle the boat at the waterline. He secured the apparatus with ropes tied to the thwarts, then helped the whole gathering of spectators one by one down off the wharf into the boat, which sank lower and lower with each new passenger.

"I'd sooner have one of those bladders under each arm," someone said.

A thin sheet of water began spilling in over the gunwales. There were laughs and startled screams.

"Twenty-three people aboard," Cartwright said loudly. "Now this is the point I want to prove. Even filled with water, it can't sink. Don't panic. You're all safe."

John was standing on one of the thwarts in the bow, his hands on Frances-Dorothy's shoulders, speaking to a Mr. Rice. "What we have today is continental despotism, not parliamentary democracy. The King has stationed a mercenary army in Nottinghamshire to put down the starving labourers there. Until they have representation through parliamentary reform, we are no better than Turks."

More water rushed in, the passengers were knee-deep in it. There were gasps, people clutched one another. Now only the bobbing corks and bladders defined the outline of the boat.

"We won't sink any further," Cartwright announced. "The flotation device is holding us up."

"I think we're on the bottom actually," Edmund said. "The pond's very shallow here."

✧

In 1817, at the age of seventy-seven, Cartwright retired from his position as barracks master in Nottingham, took up residence in The Turk's Head in Mansfield, and devoted himself to hawking and slow horseback rides. In all of Nottinghamshire he was the only person still practising falconry. "Old Labrador!" the urchins along the Nottingham road cried when he rode past; and they sometimes threw stones. Most of his old acquaintances had died. So had his brothers William and Charles, and his sisters Anne, Elizabeth, and Dorothy. Cartwright had long been the only one of his family left in the area, and, as he now travelled less to London and Kent, and as his remaining brothers and sisters rarely came up to Mansfield, he was often alone.

Near the middle of May, two years after retiring to Mansfield, Cartwright became ill. He had noticed in recent weeks, when mounting his horse or carrying Kaumalak on his wrist, that his strength was diminishing. Then breathing became difficult, as though his chest were filling with fluid, and he only wanted to stay in bed. The doctor who examined him wrote to John, and John came by himself to Mansfield.

John was disturbed by Cartwright's sunken appearance and by the shabby, impersonal room that was now his home. He sat by his brother's bedside, his hat on his lap. What did Cartwright do for meals, John asked, glancing around at the empty glasses and plates on the floor. Under his blanket, Cartwright shrugged limply. The taproom downstairs made lunches, he said.

"You need nourishing soups, lamb stews with barley and vegetables!" John exclaimed. Taproom food wouldn't do. He left the room, saying he'd make arrangements for proper meals. But John himself was old, and he couldn't afford to travel with a servant anymore – someone to manage things for him – and it was night, and Mansfield was unfamiliar. He came back with a quart of beer and a plate of bread and cheese from the taproom – the same meagre fare that Cartwright had largely been living on for the past two years.

Cartwright knew it was likely to be his last sickness, even though it offered no unfamiliar agonies, no revelations of any kind.

John held the beer to Cartwright's lips, but the smell and taste were repugnant to him. He shook his head at the proffered cheese.

John's eyes and his briefly met. Still dodging each other's reach.

John dozed in a chair, and Cartwright drifted uncomfortably in the flickering light, feeling water-logged, scarcely able to breathe – then at last fell asleep. He awakened in daylight, seemingly well again; but completely alone. And that was the way he stayed.

✧

In the early light, Cartwright listens to the creak of the shutters, smells the damp soot, the old ash in the fireplace, and reflects that these sounds and smells have the presence and force of personalities. If he had been confined here with several people, their habitual sayings, their gestures and facial expressions by now would seem no more complex, no more spontaneous and charged with intention than the sounds and smells of his room.

Without doubt, the colours and movements framed in his window are human.

Why should he feel lonely then?

He looks at Kaumalak, her shapely black eyes thinly outlined in yellow plumage. "Shall we go again?" he asks. "My queen . . . there will be doves in the sky."

He brings Thoroton to a stop at the top of a meadow and releases his hawk. She spirals upward and waits on, high overhead, shuddering in the wind like a kite.

He takes his eyes from her and glances west, thinking he sees pigeons rising in a flock. It's the roofs of Chesterfield glittering in the sun. Beyond them, as though down a long valley are the roofs and chimneys of Manchester, the black plumes. And beyond, Liverpool, Ireland, the blue misted sea.

He is higher than Kaumalak. He looks back and down, but has lost her. To the west are the Gannet Islands, the black humps of Labrador. He has never seen them like this before. Sandwich Bay and the Lookout are right below him, Maria's grave, the small cairn just as they'd left it, the roof of Caribou Castle. He sees a silver cup that he once lost, greenish and rippling, on the bottom of Dykes River, and across the bay the mouth of the Eagle River opens and he glides up its valley, strangely, without Thoroton now, the river passing beneath like a black silk scarf shot with white thread.

The bear pool, the falls, is where he comes down, touches the actual rock ledge with his feet and hands, the rough grainy stone; the sleek water swooping beside him, arrowing into its dive. The roar that erases all sound is around him, the slight constant shaking, like excitement in the earth. The sun biting his skin. Where are Kettle and Jack, he wonders. He looks down the pool past the bears, plunging and gleaming, tossing up fish, and expects to see his men emerge from the trees any minute. He has only three balls left, his ramrod is broken, two of the bears he's shot are in sight at the edge of the pool.

He sees a movement and turns on his seat to the right, aiming his rifle, elbows on knees, as a large male bear comes out of the brush, sniffing his trail. He watches it over his sights, its head low, its eyes looking at him, watches its thick legs fluidly moving, loose strings of water dangling from its fur. He watches, letting his rifle down to the left. Whose eyes does it have? It knows him in any case.

When the bear takes up his foot in its teeth, Cartwright goes down on his back, hurting his elbows and head. His foot is a house burst into flames, tongues of fire shooting from windows and doors.

He watches and, incredibly, feels no pain, feels instead the satisfaction of feeding a fierce hunger. He has been starving for so long. And with each bite, as more of him vanishes, a feast of new beauty appears. Small ferns and mosses curly as hair spring from the cracks in the rock where he was sitting.

The bear devours one leg as far as the thigh, then the other, turning its head sideways like a dog to crunch the bones in the back of its jaws.

Then it plunges its snout between Cartwright's legs, up through his hips, burrowing under his ribs. The bear's white head is a wide pointed brush, moving from side to side, painting him out, painting the river, the glittering trees in.

AUTHOR'S NOTE

This novel grew from my reading of George Cartwright's *A Journal of Transactions and Events During a Residence of Nearly Sixteen Years on the Coast of Labrador*, an eighteenth-century English gentleman's account of exploration, commercial venture, and hunting for sport in a corner of North America that until his time had been largely unknown to Europeans.

In my recreation of Cartwright's story, I have in places reproduced passages from his writings more or less verbatim. While my novel springs from Cartwright's own account of his life, his story grew as I handled it, following its own inherent tendencies as well as mine. Time has been compressed or expanded and events invented or altered according to the narrative's needs. What I've written is fiction, not history.

Parts of Chapter 10 first appeared in *The Fiddlehead*. My thanks to the editors, Don McKay and Bill Gaston.

For their kind help I wish to thank David and Antonia Chater, Ralph and Eve Bates, Klaus and Marlene Pfeiffer, Olaf Janzen, Jim Greenlee, Sarah Gillott, Ken Donovan, David Morrish, Elizabeth Behrens, and Constance Rooke; also Ingeborg Marshall and Marianne

Stopp, who permitted me to use their George Cartwright manuscript material. I particularly thank Julian Nedzelski and David Rowed for making it possible to complete this project.

For their assistance I am grateful to the Canada Council and to Memorial University's Sir Wilfred Grenfell College.

I am especially indebted to Shawn Steffler for her personal support, and to Ellen Seligman for her generous and skilled editorial advice.

In *The Afterlife of George Cartwright*, I have pulled together ideas and information from a number of books and articles in addition to Cartwright's journals. Among them are: *Captain Cartwright and His Labrador Journal*, edited by C. W. Townsend; G. Story's "'Old Labrador': George Cartwright, 1738-1819"; *The Life and Correspondence of Major Cartwright*, edited by F. D. Cartwright; G. Schott's *Life of Edmund Cartwright*; M. Strickland's *A Memoir of Edmund Cartwright*; A. M. Lysaght's *Joseph Banks in Newfoundland and Labrador, 1766*; P. Crowhurst's *The Defence of British Trade*; J. P. Lawford's *Britain's Army in India*; D. Kincaid's *British Social Life in India, 1608-1815*; J. C. R. Child's *Armies and Warfare in Europe, 1648-1789*; and R. Savoury's *His Britannic Majesty's Army in Germany During the Seven Years' War*.

John Steffler
Corner Brook, Newfoundland
December 1991